T0385181

Books by Jayne Ann Krentz

Cutler, Sutter & Salinas Novels:
By Jayne Ann Krentz

When All the Girls
Have Gone
Promise Not To Tell
Untouchable

Burning Cove Novels:
Writing as Amanda Quick

The Girl Who Knew
Too Much
The Other Lady
Vanishes
Tightrope
Close Up
The Lady Has a Past
When She Dreams
The Bride Wore White

Arcane Society Novels:
Writing as Jayne Ann Krentz, Amanda Quick & Jayne Castle

Second Sight
White Lies
Sizzle and Burn
The Third Circle
Running Hot
The Perfect Poison
Fired Up
Burning Lamp
Midnight Crystal
In Too Deep
Quicksilver

Harmony (Ghost Hunters) Novels:
Writing as Jayne Castle

After Dark*
After Glow*
Ghost Hunter*
Silver Master*
Dark Light
Obsidian Prey
Midnight Crystal
Canyons of Night
The Lost Night
Deception Cove
The Hot Zone
Siren's Call
Illusion Town
Guild Boss
Sweetwater and the Witch
People in Glass Houses
It Takes a Psychic

Ladies of Lantern Street Novels:
Writing as Amanda Quick

Crystal Gardens
The Mystery Woman

Dark Legacy Novels:
By Jayne Ann Krentz

Copper Beach
Dream Eyes

Whispering Springs Novels:
By Jayne Ann Krentz

Light in Shadow
Truth or Dare

Vanza Novels:
Writing as Amanda Quick

With This Ring
I Thee Wed
Wicked Widow
Lie By Moonlight

Fogg Lake Novels:
By Jayne Ann Krentz

The Vanishing
All the Colours of Night
Lightning in a Mirror

Other titles by Jayne Ann Krentz
Writing as Amanda Quick

The Paid Companion
Wait Until Midnight
The River Knows
Affair
Mischief
Slightly Shady
Otherwise Engaged
Garden of Lies
'Til Death do Us Part

JAYNE ANN KRENTZ

Writing As
JAYNE CASTLE

IT TAKES
A PSYCHIC

PIATKUS

PIATKUS

First published in the US in 2025 by Berkley,
An imprint of Penguin Random House LLC
Published in Great Britain in 2025 by Piatkus

1 3 5 7 9 10 8 6 4 2

A CIP catalogue record for this book
is available from the British Library.

ISBN 978-0-349-44183-2

Printed and bound in Great Britain by
Clays Ltd, Elcograf S.p.A.

Papers used by Piatkus are from well-managed forests
and other responsible sources.

Piatkus
An imprint of
Little, Brown Book Group
Carmelite House
50 Victoria Embankment
London EC4Y 0DZ

The authorised representative
in the EEA is
Hachette Ireland
8 Castlecourt Centre
Dublin 15, D15 XTP3, Ireland
(email: info@hbgi.ie)

An Hachette UK Company
www.hachette.co.uk

www.littlebrown.co.uk

For Roxy:
licensed emotional support dust bunny
and fashion icon

A NOTE FROM JAYNE

Welcome to my Jayne Castle world—Harmony. If you are new to this series, let me give you a quick tour.

Here's how it went down: Late in the twenty-first century a vast energy curtain opened in the vicinity of Earth, making interstellar travel not only possible but practical. In typical human fashion, thousands of eager colonists packed up their stuff and headed out to create new homes on the unexplored planets that were suddenly within reach. Harmony was one of those worlds.

The First Generation colonists who settled Harmony brought with them all the comforts of home—sophisticated technology, centuries of art and literature, and the latest fashions. Trade through the Curtain flourished and allowed people to stay in touch with families back on Earth. It also made it easy to keep the computers and other high-tech gadgets functioning in the psi-heavy atmosphere of Harmony.

Humans had no trouble adapting to the strong paranormal forces on the planet, but that kind of energy proved to be murder on Old World tech.

Things went swell—for a while.

One day, without warning, the Curtain closed, vanishing as mysteriously as it had appeared. Cut off from Earth, no longer able to obtain the equipment and supplies needed to maintain their modern, high-tech lifestyle, the colonists were abruptly thrown back to a far more rustic existence. Forget the latest fashions; just staying alive suddenly became a major problem.

But on Harmony, people did one of the things humans do well—they hunkered down, struggled, and survived. It's now been two hundred years since the closing of the Curtain. It wasn't easy, but the descendants of the First Generation colonists have succeeded in fighting their way back from the brink of disaster to a level of civilization that is roughly equivalent to the twenty-first century on Earth—with a few twists due to the aforementioned paranormal environment.

The four original colonies have grown into four large city-states united under the umbrella of a federal government. With no enemy nations to worry about, there is no standing army. But every society requires some form of policing. On Harmony those tasks are performed by three different agencies. Aboveground, the various police departments and the Federal Bureau of Psi Investigation (FBPI) take the lead. In the ancient Alien ruins belowground, law enforcement and general security are handled by the powerful Ghost Hunters Guild.

Vast stretches of Harmony have yet to be explored and mapped, both aboveground and down below in the amazing, mysterious maze of green quartz tunnels that was constructed by the long-vanished Aliens who first colonized Harmony. No one knows why they disappeared, but they left the lights on—literally. The ruins belowground as well as on the surface were abandoned centuries ago, but they are still luminous thanks to the paranormal radiation emitted by the acid-green quartz used to construct them.

Interestingly, a wide variety of psychic powers have appeared in the human population. The high levels of paranormal energy in the environment are bringing out the latent talents in the descendants of the colonists.

Harmony holds many mysteries, wonders, and dangers. But, as usual, the real trouble is caused by humans.

IT TAKES
A PSYCHIC

CHAPTER ONE

The dust bunny chortled from underneath a nearby display stand.

Leona Griffin paused her examination of the curiously shaped crystal object she had just removed from one of the glass cases and looked around the heavily shadowed gallery.

It had been a long evening and the annual reception of the exclusive Antiquarian Society was far from over. In a desperate attempt to stave off boredom, she had left the crowded ballroom to check out the organization's impressive collection of paranormal antiquities. The realization that a dust bunny had found its way into the private museum was a lot more interesting than the small sculpture she had just plucked from the case.

She did not see any movement in the shadows, but the dust bunny chortled again, more insistently this time.

She put the crystal artifact back into the case. The label claimed it was Old World, circa the nineteenth century. The dating was accurate, in her professional opinion. She was never wrong when it came to authenticating artifacts and antiquities. It was one of her talents, the one she used to make a living as a para-archaeologist. There was a vibe of paranormal energy in the crystal. That was what had qualified it to be displayed in the gallery. Only artifacts of power were acquired by the Society's museum. Every object in the dimly lit space had a paranormal provenance. The result was that the atmosphere in the room was infused with a buzz of energy that lifted the hair on the back of her neck.

She was sure the object had been stolen, most likely from a private collector who had not reported the theft for fear of drawing attention to other objects of questionable provenance in their collection. The trade in illegal artifacts was a booming business, and it was accompanied by the equally profitable side hustle of collector-on-collector crime.

The dust bunny chortled again. Not a cheerful chortle, she decided. It sounded more like a plea. Maybe a cry for help.

"Where are you?" she asked. "I can hear you but I can't see you."

Sensing that she was paying attention, the dust bunny fluttered out from under a glass case.

"There you are," Leona whispered.

The dust bunny came to a stop directly in front of her and rose to its full height on its hind paws. She was not a tall woman but she was wearing very high heels tonight. The top of the dust bunny's head, with the tips of two ears poking through the gray fur, did not even reach her knee.

Dust bunnies were cute. Until they were not. As the saying went, *By the time you see the teeth, it's too late.* They were small, but they were omnivores—not vegetarians.

The good news was that the one in front of her was in what she thought of as adorable mode—fully fluffed with only its bright blue eyes open. It was not sleeked out, and the other two eyes—the ones used for hunting—were closed. If it weren't for the blue eyes and the six little

2

paws peeping through its gray fur, it could have been mistaken for a large wad of dryer lint.

It chortled again. Leona whisked up the skirts of her ankle-length evening gown and crouched in front of the dust bunny. It was not an easy maneuver, given the four-inch heels. For some reason—there was no obvious physical evidence because of all the fur—she decided she was dealing with a female.

"What's wrong?" she asked. "You don't look like you're injured or sick. Are you trapped in here? I'll bet you want me to find a door and open it so you can leave. No problem. I wish I could go with you. Rarely have I been so bored."

Aiding and abetting the dust bunny's escape would be a trifle easier said than done, because the entire mansion was a fortress protected by sophisticated quartz-tech security and cameras. But she was good when it came to that sort of stuff. She had a talent for picking locks.

She stood and checked the time on her low-tech, amber-powered watch. Her work as a para-archaeologist took her into the Underworld, where high-tech devices, such as quartz-powered watches, did not function. The sturdy timepiece was not a stylish look with the formal evening gown, upswept hair, and heels, but she had refused to buy a more fashionable one for the evening.

The rest of her accessories were equally functional—amber earrings, a small amber-trimmed evening bag, and an amber-studded bracelet. All of the amber was tuned and could be used in an emergency to navigate the psi-heavy atmosphere of the Underworld. When your work took you down into the tunnels on a regular basis, you got into the habit of carrying plenty of nav amber.

The only other piece of jewelry was the small yellow crystal pendant she wore around her neck. But it was tucked out of sight beneath the draped bodice of the gown.

"I've got time," she said to the dust bunny. "I'm not due onstage for another fifteen minutes. I'm the entertainment, you see. That's because I'm temporarily famous."

The dust bunny did not appear interested in her status as the star attraction of the evening.

Leona glanced at the closed door of the gallery. The muffled rumble of voices and laughter infused with alcohol and the egos of a couple of hundred wealthy, obsessive, highly competitive collectors reverberated through it. The reception was in full swing. No one would miss her, not until it was time for her to go onstage. She was not a member of the Society. She was a lowly assistant professor in the Department of Para-Archaeology at Hollister University. In the eyes of the reception guests, she ranked a notch or two above the caterers and the valet parking staff but well below the elite people gathered in the mansion tonight.

She turned and started toward a hallway on the far side of the gallery. "Follow me. There's an emergency exit at the end of that corridor. Don't worry, I can override the alarm system."

The dust bunny growled. Startled, she looked back. The creature chortled approvingly and hustled off toward another darkened hallway.

The message was clear. *Follow me.*

She hesitated and then hurried after the dust bunny.

"Okay, I'm coming."

With one last glance over her shoulder, she followed the dust bunny into the shadowed hallway. There was a door at the far end. It proved to be secured with a high-tech psi-lock. There was also a sign emblazoned with the words UNAUTHORIZED ENTRY PROHIBITED. ALARM WILL SOUND. VIOLATORS WILL BE PROSECUTED.

The dust bunny stopped and chortled, pleading this time.

"Well, crap," Leona said. "This is probably not a good idea."

The dust bunny trembled. It took a lot to frighten a dust bunny.

"All right," Leona said. "I'll open the door, but I swear, if this is all

4

about getting you inside that room so that you can find a shiny new toy, I'm going to be very annoyed. You do realize I will be arrested if I get caught, right?"

The dust bunny scratched at the door.

Leona took a deep breath. There was no point in dithering. She had made her decision a moment ago when she had followed the dust bunny into the hallway.

She touched the lock with her fingertips and focused her senses. The vibe of the paranormal mechanism registered immediately. She found the pattern and gently probed for the anchor vibe. It took only a few seconds to flatline it.

There was a faint click as the hidden bolt slid aside. The dust bunny bounced up and down, more agitated than ever.

"Shush," Leona said. "No noise. We don't want anyone to hear us."

She eased the door open. The dust bunny squeezed past her and fluttered into the darkened room. She heard muffled chortling—but not from her newfound companion. There were more dust bunnies inside the chamber.

She could make out only the shadowy outlines of what looked like a couple of laboratory benches. She took her phone out of her purse, rezzed the flashlight, and swung the beam around the room.

Her initial impressions were confirmed. She was in a laboratory stocked with state-of-the-art equipment and instruments. She recognized the various items immediately. She worked with similar devices in the lab at Hollister University.

It was not surprising that the Society possessed its own antiquities research lab. The shocking discovery was the large glass cage on one side of the room. There were three dust bunnies inside. They were sleeked out, all four eyes and a lot of teeth showing. When she went toward them, they immediately fluffed up and chortled hopefully.

"Keep it down, guys," she whispered. "Don't worry, I'll get you out."

The dust bunnies evidently got the message. They went silent, shivering with anticipation as she approached the cage.

"How in the world did they manage to catch you?" she asked. Then she saw the empty pizza carton on the bottom of the cage. "Okay, I guess that explains a few things."

The psi-lock was relatively simple. It had been designed to keep the dust bunnies inside, not to keep humans from opening it. She touched it with her fingertips, rezzed her senses, and unlocked the door.

The dust bunnies tumbled out. They bounced up and down in front of her—she got the feeling she was being thanked—and then all of them—including the one that had gotten her attention in the gallery and led her to the lab—dashed out the door and vanished into the dark hallway. Evidently they didn't need her help to escape the mansion.

"Guess my work here is done," she said under her breath.

But the discovery of the imprisoned dust bunnies put a new light on the Society. She had been well aware that the organization was one of the university's major donors—that was why she had been sent to the gala—and she'd suspected that several of the members dabbled in the gray market. Avid collectors were obsessive by nature. They rarely went out of their way to ensure the legal provenance of valuable artifacts.

But discovering that the Society was conducting research using dust bunnies as test subjects was too much. It could not be overlooked. She would report the news to the director of the para-archaeology department when she met with him in the morning. Morton Bullinger might be willing to ignore issues of sketchy provenances, but even he could not ignore this. He would have to take the information to the university's board of directors and they would be forced to confront the endowment fund people. There was no way the institution could continue to accept money from the Society.

She started toward the door. She was tempted to examine some of the more interesting artifacts on the workbenches, but she had taken enough risks. She could not afford to get caught inside the lab.

She changed her mind when the beam of her flashlight swept across a gracefully curved black crystal bowl in a glass case. She could feel the disturbing vibe of power in the object from across the room.

Curious, she went closer and rezzed her senses a little. The bowl was definitely Alien in origin and there was a lot of energy locked in the object. Fascinated, she put her fingertips on the lock of the glass case.

A sharp frisson of awareness sparked across her senses, rattling her already tense nerves. She was no longer alone. She whirled around, struggling to come up with a believable explanation for her obviously illicit presence in the lab. She was good at thinking on her feet but there were not a lot of options here. Something along the lines of the classic *I was looking for the restroom* would have to do. It was weak, but combined with her *temporarily famous* status and her connection to the university, it might work.

She opened her mouth to start talking very fast but she went blank when the beam of her flashlight illuminated the man in the slightly rumpled tux standing in the doorway. She recognized him immediately. She had picked him out of the crowd earlier in the evening when she realized she was being watched. Somehow she had known he was the one who had been keeping an eye on her. She had concluded that he was either undercover security or a professional antiquities thief. The one thing she had been certain of was that he was not the boring, harmless-looking collector he was pretending to be.

Oh, shit.

"Good evening, Dr. Griffin," he said. He adjusted his black-framed glasses. "I thought I'd lost you. Are you selecting a little souvenir to take with you when you leave tonight? I don't blame you. There are some very nice items in the Society's collection."

CHAPTER TWO

He thought she was a thief.

Under the circumstances, that made sense—after all, she was not supposed to be in the lab. But that left his own status unclarified. Was he a security guard, or did he plan to steal one of the artifacts himself? If she were a betting woman, she would have put her money down on the latter possibility. She was quite sure she was dealing with a professional thief. He probably saw her as competition and, maybe, a threat.

There was nothing notable about him—nothing at all—and that was precisely what had given her goose bumps. A man like this one ought not be the sort who got overlooked in a crowd, yet that was exactly what had happened out there in the ballroom. He had moved through the throng of well-dressed guests as if he were a ghost.

Not that he went completely unnoticed. On a subconscious, psychic level, people were aware of him. She had watched, intrigued, as individuals moved out of his way when they sensed his aura. A powerful energy field had that effect on others.

As far as she could tell, she was the only one who had really paid attention to him. She was pretty sure there was only one explanation for his near-invisibility—he possessed some serious talent. Yet he was going out of his way to try to conceal it. His ability to do that was even more interesting.

At one point he had cruised past her while she sipped a glass of sparkling water and pretended to admire a statue of the Society's founder. She'd caught a glimpse of specter-cat eyes behind the lenses of the black-framed glasses and picked up the vibe of his powerful energy field. It would be very easy to underestimate this man. She would not make that mistake.

It paid to be careful around individuals who possessed a serious degree of paranormal power. She ought to know. She was one of those people.

She had to get control of the situation immediately. She could do that. She might be a lowly, untenured assistant professor but she was rapidly climbing the slippery, extremely treacherous academic ladder. One did not survive the ascent unless one could think on her feet. The first rule was *show no weakness*.

"I assume you are either security working undercover or an antiquities thief," she said, going for the cool, assured tones she used when she was making a presentation to a room full of other academics. "Regardless, I suggest you get out of my way before I decide to scream. We both know that if I do, a lot of people, including some very real and no doubt very well-armed security guards, will come running."

"I'm not security. Would you mind lowering the flashlight? It's hard to have a civil conversation when you can't see a damn thing."

She hesitated and then aimed the beam of her light toward the floor.

"Thanks," he said.

He folded his arms and propped one shoulder against the doorframe. If he was trying to appear nonthreatening, it wasn't working. His voice was too dark, too compelling, and infused with way too much curiosity. He watched her as if she were a very interesting artifact.

"If you're not security, that leaves the other alternative, doesn't it?" She swept out a hand. "Don't let me stop you. Help yourself to whatever takes your fancy. I'd warn you that the locks on the display cases in the gallery are quite sophisticated, but I'm sure that, as a professional, you're already aware of that."

"Evidently the Society's locks haven't been a problem for you."

"I'm not a fan of the Society's acquisition practices. I couldn't care less if they get ripped off tonight. They deserve it. But for your information, I'm not a thief. I just want to do the job my boss sent me here to do and then go home."

"Your boss being Morton Bullinger, the head of the Department of Para-Archaeology at Hollister University."

Her identity was no secret. Videos and photos of her had been all over the Illusion Town media for weeks after she and two of her colleagues had been kidnapped by antiquities pirates and held captive in the Underworld. Fortunately, the press had quickly lost interest after the dramatic rescue. Nevertheless, she had not yet sunk back into complete anonymity. Her temporary fame was the reason the Society had requested her services tonight.

"You obviously know who I am," she said. "The least you could do is introduce yourself."

"Of course. Oliver Rancourt."

"I've never heard of you."

"That's not a surprise. I don't get out much." Oliver glanced at the empty glass cage with its open door. "Was freeing a bunch of dust bunnies one of the things Bullinger sent you here to do tonight?"

"Nope, that was a freebie. I'm sure Bullinger wasn't aware that the Society was engaged in illegal research using dust bunnies."

"Whoever locked up those little guys should be tossed into the tunnels without any nav amber."

"Well, at least we agree on that," she said.

"Yes." He seemed pleased. "Now, I suggest we both return to the ballroom before someone notices that you're missing and decides to come looking." Oliver straightened away from the doorframe, took out his phone, and switched on his flashlight. "We can continue this conversation— Huh."

She realized he had been distracted. She turned her head slightly and saw that the beam of his light was focused on the Alien artifact in the glass case.

"That looks interesting," he said.

"Yes, it does. If I'm right, it qualifies as an artifact of unknown power. It should have been turned over to the authorities when it was discovered."

"I'm shocked, of course, to discover it here in the private lab of an organization run by and for obsessive collectors who will pay any price for AUPs."

She watched him walk closer to the artifact. "I wonder if they were planning to run experiments on the dust bunnies with it."

He stopped in front of the case, clearly intrigued. "Think it's a weapon?"

"It might not have been intended as such, but when it comes to Alien artifacts, who knows? Even something as simple as a child's toy could prove lethal to humans."

"True." With a small sigh of regret, he turned away from the artifact and moved toward her. "Evidently neither one of us is here to take possession of that object. We both have other priorities tonight. We should get back to the ballroom."

"I'm not arguing."

Neither one of us is here to take possession of that object? The obvious inference was that he was here to grab one of the other artifacts. That settled it. Rancourt was definitely not security. He was an antiquities thief.

She whisked through the doorway, the skirts of her gown sweeping around her ankles. Oliver followed her out into the hall, pausing long enough to close the door. She heard the automatic lock click. They both de-rezzed their flashlights.

"The security in this place is very, very good," Oliver said quietly as they made their way through the shadowed gallery. "I'm impressed that you were able to get into that lab without rezzing alarms. I had no idea lock picking was being taught in para-archaeology classes these days."

"It isn't. I was homeschooled in that particular skill. My moms believed in giving their daughters a well-rounded education."

"Your mothers being the proprietors of Griffin Investigations."

"You have done your research."

"You've been in the news a lot recently."

"Who knew that getting abducted by pirates and forced to work an illegal archaeological site would make so many headlines?"

"Are you kidding?" Oliver was clearly amused. "The story had it all. Drama. Danger. Alien archaeology. Artifacts of unknown power. It even had pirates and a heroic dust bunny."

She smiled at that. "Pretty sure it was the dust bunny that brought in the big headlines at the end."

"Everyone loves dust bunnies."

"Except creeps who use them to test Alien artifacts."

"Creeps like the members of the Society," Oliver concluded.

"Trust me, I'm going to make sure Bullinger knows what I saw in that lab. The endowment fund and the board will have to sever their connections to the Society."

"Are you always this optimistic?"

"It's not a question of optimism. It's a matter of professional ethics."

"Uh-huh."

There was a suspicious note of cynical amusement in his voice. She glanced at him over her shoulder.

"You don't think the university will act?" she asked.

"Let's just say I wouldn't hold my breath."

She was about to deliver a short lecture on the rules and regulations that governed endowment funds, but they had reached the door that opened onto the hallway that led to the ballroom. She stopped.

"Why don't you go first?" she said. "It would probably be best if we aren't seen coming out of the gallery together."

"Don't worry, no one will notice us."

Before she could ask him what made him so certain of that, she felt his hand wrap around her arm, strong and firm. She sensed a subtle shift of energy in the atmosphere and knew that he had just rezzed his paranormal senses.

He opened the door and steered her down the hallway and into the crowded ballroom.

Not a single head turned. No one appeared to notice them. She was fascinated. Oliver was powerful enough to envelop her in the cloak of his energy field. For all intents and purposes, they might as well have been invisible.

"That," she said quietly, "is a very useful talent, given your line of work."

"Comes in handy," he agreed. "But what interests me is that you saw me this evening."

"It's not like you are actually invisible. You're just very good at fading into a crowd."

"Not that good, apparently. Everyone else was ignoring me, but not you."

"Oh, I see what you mean. Well, I knew you were watching me. That made me curious."

"See, that's the part that I find fascinating," he said. "You knew I was watching you."

She waved that aside. "There's no mystery about it. I got that vibe you get when you know you're being watched, that tingle on the back of your neck."

"Most people would not have gotten it. Not when I'm the one doing the watching."

"You're that strong?" she asked, amused.

"That's not the point."

"What is the point?" she asked.

Before he could respond, the chandeliers dimmed three times. An expectant hush fell over the crowd.

"Finally," she said. "That's the signal. This is the part where I do my job. As soon as I'm finished, I'm going home."

"Need a ride?"

"No, thank you," she said, aware of a small pang of regret. It would be interesting to see what kind of car an antiquities thief drove. Actually, it would be even more interesting to spend a little more time with this particular thief. "The Society booked a limo for me."

"You can tell whoever asks that you made other arrangements."

She thought about that. "I suppose I could. On the other hand, if you get caught tonight and I happened to be with you, my entire career would explode in my face."

"You already risked your career once this evening by breaking into the lab and freeing the dust bunnies."

She winced. "There is that."

"Don't worry, I won't get caught."

She was about to point out his faulty logic—there was no way he could know for certain he wouldn't get caught—when a tall, lean thirty-something man in an elegantly tailored tux loped easily up the steps at the side of the stage and stopped in front of the curtain. He did not have to introduce himself. Everyone in the room knew who he was. Preston Tripp, wealthy tech-bro entrepreneur, the founder and CEO of a wildly successful start-up focused on gaming apps.

"Good evening, members of the Society," he intoned. "I am honored to act as your master of ceremonies tonight. In that role, I am pleased to announce that we have come to the moment everyone, especially the candidates for membership in the Society, has been waiting for—the judging of the submissions."

A ripple of anticipation and applause interrupted him. When the room quieted again, he continued.

"As you know, each candidate has offered an artifact for consideration. The objects have all been deemed authentic and of extraordinary rarity by our own museum curators. But in order to confirm their opinion and reassure everyone involved, the board requested that Hollister University provide us with an expert from their academic staff."

Oliver leaned in very close to Leona and whispered in her ear. "How did you get so lucky?"

"Haven't you heard?" she muttered. "I'm temporarily famous."

"Not just any expert," Tripp continued, "but a very special member of the Department of Para-Archaeology, none other than Professor Leona Griffin. You will all recognize the name. Dr. Griffin was one of three scientists on the ill-fated Hollister Expedition. She is credited with protecting her colleagues and a cache of unique artifacts while they waited for rescue."

There was a round of polite applause. The audience was getting impatient. Leona gritted her teeth. *Not much longer.*

Tripp smiled down at Leona and gestured toward the steps. "If you will be so kind as to join me on the stage, Dr. Griffin?"

"Wish me luck," she murmured to Oliver.

"You'll be fine," he said.

She started toward the steps but hesitated when she felt his hand on her elbow. For a chaotic few seconds she wondered if he was planning to make both of them invisible again.

"What are you——?" she began.

But Oliver did not rez his talent. Instead, he escorted her to the bottom step, released her, and stepped back. When she made it to the stage she glanced back. He had not exactly vanished into the crowd, but those around him were ignoring him. He really was the perfect thief, she thought. You would never see him coming.

Once again she had to remind herself that she was a trained para-archaeologist, dedicated to the preservation and study of important artifacts. People in her profession did not admire antiquities thieves. On the contrary, they helped the authorities catch them whenever possible.

There was no more time to contemplate her mixed feelings about Oliver Rancourt, because Tripp was greeting her and signaling to the stage crew.

"The curtain, please," he ordered with a dramatic gesture.

The heavy amber drapes slid aside, revealing five transparent display stands. An object draped in black cloth was positioned on top of each of the stands.

"Uncover Submission Number One," Tripp commanded.

Two people—members of the Society's staff, judging by their formal attire and white gloves—stepped forward to raise the first black cloth. A large, round, elaborately faceted gray crystal was revealed.

"If you please, Dr. Griffin?" Tripp urged.

She stepped forward, kicked up her senses a little, and confirmed what she had already concluded with an initial visual exam.

"A fine example of crystal unique to the Ghost City ruins," she said, automatically sliding into her authoritative academic voice. "Alien tuning. There is definitely power locked inside. Purpose unknown."

She did not add that Hollister's museum had a dozen similar objects securely stored in the basement vault—which was where this one should be. True, objects of power that had been engineered by the Aliens were notoriously difficult for humans to activate. That was a good thing, because such artifacts were inherently unpredictable and dangerous. Still. They should be in safekeeping. There were laws.

But everyone knew the laws were routinely flouted and ignored by collectors. Artifacts judged to contain any degree of energy were sought after on both the legitimate and the black markets.

"Thank you, Dr. Griffin," Tripp said. "Candidate Number One is hereby accepted into the Society."

More applause.

The drapery was removed from the next pedestal, revealing a brilliant quartz mirror. In spite of her desire to finish her job and leave, she could not resist a smile of appreciation.

"Very nice," she said. "Definitely of Alien origin. There is some power inside. As usual, purpose unknown."

"Candidate Number Two is hereby accepted into the Society," Tripp declared.

There was another wave of polite applause.

The drape was removed from the third pedestal. Leona took one look at the very charming blue amber necklace and winced.

"A pretty piece," she said. "But it is, to put it politely, a reproduction."

"A fake," Tripp stated.

"I'm afraid so."

Tripp looked pleased. "Your opinion confirms that of our in-house experts, Dr. Griffin."

This time there was a roar of laughter from the audience. She sighed. Obviously the fake relic had been inserted into the lineup as a test to see if she knew what she was doing. If she hadn't already been pissed off because of the captive dust bunnies, the disrespect would have triggered her temper. She reminded herself that her job was to finish the authentication process and go home—in a limo that had been paid for by the Society. Maybe she would dismiss the ride and accept Oliver's offer.

She dealt with the fourth submission—a decent example of dreamstone sculpture—and moved to the last pedestal.

She sensed the vibe before the drapery was removed. There was only a thin trickle of energy, but when she rezzed her talent, the frissons struck her senses like small shocks of lightning.

Whatever was under the drape was Old World in origin, not Alien. It was also powerful.

As badly as she wanted to leave, she knew she could not have walked away from object number five without satisfying her professional curiosity. She had to know what was under the drape.

At Tripp's command, the attendants removed the cloth. Whispers of surprise followed by astonishment swept across the audience. She did not blame the onlookers for being startled by the sight of the seemingly unimpressive artifact. She was, too.

At first glance it looked like a solid brick of opaque blue-green glass. Approximately ten inches long, perhaps six inches wide, and three inches tall, the object reflected light in a way that made it difficult to see the subtle wavelike pattern in the stone.

Not a glass brick, she thought. *A glass box. And not just any box.*

A thrill of knowing dazzled her senses. Fortunately her back was turned to the audience. That gave her a few seconds to get her expression under control.

"Well, Dr. Griffin?" Tripp prompted.

She made a show of walking slowly around the pedestal, examining the relic from all sides, giving herself another moment to decide just how much to say. She was fairly certain that the individual who had submitted the box knew its true value. She had to assume the Society's experts had also identified it, so there was no point trying to pretend it was an unimpressive artifact.

"A most unusual object," she said in her best lecturing tones. "Old World origin, not Alien, of course."

Tripp's eyes glittered with anticipation.

"Can you offer any further information on the object?" he prompted.

He sounded impatient. That confirmed her conclusion—the higherups in the Society were well aware of the true value of the box. There was no point finessing her professional opinion.

She turned to face the audience. Time to go for the drama. That was, after all, what everyone wanted from her.

"I must congratulate the Society," she said. "Candidate Number Five has presented you with a truly remarkable Old World artifact, the object known as Pandora's box. Circa the early twenty-first century, Old World date." She smiled a cool smile. "Not the box of the ancient myth, of course. This is most certainly an example of human engineering, but it is a legend in its own right."

Stunned shock froze the audience for a couple of beats. But Tripp's expression was one of cool satisfaction.

"Nice work, Professor," he said under the cover of applause.

"It belongs in a museum," she snapped.

"Agreed. Don't worry, it will be safe inside the Society's vault."

"Where no one except members of the Society can see it or study it."

Tripp pretended he hadn't heard her.

"Can we discuss provenance?" she asked sweetly.

Tripp ignored her again.

While she waited for the crowd to settle down, she glanced toward the side of the stage, looking for Oliver. She was interested to see how he was taking her verdict.

He was nowhere in sight.

She heightened her talent again, trying to pick him out of the throng of excited people near the stage. He was not in the vicinity. He truly had vanished.

It occurred to her that a smart thief would probably take advantage of the distraction caused by the crowd's excitement to return to the gallery and help himself to whatever he wanted to steal. That, she thought, was what she would have done—if she were an antiquities thief.

Considering the fact that many of the items in the Society's museum had been acquired under suspicious circumstances, she felt no obligation to alert Tripp or the security guards.

Tripp took charge of the room, gradually bringing things under control.

"Thank you for confirming the analysis of our in-house experts, Dr. Griffin. The Society is delighted to accept the Old World object known as Pandora's box into our collection, and Candidate Number Five is hereby admitted to our organization."

"Happy to have been of service," Leona said through her teeth.

She turned to make her way off the stage. She had done her job. Now she could go home. For some ridiculous reason she found herself wondering where Oliver Rancourt called home. Common sense warned her that it was probably not a good idea to indulge her curiosity about him, but curiosity was one of her defining personality traits. Everyone in her family said so.

"One moment, please, Professor," Tripp said. "We're not quite finished."

Reluctantly she stopped at the top of the steps and looked back at him. "What now?"

"To celebrate the occasion and to thank you for your professional opinion, Candidate Number Five requests that you have the honor of opening Pandora's box for us."

An icy chill stopped her breathing. This was not good. She was not certain what was happening but her intuition was slamming into the red zone. Not many people knew she had a talent for locks. It was not the sort of skill you advertised.

"I appreciate the gesture," she said. "But while that artifact is Old World in origin, it's sealed with a rather sophisticated psi-lock. I'm afraid you'll need a quartz-tech lock pick to open it."

Tripp chuckled. "Which I just happen to have with me." He plucked a pen-shaped device out of his pocket and held it aloft for the crowd to see. There was a roar of appreciative laughter and applause. "If you please, Dr. Griffin."

Anger flashed through her. She thought about the dust bunnies in the cage and the illegally acquired antiquities in the Society's collection and then she gave Tripp an icy smile.

"Open it yourself," she said.

She turned and went quickly down the stage steps before anyone could react. Her intuition was flashing warning signs. She needed to leave. Immediately.

Her instinct was to run, not walk, to the front door and escape in the limo. She had a fleeting vision of herself fleeing down the steps, long skirts whipping out behind her as she dashed to her carriage before it turned into a large orange squash. But that particular scenario required a Prince Charming standing in the doorway of the castle, a high-heeled crystal shoe in his hand.

Mentally she stomped on the romantic scenario she had conjured. Her Prince Charming tonight was an antiquities thief. People in her profession did not have romantic fantasies about antiquities thieves.

The sensible thing to do would be to slip through the crowd while it was paying attention to Tripp and then exit through a side entrance.

A few heads turned her way as she reached the edge of the crowd, but most of the audience was focused on Tripp.

"I have just been informed that Candidate Number Five, who presented us with Pandora's box, will not be going through the ceremony with the others," he announced. "The individual has retracted the application for membership and has withdrawn the artifact from consideration. Therefore, Pandora's box will not be opened."

There was an audible gasp from the crowd, followed by a tide of disbelief.

Okay, that was weird, Leona thought. Membership in the Society was highly coveted in the collecting world. But everyone knew collectors were frequently off-the-charts eccentric. She hated to see the box vanish back into someone's private vault, but if the Society had taken possession of it, its fate would have been the same. It would have ended up in a private vault.

She took one last look around to make sure no one was paying attention to her and then slipped into the shadowed hallway marked *Restrooms*. Earlier, when she had used the facility to freshen up, she had noticed an emergency exit sign at the end of the corridor. She would override the alarm system long enough to slip outside without being noticed, make her way around to the sweeping driveway in front of the mansion, and locate the limo that had been booked for her.

She reached the end of the hallway, turned the corner, and saw the exit. There was a large sign. **OPENING DOOR WILL SOUND ALARM.**

She was almost at her destination when she saw the stream of blood on the floor.

Stunned, she stopped short and traced the crimson river to its source. It was seeping out from underneath a closed door. She stilled. The very last thing she wanted to do was open the door. But she had no choice. Someone was inside, someone who desperately needed help.

Trying to keep her shoes out of the blood stream, she gripped the handle and opened the door. She found herself gazing into a large vintage pantry. There were no canned or packaged goods on the shelves, but there was an array of dishes, kitchen utensils, and cutlery.

The body of a woman was sprawled on the floor. She was wearing a caterer's uniform. A bloodstained knife lay nearby.

CHAPTER THREE

With a furious effort of will, she yanked herself out of the shock-and-horror-induced trance and edged into the pantry, trying to avoid the blood trail. She crouched beside the body and felt for a pulse, not expecting to find one.

She felt nothing but cooling skin and the utter stillness of death. Given her own pounding pulse and shaking fingers, however, she could not be sure. She fumbled with the buttons of the blood-soaked jacket, got them undone, and raised one edge to search for the wound.

She was startled by the sight of the metal disc that hung from a chain around the woman's neck. The disc was emblazoned with a notorious emblem familiar from history books and old videos. A transparent crystal was embedded in the pendant. The words VINCENT LEE VANCE WILL RETURN were inscribed around the outer edge.

The waiter had evidently been a member of a Vance return cult.

Focus, she thought. There were two terrible slashes in the bloody white shirt. The bleeding had stopped. The energy laid down by violent death was already soaking into the floor beneath the body. It would remain there indefinitely, evident to those who possessed the psychic sensitivity to detect it. There was no scrubbing away that kind of evidence.

She let the jacket fall back over the pendant and the wounds and got to her feet. So much for slipping away from the reception unnoticed. She had to alert the security staff.

She took a step toward the door and froze. Muffled yells and shouted commands erupted from the direction of the ballroom, reverberating down the hallway. She could hear sirens now as well as the thuds of stampeding feet.

Out in the ballroom someone bellowed through a bullhorn.

"FBPI. Nobody move."

Energy shifted in the hall outside the pantry. A familiar figure appeared in the doorway. She remembered the old saying about criminals returning to the scenes of their crimes. Panic electrified her senses.

"What are you doing here?" she whispered.

"What the hell?" Oliver looked at the body. "Is she dead?"

The shot of panic receded. Her intuition told her that Oliver had not murdered the woman. For one thing, there was no blood on his clothes. Whoever had butchered the waiter would almost certainly have been splattered with some of the evidence. There was another factor that reassured her as well. If Oliver had killed the waiter, he would have done it in a much neater, more efficient way.

"Yes. I was going to slip out through the emergency exit. But I found her. I have to tell security. Or the police. Someone. What is happening out there?"

"A raid. The planning has been in the works for months. Let's go. We need to get out of here."

"We can't leave her here. We have to tell someone."

"Trust me, the agents will find her very soon, and if they also find

24

you standing over the body, your hands covered in blood, guess who's going to get arrested?"

"But I didn't kill her."

"I believe you, but the situation out in the ballroom is complicated."

The pandemonium was escalating. A small muffled explosion reverberated from some distant quarter of the mansion. A series of shots quickly followed.

No question about it, the situation had descended into chaos.

"Follow me," Oliver said.

He turned to go down another hallway. That was when she saw the pack slung over his left shoulder. She wondered which artifact he had helped himself to on his private tour of the gallery.

She glanced at the alarmed door. "We can use the emergency exit."

He glanced back over his shoulder. "Too risky. There are agents and cops stationed outside the house, watching for anyone who comes through the emergency doors. There's another way out."

She hoisted her skirts, realizing belatedly that the lower portion of her gown was soaked with blood and her hands were smeared with the stuff. A wave of lightheadedness came over her. *If I had left the ballroom a few minutes earlier, I might have been able to save the waiter . . .*

For a beat she was afraid she might faint. She never fainted.

And then a firm hand closed around her arm, steadying her.

"Breathe," Oliver said.

"If I had come down that hallway a few minutes earlier, I might have been able to save her . . ."

"I said *breathe.*" This time it was an order.

Instinctively, she obeyed. Her head cleared, but now she felt nauseous. *So much blood.* She looked at the sign on a nearby door. **RESTROOM.**

"I'll be right back," she managed to whisper.

"We don't have time."

"I understand. Go without me. I can take care of myself."

She pushed open the swinging door and dashed to the first in a long row of sinks. She rinsed her hands as quickly as she could, yanked some paper towels out of the dispenser, and rushed back out into the hallway. She was shocked to see that Oliver was still there.

"You waited," she said in disbelief.

"Not like I had anything better to do." He turned away and started down the hall. "Let's move."

She hurried after him. When she got closer, she picked up a faint, familiar trickle of energy. She looked at the pack on his shoulder in disbelief.

"You stole Pandora's box?" she asked.

"I didn't steal it. I recovered it. The artifact is why I'm here tonight."

She decided this was not a good time to debate the semantics of the words *theft* and *recovery*.

He turned another corner and led her down a narrow, cramped corridor. Halfway along the hall he stopped in front of what looked like a blank wall. He rezzed a concealed button. A panel slid aside.

Leona looked past his shoulder and saw a well of darkness. Underworld energy wafted up a cracked concrete staircase. With it came the dank smell of a deep basement.

Oliver rezzed his phone flashlight. "There's a hole-in-the-wall entrance to the tunnels down there."

"Why aren't the members of the Society using it to escape the raid?"

"Because they don't know about it. They are trying to escape through another hole-in-the-wall but the task force team is guarding it. Let's go. Close the panel behind you."

He went easily down the steps, apparently assuming she would follow. She hesitated, but when another round of shots rumbled in the distance, she followed him, sliding the panel shut.

They reached the bottom of the steps and, guided by the flashlight, crossed the darkened basement. Oliver stopped in front of a mag-steel vault door.

"Don't worry, I can open it," she said.

"So can I."

He took a small gadget out of the inside pocket of his jacket and rezzed it. There was a muted hum from the interior of the door and then a sharp click.

She wondered if she had offended him by her offer of assistance. Probably. She had a list of exes who had indicated that she had an annoying habit of telling them what to do and how to do it. During the course of the recent—unfortunately, explosive—breakup with Matt Fullerton, he had made her faults quite clear.

She put the issue aside. It wasn't as if she was trying to fire up a romantic relationship with Oliver. They were temporary partners in crime. Sort of. And she had to admit, the fancy lock pick was impressive.

"Cool gadget," she said. "Where did you get it?"

"Company labs."

She decided it would be best not to ask the name of the company. If he had stolen the lock pick, she would just as soon not know the details.

"Amber check," he ordered.

"Right."

First things first. Rational people did not go into the Underworld without making sure their navigation amber was properly tuned. To do otherwise was to take a risk that was borderline suicidal.

She rezzed a little energy and got the reassuring feedback from the amber in her jewelry that told her it was functioning properly.

"I'm good," she said.

"So am I."

He pulled open the vault door, revealing the glowing green quartz tunnel on the other side. The powerful currents of paranormal energy that flowed throughout the vast maze of underground corridors stirred her senses. It always did. The flash of sheer, unadulterated wonder that she experienced in the ruins never got old. There was so much to learn, so much to discover, among the antiquities the long-vanished Aliens had left behind.

Oliver moved through the opening, waited for her to follow, and then pulled the vault door closed.

The jagged opening in the tunnel wall was taller than a normal door but narrower. Oliver had to turn sideways to get his broad shoulders through it. The experts had plenty of theories about the forces that had been powerful enough to rip holes in the seemingly indestructible quartz—nothing human engineering had produced could even chip or dent the stone—but no one knew for sure what had caused the cracks and fissures. Currently the most popular notion was that nothing less than massive natural forces deep inside the planet—tectonic plates or underground volcanoes—could have created the openings. But who knew?

Inside the tunnel, Oliver switched off the flashlight. There was no need for it. The green quartz the Aliens had used to construct the sprawling network of passageways was infused with an eerie radiance that glowed day and night.

"Stay close and stay focused," Oliver said. "Don't get distracted."

She tried to ignore the cold, *I'm in charge here* attitude, but now she was the one who was offended. She was no newbie in the Underworld.

"Distracted by what?" She waved a hand at their surroundings. "The energy down here? The scenery? Don't worry. This is not my first trip into the tunnels. I'm a professional para-archaeologist, remember?"

"A professional para-archaeologist whose last expedition did not end well."

That stung. It also sent a jolt of anger across her senses. She did not need the guilt trip. She had been hard enough on herself as it was in the wake of the abduction and rescue. Lately her anxiety-ridden nightmares were threatening to turn her into a full-blown insomniac.

"The Hollister Expedition disaster had nothing to do with being distracted," she said in her iciest voice. "My colleagues and I were kidnapped. You can't blame that on me."

But maybe if I had been paying more attention to the actions of the security team . . . just as I should have been paying more attention that long-ago day at the orphanage . . .

"Listen up," Oliver said. "I'm not blaming you for anything. I'm making the point that we're not in the clear yet, so pay attention. Obviously you don't take orders well."

She refused to dignify that with a response.

"Think of my suggestions as well-intentioned advice," he added.

She reminded herself that she had been told she had a tendency to give others the benefit of her advice even when it was not always appreciated.

"Can I assume you have a plan?" she asked.

"Always. And a backup."

She vowed not to get drawn into an argument. There was no good reason to complicate their already messy relationship, at least not until she had a plan of her own.

No, not *relationship*. What she and Oliver had was a temporary *association*. Big difference.

"In that case, thank you for the advice," she made herself say, keeping her tone exquisitely polite. "No distractions. I will keep that front of mind."

She could have sworn the edge of his mouth twitched ever so slightly. A tell of some sort, she decided, but she wasn't sure what it meant. It had better not indicate amusement. This was not an amusing situation. Also, she really, really did not want to be a source of *amusement* for Oliver Rancourt.

They started down a tunnel lined on either side with vaulted entrances to chambers of various sizes. The energy spilling out of one of the doorways hit her with the force of a thunderstorm. She knew objects of power when she got near them. She glanced inside the room and saw dozens of museum storage crates piled high around the space.

"Some of whatever is in those crates came from the Glass House sector," she said. "I can sense the vibe. They shouldn't be here. That entire region is controlled by the federal government. It has not been approved for open exploration because it has not been mapped and cleared. The removal of any artifacts is against the law."

"I warned you not to get distracted."

"When we get back to the surface, I'm going to report this."

"Suit yourself, but if you're as smart as I think you are, you'll keep quiet."

"Why?"

"Because there's no good reason to get involved. In fact, it would be spectacularly dumb to do so."

"Why?" she said again.

"Do you always ask questions at inconvenient times?"

"Always. And I usually have a backup question, too."

He winced. "Moving right along. I told you, there's an FBPI raid going on back there. The Feds have been planning the operation for months. They scheduled the takedown for the one night of the year when the Society and its members are most vulnerable."

"The annual reception," she said quietly.

"There will be a lot of arrests tonight. There will also be a thorough search. The authorities will find the body of the waiter and the artifacts stashed down here. There's no good reason for them to link you to either of those two problems. It would not look good on your résumé."

She got a ping. Her intuition kicked in. With it came a rush of certainty. "You're working with the FBPI, aren't you? You were the inside contact, the one who gave them the signal to move in. Are you a confidential informant? Did they pressure you to be their spy tonight? Threaten to put you in prison if you didn't cooperate? There's an old saying, *It takes a thief to catch a thief.* What have the Feds got on you?"

"I am devastated to discover that you hold such a low opinion of me."

"My current opinion of your character is based on available facts." She flashed him a very shiny smile, the one she used when she was trying to persuade obsessive collectors to donate their best pieces to the university's collection. "If you want me to change that opinion, you'll have to supply new information."

"It's true I agreed to do the Bureau a favor tonight."

"Because you had your own agenda," she said, satisfied with the way her intuition was connecting the data points. "The raid certainly worked nicely with your personal plan, didn't it?"

"Yes, it did." He sounded pleased.

"Hah. I thought so. Do the Feds know you stole one of the artifacts?"

"I thought I made it clear that I did not steal the damned box," he said. "I recovered it."

The edge of amusement was gone. He was getting irritated. Served him right.

"I forgot," she said. "You're a repo agent."

"The box was stolen from a private museum. I was tasked with retrieving it. My sources indicated it would be on display tonight. And yes, my goal was aligned with the Bureau's decision to raid the Society."

"And you knew about the happy coincidence of the timing because?"

"It's not the first time I've coordinated with the FBPI."

"I see," she said. She glanced at the pack slung over his shoulder. "Do you know who stole the box from this—ahem—so-called private museum?"

"No," he said. "But I'm going to find out."

He was beyond both amusement and irritation now, she realized. In their place was a cold determination that sent a chill across her senses. He was serious. Resolute. Focused on the objective. A man with a mission.

Earlier she had concluded it would not be a good idea to underestimate Oliver Rancourt. She suspected whoever had stolen Pandora's box had made that mistake and would live to regret it.

He led her across a wide rotunda and into one of a dizzying number of branching tunnels. A few steps past the entrance he stopped and motioned toward a sled.

"Your carriage awaits," he said.

The simple amber-fueled sleds resembled golf carts. They didn't move fast—at top speed they could barely outpace someone who was running—but they were the only means of transport in the Underworld. More sophisticated, more powerful engines did not function in the psi-heavy environment.

For some reason, she was now the one who was amused. "You know, I arrived at the reception in a limo tonight. I had intended to leave the same way."

"Sorry I can't offer more impressive service, but I'll be happy to give you a lift back to the Dark Zone."

She froze. "You know where I live?"

"I always do my research. You were the anomaly at the reception tonight. The unknown quantity. I needed to know if you might prove to be a problem."

The anomaly.

Not exactly the provocative, mysterious, sexy image a woman in an evening gown and heels wanted to project.

"You should have asked me," she said. "I could have told you the answer to that question is yes."

"Believe it or not, I figured that out right off. Do you want a ride or not?"

The alternative involved finding the nearest exit from the tunnels on her own. She would probably end up in an unfamiliar neighborhood, one in which walking down the street in high heels and a bloodstained evening gown at midnight might be a very good way to get arrested.

"I suppose that if you intended to murder me to keep me from telling the authorities that you stole a rare artifact, you would have done so by now," she said. "Yep, I accept your offer of a ride."

"Keep this up and you're going to hurt my feelings."

"Wouldn't want to do that, considering that you're the one with the sled."

"See? I knew you were pretty smart."

She whisked up her bloodstained skirts, stepped onto the platform, and sat down at one end of the front bench. Oliver slipped off the pack and set it on the rear bench. He got behind the wheel and rezzed the motor. There was a quiet confidence in every move he made.

She was suddenly conscious of just how close he was now. He was not a big man but he dominated the space around him. It was his energy field, she thought. So much chained power.

"You told me you always have a plan and a backup," she said on impulse.

"Right."

"Obviously I wasn't a factor in your original plan. So, are we now going with your backup plan?"

"No. I also believe in having a very flexible plan A. My original plan included leaving on the sled, and that's what I'm doing. The only difference is that I'm not leaving alone."

"In other words, I'm excess baggage?"

"I was thinking more along the lines of a souvenir." An enthusiastic chortling stopped him just as he was about to step on the accelerator. "What in green hell?"

Startled, Leona turned on the seat and looked back. A large wad of dryer lint with six paws and a couple of bright blue eyes was bustling toward the sled.

"It's the dust bunny," she said, delighted.

"Which dust bunny?" Oliver asked, glancing over his shoulder.

"The one that got my attention in the gallery and led me to the lab to rescue her pals."

"How can you be sure it's the same dust bunny?" Oliver's brows rose. "Or that it's a female?"

"I can't explain it." She smiled. "I guess there's some sort of connection between us now." She broke off. "Uh-oh."

"What?"

"She's got something in her paws. A little crystal sculpture. Pretty sure I recognize it."

"Does it belong to you?"

"No. I noticed it earlier in one of the glass cases in the gallery. Dust bunnies are very attracted to bright, shiny objects."

"Those cases are securely locked. How did she get it?"

"I unlocked the case to get a better look at the artifact. I may have left it open."

"Got it. You were planning to take a little souvenir yourself."

She glared at him. "I was distracted by the dust bunny. It was obvious she needed help."

Oliver's mouth twitched again. "Distracted?"

"Oh, shut up."

The dust bunny hopped up onto the sled platform and then bounded onto the rear bench. With a cheery chortle, she offered the object to Leona.

"Thanks." Leona took the object and stifled a sigh. "Really? Of all the valuable objects that were in the gallery, you picked this one to give me as a thank-you gift?"

The dust bunny had lost interest. She was braced expectantly on the rear seat.

Oliver gestured for her to hop off the sled. "Time to bail. We're leaving now."

The dust bunny chortled and made no move to leave.

"Suit yourself," Oliver said.

He stomped on the accelerator. The sled moved forward along the glowing tunnel, picking up speed. The dust bunny bounced up and down, chortling enthusiastically.

"Dust bunnies like to go fast," Leona explained. "They're little adrenaline junkies."

"Yeah?" Oliver studied the location indicator on the dashboard and steered around a corner. "How do you know that?"

"My sister is pals with one. She calls him Newton. He gets very excited in a car or a sled."

Oliver glanced at the crystal object in her hand. "What is that?"

She cleared her throat and dropped the artifact into her evening bag. It barely fit. "It's an interesting little sculpture. Old World. Circa the nineteenth century, I think, although this isn't my area of expertise."

"Yeah, but what is it?"

"I believe the technical name for this type of sculpture is *personal intimacy aid*."

"Thought so. A hot dildo."

CHAPTER FOUR

Leona started to shiver. She could not blame a drop in the ambient temperature, because that never changed in the Underworld. It took her a moment to realize she was coming off an adrenaline jag. *Breathe.*

She looked down at the bloodstains on her dress and then yanked her attention away from the disturbing sight. She longed for a hot shower and a change of clothes. *Like that's going to change what happened. Breathe.*

She forced herself to focus.

"I wonder who she was and why she was murdered," she said.

Oliver slowed for another sharp corner. "The FBPI will find her body. When they do, they'll identify her and launch an investigation."

"She was a member of one of those weird Vincent Lee Vance return cults."

Oliver glanced at her. "Are you sure?"

"She was wearing a necklace with a metal disc inscribed with '*Vincent Lee Vance Will Return.*' There was a small crystal set in the pendant. It looked like an exact replica of the pendants Vance distributed to his followers."

"They say no one ever went broke running a cult. There have always been idiots who buy into the old conspiracy theory about Vance not dying in the tunnels. They're convinced he was frozen with some sort of mysterious Alien cryogenic technology and that one day he'll return to lead another revolution."

"I know. It's hard to kill off a conspiracy theory." Leona hesitated. "The crystal in that cult pendant was hot, Oliver."

He frowned. "Tuned?"

"And locked. I didn't get a chance to examine it, but I can tell you it was not some cheap knockoff of the old Vance pendants. It was sophisticated work. Whoever did it is serious about firing up another Vance return cult."

"Think the tuning was the kind of identification or signature vibe that people use to indicate they belong to certain clubs or organizations?"

She thought about that for a moment. "I don't know. Maybe. I'm good with psi-locks but I'm not a crystal tuner. That's my sister's area of expertise."

"Don't worry, the FBPI will be able to crack the code. Once they do, they'll have a lead on whoever gave the pendant to the dead woman. With luck, that will provide a clue to the identity of the killer."

"Maybe, assuming she was murdered because of her connection to a cult."

"Even if there wasn't one, her associates will know something about her that will provide a lead. Someone always knows something."

Cheered by that thought, she tried to push the searing memory of the dead woman aside. Just another scene to add to her nightmares. Oliver was right. There was nothing more she could do. The murder investigation was in the hands of the Bureau.

She rezzed her senses a little to pick up the invigorating buzz of the tunnels and once again became aware of the faint trickle of energy seeping out of Oliver's pack.

She looked at him. "Why did you help me escape the raid tonight?"

He was unfazed by the question. "Maybe I'm a nice guy?"

"It's a possibility," she allowed. "But there is another one."

"Such as?"

"You knew I was going to authenticate the submissions tonight. Maybe you decided to use me as an unpaid antiquities consultant to verify the authenticity of the box before you took the risk of stealing it. Later you felt obligated to get me away from the raid."

"That would have been a sharp move on my part. But as it happens, I didn't need your expert opinion. I knew the box was authentic."

"I see." She realized she believed him. He would not have left the question of the authenticity of the box to chance, not when he had planned out so many other details of what he was pleased to call a repo job.

"Are you always this suspicious?" Oliver asked. He sounded intrigued, not wary or offended. Just curious.

Her jaw tightened. "It wouldn't be the first time someone has used me to get what they wanted."

"I sense bitterness."

"The incident happened quite recently, so yes, I'm still pissed. Enough about me. You said you're going to return the box to its rightful owner, a private museum. That means it will once again disappear into a vault, perhaps never to be seen again by the public or academics who would give a great deal to examine it."

"The private museum is maintained by a foundation that has a long history of paranormal research. Qualified members of the staff are free to examine the collection."

"What about qualified outsiders?"

"Like you?"

"Yes."

"Sometimes. Under strict supervision."

"I know how to handle artifacts like this one," she said.

"You do realize there may be a reason it's called Pandora's box?"

"The story of Pandora's box is just an ancient Old World myth. Our artifact is definitely human engineered."

"*Our* artifact?"

She flushed. "You know what I meant."

"Why didn't you open it tonight when you were onstage?"

"Because I was furious at the Society for imprisoning the dust bunnies and annoyed by that gallery full of illegally acquired artifacts. I had done what I was sent there to do. I had authenticated the artifacts. I saw no reason to unlock the box for the Society."

Oliver nodded. "I thought that might be it. Understandable. Think you can unlock the box?"

"No problem. It's pretty sophisticated, but nothing I can't handle."

Oliver looked at her. She knew he was remembering how she had dealt with the quartz-tech security in the Society's lab. She got the feeling he was making a calculated decision.

"Okay, after what you've been through tonight, you deserve a look inside the box," he said. "Go ahead, open it."

She did not hesitate. Twisting around, she plucked the pack off the rear bench. The dust bunny chortled and bounced a little. She took that as encouragement.

She unzipped the pack and removed the artifact. Now that she had physical contact with the relic, she was much more aware of the energy whispering from it. She could not wait to examine the contents.

"Do you know what's inside?" she asked.

"There should be six human-engineered crystals in the box. All Old World tech."

"What were they created to do?"

"That's a more complicated story."

"Translation, you're not going to tell me."

"Open the box, Leona."

She got a ping that sent a flicker of awareness across her senses. He was telling her the truth, she decided, but there was something missing. She needed context. One thing was certain: whatever else was going on here, this was much more than a simple repo job. The box was important to him. This was personal.

A thousand questions sprang to mind but she decided to go with the subtle approach. "What, exactly, is this foundation you mentioned?"

"Let's discuss that some other time. It's not important tonight. Open the box."

So much for subtlety. It was not her strongest suit.

"You don't think I can open it, do you?"

"Do it."

She rezzed her senses, feeling her way into the psi-code. The lock had been installed by someone who had a real talent for the work. It should have been resistant to all but a high-tech quartz lock pick, one capable of jamming the paranormal frequencies. But she had a very high-rez talent.

She concentrated. It was a more complex lock than the one that had secured the Society's lab, but the basic principles of picking a psi-lock did not vary. Step one, locate the anchor frequency. Step two, flatline it.

There was no satisfying click or snick or snap when she neutralized the currents of the anchor, but the lid of the box popped open.

"You are very, very good," Oliver said softly.

There was sincere respect in the words, she realized. His professional admiration warmed her for some reason.

She looked down at the contents of the box—and almost stopped breathing.

As Oliver had predicted, there were six lab-grown crystals inside. Each was round—a couple of inches in diameter—and faceted. Each stone rested in a velvet-lined pocket. They were arranged in two rows.

The crystals were all highly polished and charged with heavily locked power. She knew intuitively it would not be easy to release the energy in the objects.

But as intriguing as the six crystals were, they were not what made her catch her breath. A fresh jolt of adrenaline flooded her veins and briefly sent her senses spinning into stunned chaos.

Oliver glanced into the box and frowned. "There's a seventh crystal?"

Leona pulled her scattered senses together. She could not allow him to see just how shaken she was. Priorities. "Yes. I gather you were not anticipating that."

"No." Oliver went back to his driving. "I wasn't. This is . . . interesting."

"Yes, it is," Leona said faintly.

The seventh stone looked out of place in the box. It was palm-sized and cut in the shape of a pyramid. There was no special pocket for it. Instead, it sat alone between the two rows of round crystals as if someone had tucked it inside for safekeeping because there was no other place to put it. Or maybe no other place to conceal it.

She could sense the power in the pyramid but it was secured with an unusually elaborate psi-code. Given time, she could flatline the lock, but that was not what fascinated her. What mattered was that she could feel a faint whisper of energy from the yellow crystal she wore beneath the bodice of her evening gown. The pendant was resonating with the pyramid.

She had no clue what that might mean, but one thing was crystal clear—the pyramid was a direct link to the Griffin Family Secret, the dangerous secret that she and Molly and their parents had vowed to conceal.

This changed everything. She could not let the crystal pyramid vanish back into the vault of a mysterious private museum.

CHAPTER FIVE

She realized that the dust bunny had gone very still on the rear bench and was now gazing into the box with an intent air.

Oliver took another look at the pyramid. If anything, he looked more riveted than the dust bunny. "What do you think? Old World like the other crystals in the box?"

She had to stay cool and collected. The last thing she wanted to do was let him see that she was desperate to get her hands on the pyramid.

"Yes," she said, leaning into her well-honed academic-expert persona. "Definitely Old World. Also, lab-engineered like the others."

"Tuned?"

"Oh, yes." She cleared her throat and stuck to her cool, professional-interest-only image. "Any idea of the purpose of the crystals in this box?"

"The archives are not entirely clear about that, but all things considered, it would be best to assume they are potentially dangerous."

He was not lying, she decided, but he was definitely finessing his answer. He knew a lot more about the purpose of the six round crystals than he was saying.

"I agree," she said.

"Can you unlock them?" he asked.

"Yes, but it would be stupid to do so outside of a properly equipped lab." She gave Oliver a stern look. "This artifact should be turned over to the FBPI."

"I'll make a note of your thoughts on that subject." Oliver checked the rearview mirror and pressed harder on the accelerator. "Meanwhile, we've got other problems."

"What?" Startled, she twisted around on the bench. A sled was closing the distance between the two vehicles. There were two men on board. One was at the wheel. The other had a high-powered flamer, the type that law enforcement carried in the Underworld, where mag-rez weapons did not function. "Let me guess. Those are not some of your FBPI pals."

"No. They aren't." Oliver slowed for a corner and then stomped hard on the accelerator. "Those are a couple of the Society's private security goons. Ex-Guild, probably. How in green hell did they track us? I swept the sled for tracking devices. It's clean."

The dust bunny chortled excitedly. She lost interest in Pandora's box and bounded forward and up onto the dashboard, evidently trying for a better view. She was clearly thrilled.

"What about the artifact?" Leona studied the box. "Maybe it was tagged with a locator code."

"It was, but I neutralized it when I took it out of the display case. It's clean, too." Oliver sped around another turn and shot a speculative glance at the dust bunny. "It's got to be something I didn't have a chance to check."

"Not the dust bunny," Leona protested, overcome with a ridiculous need to defend the creature. "Don't throw her off the sled. She'll get hurt."

"Not the dust bunny," Oliver said grimly. "The crystal dildo."

Leona set Pandora's box on the floor of the sled behind the front bench and scrambled to dig the small sculpture out of her evening bag. She held it in her palm and opened her senses. "Oh, shit. You're right."

"Get rid of it," Oliver said.

She flung the sculpture out of the sled. The dust bunny did not seem to mind that her souvenir gift had been discarded. She chortled exuberantly, evidently considering the chase a great game.

Leona watched the crystal bounce on the tunnel floor. The oncoming sled did not pause.

"They didn't slow down to pick up the artifact," she reported. "They've got visual contact, though."

"As long as they can see us, they can follow us," Oliver said. "We need a distraction, anything that will buy us a little time so that we can get out of visual range. According to the locator, there's a rotunda up ahead. If we can get far enough ahead of those guys in the sled, we can turn in to one of the branching tunnels without them seeing us."

The passenger in the pursuing sled raised the big flamer and fired twice. The jets of fire fell short, but just barely.

"They're serious," Oliver said. "Any chance you know how to use a flamer?"

"Sure. Griffin women can take care of themselves. But I had to leave mine behind tonight. It didn't fit into my evening bag. Got one on board?"

Oliver smiled. "In the console."

She opened the cabinet and retrieved the flamer.

The weapons were simple amber-based firearms that produced bolts of fire. They had an extremely limited range—power and accuracy diminished rapidly over distance in the Underworld because of the heavy paranormal atmosphere—but when set on the highest level and used at close range, they could be lethal.

"Buy me a little time," Oliver said. "I just need a few minutes to get us out of this tunnel and out of visual range."

"I understand."

She hiked up her skirts and swung her legs around on the bench so that she was facing the pursuing sled. She checked the flamer charge, aimed, and rezzed the trigger. The jet of fire fell short of its target, but the other sled dropped back a little.

The dust bunny chortled.

"Right," Oliver said approvingly. "Like that."

The enforcer in the passenger seat of the other sled fired a couple more shots. She replied with two of her own.

"I can keep them at a distance as long as I've got a charge," she said, "but this flamer is sort of dinky. It isn't going to last long."

"Dinky?" Oliver sounded offended. "That is a top-of-the-line, customized Igniter, Model 240 Compact."

"Petite? Smallish? Like I said, dinky. Forget it—my point is, do you have another one?"

"No."

"That's unfortunate, because I've got a feeling the guys following us have a couple of backup pieces."

"Next time, bring one of your own."

"I'll do that. Meanwhile, I've got an idea."

She set the flamer down, reached behind her back, and unzipped the bloodstained gown.

"What are you doing?" Oliver asked as she peeled off the long sleeves and lowered the bodice of the dress.

"We need more firepower. I'm going to create some. I hope."

She stood and shimmied out of the gown, leaving herself clad in panties, bra, and heels. When she was free of the yards of fabric, she picked up the flamer and fired a short burst of flame at the hem of the gown.

The delicate material caught fire immediately. Driven by the thick currents of energy in the tunnels, the flames leaped high—a lot higher than she had anticipated.

Fire was one of the elemental forces. That meant it traveled across the normal spectrum and into the paranormal end. She was suddenly holding a torch.

"Shit," she yelped.

Frantically she hurled the burning dress out of the sled, seized the flamer again, and fired two more shots into the blazing fabric as it fell to the ground.

The thick psi flowing through the tunnels did the rest. Fed by the intense energy, the flaming dress exploded into a full-blown firestorm between the two sleds. It would not last long, but while it burned, it was an impassable barrier.

There was a lot of yelling and some furious shouts from the pair in the pursuing sled. The driver stomped on the brakes to avoid plowing into the firestorm, but it was too late. Detecting fresh fuel, the ravenous flames surged around the vehicle.

Leona watched through the wall of fire as the two enforcers leaped off the back of the sled's platform, barely escaping the conflagration. Screams that sounded a lot like *Fuck you* and similar farewells could be heard, but they were muffled and distorted by the atmosphere and the roaring flames.

The dust bunny chortled enthusiastically. She bounced down from the dashboard and bounded onto the rear seat to get a better view of the fire. She was obviously buzzed on dust bunny adrenaline.

She was not the only one flying high. Oliver slapped the steering wheel with one hand and whooped with laughter.

"That was *brilliant*," he said. "I gotta tell you, my evenings aren't usually this exciting. We should do this more often."

Leona was suddenly very aware of the breeze created by the moving sled. She was almost naked.

"Easy for you to say," she muttered. "You're not the one who will have to walk home through the Dark Zone in her underwear."

He glanced at her. Heat flashed in his eyes. He quickly returned his attention to his driving.

"Sorry about the dress," he said.

"I would have burned it anyway. Not like I was ever going to wear it again. The bloodstains."

"Right." With an easy motion, he shrugged out of his jacket and handed it to her. "Here, take it. You're not very tall. I think it will give you plenty of coverage."

"Thanks."

He paused, taking a closer look at her chest. Offended and disappointed—for some reason she had not expected him to be the leering type—she held his coat in front of her to shield her breasts.

Evidently aware of how she had interpreted the situation, he flushed and turned back to his driving. "Sorry. I just noticed that crystal you're wearing. It looks like the same kind of stone as the yellow pyramid in the box."

Oh. Right. The crystal.

Naturally he had noticed her pendant now that the bodice of the gown no longer concealed it. He hadn't been interested in her breasts. That was a good thing, she told herself. So why was she feeling just a tad deflated?

She got a belated ping from her intuition alerting her that it was probably not good that he had leaped to the conclusion that her pendant was the same type of crystal as the pyramid. The situation would get even more complicated if he realized the two stones had resonated.

"Yellow is not a rare color when it comes to crystals," she said, striving for a dismissive tone.

"That particular shade of deep golden yellow is uncommon. It makes me think of whiskey. What do you know about the stone you're wearing?"

He sounded far too curious. The fine hair on the back of her neck stirred. She needed to tread cautiously.

"My sister, Molly, found a couple of them when she was a little girl. She grew up with a talent for tuning crystals, so eventually she tuned a stone for each of us. It's a sisterhood thing."

"Can you focus through them?"

"Well, yes, because Molly tuned them. But they're no more accurate than standard nav amber."

Okay, that was not the whole truth, but she was not about to spill the Griffin Family Secret to an antiquities thief. Yes, he had saved her from getting swept up in the raid, but that didn't change the fact that he was a stranger—unknown and potentially dangerous. He had his own agenda.

She did not want to give him any reason to think that she might be standing in the way of his priorities, because she was pretty sure he was the kind who kept moving forward until he reached his objective. She knew the type. She had a similar streak of stubbornness.

Oliver was no longer looking at the yellow crystal, so she took the opportunity to slip into his jacket and pull it snugly around herself. The garment was warm from the heat of his body and it carried an intriguing hint of his very masculine scent. Her senses were already spiking because of the adrenaline overload and the Underworld buzz, but the coat added another layer of stimulation. She searched for a word to describe the unfamiliar sensation she was experiencing. She came up with *thrilled*.

Ridiculous.

They drove into the rotunda. Oliver whipped the sled down one of a dozen hallways and checked the dashboard locator.

"All good," he said. "We didn't even lose much time. It's way past midnight, Amberella, but I'll have you home before dawn."

She blew out a sigh of relief and suddenly remembered the artifact.

She glanced down and saw that Pandora's box was right where she had put it, on the floor of the sled. The lid, evidently jarred from the motion of the vehicle, had fallen closed. Once the artifact disappeared back into a private collection, she was highly unlikely to come in contact with it again.

Oliver was her only link to the private museum that had hired him to recover the relic. She had to start talking. Fast.

"It occurs to me," she said, "that your client has every reason to be grateful to me."

Oliver's mouth twitched at the corner. Definitely his tell, she decided. He knew she was about to bargain for something and he was willing to play the game—probably because it amused him.

She gave him a very bright smile. "Do you think you could convince the director of that private museum to allow me to examine the crystal at some point in the near future?"

"Maybe." His mouth twitched again. "I'm the director."

That stopped her cold for a beat. "I thought you said you were a recovery agent."

"In my case, recovering artifacts for the museum is part of my job description."

She narrowed her eyes. "I think you owe me a little more information about this so-called private museum."

"Such as?"

She drummed the fingers of one hand on the bench. "Does it have a name?"

"Sure. The Rancourt Museum."

"Never heard of it." She frowned. "Rancourt is your name."

"You could say the museum is one of the family businesses. A Rancourt has served as director since it was established on the Old World. In those days it was officially part of what was then called the Foundation, a front for a government entity named the Agency for the Study of Atypical

Phenomena. But here on Harmony it went private and became the Foundation for the Study of Atypical Phenomena."

"I've never heard of that, either."

"The Rancourts and the Foundation prefer to keep a low profile."

"Obviously." She considered how to proceed. "So you're in charge of the museum?"

"I am."

"Will you do me the professional courtesy of allowing me to examine the pyramid at some point in the near future?"

"I think that can be arranged." Oliver slid her a quick, searching look. "I get the impression your interest is not just academic. Sounds personal."

She hesitated and then decided to go with a bit more of the truth. "You're right. The pyramid does appear to be made out of the same type of crystal as the ones my sister and I wear. Neither of us has ever come across any similar stones. Naturally I'm curious to take a closer look at the one in Pandora's box."

"I'll make arrangements."

"Thank you. I appreciate it."

"But it will be a while before that can happen."

She narrowed her eyes. "Why am I not surprised that there's a but?"

His jaw tightened. "I'm not trying to wriggle out of our agreement. The problem is that I've got another priority at the moment. I'm not sure how long it will take to sort this other situation. A few days, with luck."

"Uh-huh."

"I give you my word I'll get you into the Rancourt Museum so that you can examine the crystal."

"Okay."

"You aren't a very trusting person, are you?"

"Depends on who I'm expected to trust. Let's face it, I've only known you for a few hours."

"You have my word on this."

"Okay."

Maybe he intended to vanish from her life five minutes after he left her in the Dark Zone, but there was not much she could do about it. She could only hope he would come through for her.

Oliver checked the locator again. "We're in luck. Looks like there's a hole-in-the-wall very close to your loft."

She glanced at the coordinates. "I know it. It's in the basement of an abandoned warehouse. You can just drop me off at the exit point."

"I'll see you home."

"That's very thoughtful of you, but I'll be fine. I know the neighborhood."

"I said I'll see you home."

It was clear he had made the decision and there was no point arguing about it. He was a man on a mission. For a time tonight she had become entangled in that mission, so he had made the decision to get her out of what was going to be a very messy situation—probably so that she would not blab to the press or the cops about his own involvement with the raid, the FBPI, and the missing artifact. In other words, he had whisked her away from the scene to keep her quiet.

That raised an interesting question, one that ought to worry her a lot more than whether or not Oliver Rancourt was going to disappear from her life.

"I wonder how Hollister's public relations department will handle the media after the news of the raid breaks," she said. "It's bound to get a bit sticky when word gets out that the endowment fund was taking huge donations from an organization that was the target of a stolen antiquities raid."

"Not your problem," Oliver said. "The university authorities will want to do everything they can to keep their involvement with the Society hushed up."

"Oh, yeah."

"Trust me, your boss and everyone else will do their best to make any evidence of a connection disappear. They definitely won't want their star para-archaeologist linked to the story."

"I told you, my status as a star is temporary, but you're right. The last thing Morty will want to do is admit that a member of the staff participated in a ceremony intended to validate stolen antiquities."

"Morty?"

She winced. "Dr. Morton Bullinger, head of the Department of Para-Archaeology."

"Right. Morty. He will definitely have to protect you in order to protect himself and the university."

She slanted him an assessing look. "What about you? Are you worried about your reputation as the director of the Rancourt Museum?"

"No one who can do any damage recognized me at the reception," he said.

Absolute confidence resonated in his voice. He was very sure of his talent for going unnoticed, she realized.

"Except me," she said dryly.

He gave that a moment's thought, as if he had just now realized she knew some of his secrets and might be a liability.

"Except you," he said. "Are you planning to tell Morty or the media that I was at the reception tonight?"

His cool tone sent a shiver across her nerves.

"Of course not," she said quickly.

"Good," he said. "I appreciate that."

She was not sure how to take his words. Perhaps he had been lying to her all along. That would certainly explain why she had never heard of the Rancourt Museum or the Foundation. Maybe they didn't exist. For all she knew, Oliver was precisely what she had assumed him to be at the start—a professional antiquities thief. That did not rule out the possibility that he occasionally did favors for the FBPI. Everyone knew that law enforcement often used shady characters for intelligence purposes.

Still, he had helped her escape what could have been a very unpleasant situation, one that had the potential to do a lot of damage to her own career. Getting arrested tonight would not have been a good look.

"Sounds like we have a deal," she said.

Oliver smiled, evidently satisfied. "It does, doesn't it?"

CHAPTER SIX

The dust bunny abruptly lost interest in the evening's adventures when the sled came to a halt at the hole-in-the-wall exit. Oliver watched her bound off the vehicle, chortle a cheery farewell, and vanish into the maze of tunnels.

"Looks like the party's over as far as she's concerned," he said.

Leona sighed. "I'm going to miss her."

He got a shock of knowing. *I'm going to miss you, Leona Griffin.*

He turned to look at her, trying to pin down exactly what he was experiencing. It was as if he had just turned a corner in the Underworld and walked into a kaleidoscope of sensations. He was getting hard. This was not a good time for that particular distraction.

Whatever was happening here wasn't just about the physical attraction, although there was plenty of that, at least on his side. She looked sexy as hell sitting there on the sled bench, his evening jacket draped around her shoulders, her gently rounded legs bare from her upper thighs all the way down to the high heels.

Her hair was the color of whiskey. It had been pinned up in a sleek, gleaming bun at the back of her neck for most of the evening, but now several tendrils had come free and danced around her ears. They framed her intelligent, watchful hazel eyes and her strong, feminine profile. He came from a family of strong women. He recognized the type on sight.

Whatever happened after tonight, one thing was clear: he would do whatever it took to see Leona again. The realization had been coalescing ever since it had dawned on him that she had *seen* him at the reception—really seen him. She had not dismissed him as just another face in the crowd even though he had used his talent to render himself socially invisible. She had sensed that he was not who he pretended to be. And she had concluded, quite rightly, that he was a potential threat.

Very few people sensed that threat. He did his best to camouflage it. *But you saw it, Leona Griffin. And you weren't afraid. I like that about you. I like it a lot.*

For a moment he wasn't sure why he liked knowing she could see him so clearly. Then it struck him that it was because he could relax when he was with her. He could drop the camouflage.

His initial reactions to her had been curiosity and fascination. There were a lot of layers beneath the surface of Leona Griffin, temporarily famous para-archaeologist.

Now he was way beyond curiosity and fascination. He was aware of an exhilarating anticipation. It was good to be in the company of a woman who saw more of the truth about him than most people did—risky, but good. Yes, they were wary of each other—each had an agenda—but they confronted each other as equals.

Reluctantly he got out of the sled, picked up Pandora's box, and inserted it into his day pack. Leona stepped down from the platform and joined him. She watched him sling the pack over his shoulder but she made no comment. Together they crossed to the ragged hole in the quartz wall.

"It isn't necessary to walk me home," she said.

"It is," he said. "For me."

She abandoned the attempt to dissuade him and moved into the rubble-strewn opening in the tunnel. He admired the way she navigated the chunks of quartz on the ground. It couldn't have been easy, not in the very high heels.

She led the way to a mag-steel vault door that sealed the entrance to the warehouse basement.

He was aware of the whisper of her briefly heightened energy field when she rezzed the lock. The sight of her enveloped in his jacket gave him an intoxicating rush. The very last thing he wanted to do tonight was take her home and leave her there while he went back to his boring, semi-furnished apartment.

"I'll give you the psi-code so you can use this gate to return to the sled," she said as the vault door swung open.

"Thanks." He decided not to mention that he could rezz the door with the lock pick. By offering up the code she had just given him a small measure of trust. He valued that too much to tell her he didn't need the gift.

They moved into darkness and the stale, faintly moldy smell of yet another old basement. He rezzed the flashlight on his phone and saw the stairs against the far wall.

They climbed the steps to the ground-level floor of an abandoned warehouse and crossed to another door. This one opened onto an alley filled with light, drifting fog.

He de-rezzed the flashlight. There was no need for the device now. The Dark Zone was built close to one of the eight massive walls that enclosed the ancient Dead City at the heart of Illusion Town. At night the neighborhood glowed with the green radiance infused into it by the ruins.

"Thank goodness for the fog," Leona said. "With luck, no one will see me in your coat."

"You're worried about the outfit? This is Illusion Town. No one will look twice at a woman wearing an evening jacket and high heels, not at this time of night."

"That might be true in some of the other zones, where the casinos and clubs are located. But the DZ is a neighborhood. My sister and I grew up here. My parents have a business here, and so does my sister. The locals know me. If one of them sees me dressed like this, walking back to my loft with a man who happens to be wearing the rest of this outfit, there will be gossip."

"I'm sorry about the jacket but it was the best I could do under the circumstances. You're the one who decided to burn the dress."

"True."

"It was a brilliant move, by the way."

"Thanks."

She walked briskly, he noticed. The tap-tap-tap of her heels on the pavement echoed in the night. She was eager to get home. Eager to get rid of him?

They reached the entrance of the alley and moved out onto the sidewalk.

"My place is just around the corner," Leona said.

She was almost trotting now. He lengthened his stride to keep up and wondered if he ought to be offended.

They had the sidewalk to themselves. Until they didn't.

A small cluster of cheerfully inebriated people spilled out of a narrow lane and into their path. They wore T-shirts emblazoned with the logo of a sports team and it was clear they were celebrating a win. Mugs of beer were raised on high as they half sang, half shouted a college song.

"On to victory, on to victory, we never stop and we never run . . ."

Leona came to a sudden halt. "Damn."

Oliver rezzed his senses, took her arm, and steered her around the small throng. "Just a bunch of kids from out of town. They aren't interested in us."

The small group went past, paying no attention to them.

"Thanks," Leona said. "That really is a handy little trick you've got there."

"It has its uses," he said.

He did not realize that he must have sounded grim until she shot him a quick, searching look.

"You don't seem too happy about it," she said.

"You know the old saying. *There's a dark side to every talent.*"

"What's the dark side to yours?"

"This isn't the time for that particular discussion."

"I understand."

That gave him pause. "Got a problem with your talent for picking psi-locks? Strikes me as a very convenient skill set."

She stopped in front of a door and gave him a cool smile. "As you pointed out, this isn't a good time to discuss the subject. If you'll give me your address, I'll make sure your coat gets returned to you."

"Keep the coat," he said. "I'll pick it up the next time I see you."

"When you invite me to the Rancourt Museum to examine the crystal? Excellent." She paused as if a thought had just struck her. "Do you live in Illusion Town?"

"I've got an apartment in the Emerald Zone. Close to work. The museum and the Foundation headquarters are located in the EZ."

Her eyes glinted with renewed suspicion. "I still find it hard to believe that I've never heard of the Rancourt Museum. Where, exactly, is it located in the Emerald Zone?"

He braced one hand against the doorframe and smiled a little. "Down below in the Underworld, of course. For security reasons."

"It's so easy to hide stuff in the tunnels."

"Even an entire museum."

"Apparently. Well, thanks, again, for the rescue tonight."

"Anytime. I'm going to be out of town for a few days."

"That priority you mentioned earlier."

"Right. But if you'll give me your phone number, I'll call when I return and we can set up a date."

"A date?" she repeated, as if the word were unfamiliar.

"For you to examine the pyramid crystal," he said, going for smooth.

"Right. A date."

She opened her evening bag and took out her phone. When they exchanged numbers, he got another little thrill. This made it all so much more real. He *was* going to see her again. Soon.

"Good night, Oliver," she said. She started to close the door and then paused. "Do you think you can find your way back to the warehouse and the hole-in-the-wall where you left the sled? The DZ can be a little confusing."

"No problem."

"Okay, then."

She closed the door gently in his face. He waited until he heard the bolt slide home and her footsteps on the stairs. Reluctantly he tightened his grip on the pack and headed back to the warehouse, savoring the energy-spiked fog.

He was going to see Leona again, but first he had a long, boring road trip ahead of him. Priorities.

Damn.

CHAPTER SEVEN

Leona reached the second floor, went down the hall, and rezzed the lock on the front door of her apartment. She let herself into the shadowed interior and stood quietly for a moment, absorbing the silence. She loved the spacious one-bedroom with its big windows and little balcony. There was a view of the massive green wall and the tops of the ethereal spires and towers of the Dead City.

She had enjoyed decorating the place to suit her personal taste for strong colors and sleek lines. Everything from the ocher walls to the jewel-toned area rugs and modern furniture was precisely as she wanted it. Yet for some reason, it seemed to be missing something tonight.

She stepped out of the high heels and went down the short hall to her bedroom. There was no need to rez the lights. The green glow of the ruins spilled softly through the windows.

When she slipped out of Oliver's jacket, she found herself reluctant to let go of it. For a moment she just stood there, gripping it in both hands while she tried to figure out why she did not want to hang it in the hall closet where she always hung guests' coats.

Her jumbled emotions made no sense. Okay, so she was attracted to him. So what? He certainly wasn't the first interesting man in her life. She was an adult, a well-educated, professional woman with a great career and a reasonably active personal life. She'd had her share of relationships—men were attracted to the idea of dating a self-declared free spirit. True, they usually changed their minds after they got to know her, so her relationships usually fizzled out fairly quickly. Still.

The exception was the recent fiasco with Matt Fullerton. Things hadn't fizzled at the end; they had exploded. She needed time to recover from the humiliating disaster. It had been unnerving to discover that she had allowed herself to be deceived by a creep who had used her to advance his own academic career while plotting to crush hers. She had vowed to never again date anyone else in the profession of para-archaeology.

It occurred to her that Oliver Rancourt was in that profession. At least he wasn't a colleague. She could modify the rule to accommodate an exception for museum directors.

She contemplated the jacket and wondered if an arrangement to view the pyramid stone at his museum constituted a real date.

She groaned and crossed the bedroom to hang the jacket in the walk-in closet—the closet she used—not the one out in the hall. When she was finished, she closed the door very firmly. Out of sight, out of mind. Except that she would see it every morning when she dressed for the day and every evening when she got ready for bed.

She skimmed off her underwear, took a shower, put on a nightgown and a robe, and headed for the kitchen. She needed a drink to help decompress.

She poured a restorative glass of brandy and went to stand at the wall of windows. The familiar sight of the glowing Dead City had a calming effect.

She was about to swallow some brandy when a shadowy silhouette appeared on the deck railing. Startled, she almost spilled her drink. At first she thought she was looking at a large night bird of some kind. But the creature hopped down to the deck and bustled to the glass door. There was a muffled chortle.

Delighted, she opened the door. The dust bunny fluttered inside and stopped, stood on her hind paws, and graciously offered an object that glowed faintly in the night.

"For me?" Leona whispered. She crouched and took the offering. "Thank you. I appreciate it. But this is probably going to cause a lot of trouble."

The dust bunny lost interest and fluttered around the loft, checking it out as if deciding whether or not to move in. Leona stood and went into the kitchen. She picked up a glass canister and shook it a little.

"I have some pretzels if you're interested," she said.

The dust bunny chortled again and bounded across the room and up onto the counter.

Leona took the top off the canister and poured some pretzels into a bowl. "Help yourself."

The dust bunny hovered over the bowl and surveyed the pretzels with an intent expression before making a decision. Selecting one, she munched enthusiastically and reached for another.

Leona sank down onto a dining stool, rezzed a light, and held up the gift to get a closer look. The pyramid crystal sparked with inner fire. She could feel the stone around her neck resonating in response.

"I wonder how long it will take Oliver Rancourt to discover that one of the crystals is missing from Pandora's box?" she said. "It will be interesting to see what he does when he finds out."

The dust bunny ate another pretzel, blissfully unconcerned. Leona smiled.

"I think it's time you got a name," she said.

CHAPTER EIGHT

Oliver waited until he was back in his apartment before he unzipped the pack and took out Pandora's box. The artifact gleamed in the light. Now that it was once again sealed, it was, to all appearances, a solid brick of high-tech opaque blue-green glass. There was no sign of a seam or a hinge, but he could pick up the vibe of the power locked inside.

He was proficient with locks—it was a useful skill in his line of work—but he did not have Leona's talent for flatlining sophisticated psi-locks. Few did. There were not a lot of people around who could have opened the artifact without a high-tech tool. It was not simply a matter of raw power. It required a certain delicacy and an intuitive sense of timing to identify the anchor frequency and neutralize it without triggering a potentially devastating rebound effect. In the end, power was useless without skill and control.

He set the box on a table and went into the kitchen to pour himself some whiskey. He took a long swallow, swirled the liquor in the glass, and returned to the table to contemplate the relic. The thought of the ease with which Leona had opened it made him smile. She was probably a double talent, he decided—a para-archaeologist and a locksmith.

Doubles usually tried to keep a low profile for good reasons. People reacted in unpredictable ways to others who possessed a single high-grade talent. Those reactions tended to range from unwholesome fascination to fear and distrust. Things could get downright weird when it came to doubles. Power in any form attracted some and repelled others. The stronger the power, the more forceful the reaction.

Triples, of course, alarmed everyone. They were assumed to be psychically unstable and often wound up spending most of their lives in locked para-psych wards or maximum security prisons. Many died young, often by suicide. The prevailing medical theory was that the human brain was not strong enough to handle the sensory overload that came with three paranormal talents.

But medical theories were subject to change, and there was another factor to consider. If doubles were inclined to be secretive about their para-psych profiles, it was logical to assume that a stable triple would be even more careful to stay under the medical and social psi-dar.

He took another swallow of the whiskey, set the glass down, and got the lock pick out of his pocket. The device was the latest and greatest in quartz technology, fresh out of the Foundation's R and D lab. It was still in beta testing, but according to Wilkins, the para-engineer in charge of the lab, it should be able to handle an Old World lock, even one that had been installed by a strong psychic talent.

It took a few tries and a bit of time—the quartz lock pick was not as fast as Leona—but the lid eventually opened on soundless, concealed hinges. The combined vibes of the six crystals inside hit his senses like a small hurricane.

Six crystals. Not seven.

The whiskey-yellow pyramid was missing.

He picked up his phone and called the newest entry on his list of contacts. Leona answered immediately.

"Obviously you were expecting my call," he said.

"I didn't steal the pyramid. Roxy took it while you and I weren't looking."

"Roxy?"

"The dust bunny and I agreed on a name. She showed up on my balcony after I got home and gave me the crystal. She thinks I ought to have it."

"We need to talk but not on the phone."

"I know, but you'll have to get in line tomorrow."

"What line?"

"I've got a busy day. It starts with an appointment with the head of the para-archaeology department. The news of the raid is already hitting the media. Morty Bullinger just texted that he wants to see me in his office first thing in the morning. After that I'll be joining my moms and my sister at a wedding boutique to choose mother-of-the-bride dresses. I believe I can fit you into my schedule around one o'clock."

"You can fit me in? I'm supposed to wait until tomorrow afternoon for the return of my stolen property? I thought I made it clear, I'm leaving town tomorrow."

"Which appointment would you prefer that I cancel? The one that directly impacts my career or the one that is absolutely essential to my sister's wedding? By the way, in case I haven't made it clear, this is a Covenant Marriage, not a Marriage of Convenience. Priorities, Mr. Rancourt."

"Well, shit."

"Thank you for your understanding. I'll call you when I'm free."

"Wait, whatever you do, don't let the dust bunny make off with the crystal again—"

The phone went dead.

CHAPTER NINE

That night she dreamed the old dream again.

"... *Molly didn't run away. Someone took her while I was on the swing. It's my fault. You have to find her ...*"

A low rumble brought Leona out of the nightmare. She woke up, nightgown damp with perspiration. Guilt and despair twisted through her. It was her fault Molly had been kidnapped that day at the orphanage. She should have been paying attention. They were *sisters*.

Maybe if she had been paying attention the day she and her colleagues had been grabbed by the pirates, she could have acted before they were all taken captive.

And maybe if she had gone down that hallway in the mansion five minutes earlier tonight, she could have saved the waiter ...

Another muttered rumble interrupted the searing, dream-enhanced memories. She turned her head and saw four eyes glowing in the shadows a few inches away. Roxy was hovering anxiously.

"It's okay," Leona said. "Just a dream."

Relief washed through her. She was not alone. That was a first. She was always alone when she woke up in the middle of the night. She did not do overnights. She was a free spirit and she had rules. But the rules applied to lovers, not dust bunnies. She sat up, reached for Roxy, and hugged her close. "Thanks for sticking around."

Roxy chortled and closed her hunting eyes, evidently satisfied that things were under control.

"I used to be able to take control of the dream," Leona explained. "For years, I rarely had it. But lately it's become a problem again. Probably stress. Maybe the moms are right. Maybe I do have some PTSD from the kidnapping. I seem to have forgotten how to rewrite the script with lucid dreaming."

Roxy mumbled encouragingly.

"You're a good listener," Leona said.

She had been dreaming the old dream almost every night since she and the others had been rescued a month earlier, but tonight's edition had been the most disturbing one yet. The guilt had been overwhelming. She had felt helpless to take control. And the nightmare had become even more harrowing. Tonight, it had included a dead woman, a lot of blood, and a knife.

She sat up on the side of the bed and glanced at the self-help book on the nightstand. She had purchased a copy of *Achieving Inner Resonance: A Guide to Finding Your Focus and Channeling Your True Potential* on impulse. It was highly rated on the rez-net. The author guaranteed success. Readers and talk show hosts raved about his techniques.

So far it wasn't working very well for her.

Perhaps she should reread chapter four, "Find Your Focus, Find Your Power." She had been feeling increasingly scattered lately. No surprise. She was awash in distractions, and distractions meant stress. The kidnapping, the breakup with Matt, the growing realization that the academic world might not offer the satisfying career she had hoped to create for herself—to say nothing of encountering a dead body and the discovery of a possible clue to the past tonight—added up to a massive amount of stressful distraction.

On top of all that, while she was happy that Molly had found joy with her future husband, it had brought home the realization that she herself was unlikely to ever know that kind of resonance with a partner.

"I need to regain my focus, Roxy."

Roxy chortled.

"I'll take that as agreement," Leona said.

She was about to reach for the book and rez the bedside reading lamp, but she paused when she became aware of the faint vibe of her pendant. She tugged the crystal out from under the top of her pajamas and looked at it. The stone was still resonating gently with the pyramid.

"I can't let go of it until I know why my crystal is responding," she whispered to Roxy.

An intense sense of possessiveness, of urgency, jolted through her. Now that the pyramid was in her possession, she was reluctant to give it back to Oliver Rancourt. Very reluctant. Sure, his claim to it might be stronger than hers—if he had told her the truth, he had the law on his side—but she really needed to know more about the pyramid.

"He promised to let me examine it but I don't know if I can trust him," she said to Roxy. "I'm certain his interest in the crystal is personal. He wasn't expecting it to be in the box but when he saw it, he got very fierce. Dangerous. I could tell he recognized it. He thinks it's important. The question is, why?"

Roxy chortled, unconcerned.

Leona got to her feet. With Roxy tucked under her arm, she padded, barefoot, to the walk-in closet, opened the door, stepped inside, and unlocked the small wall safe.

She extracted the black velvet pouch and undid the cord that secured it.

The pyramid crystal pulsed gently. She not only sensed the resonance but recognized it on some deep level. The longer it was in her possession, the more certain she was that it held the key to at least some of the secrets of the past.

"See, here's what's starting to bother me, Roxy. The more I think about this situation, the more I have to wonder if it was a genuine coincidence that a yellow crystal like the one Molly and I wear popped up in an artifact that I was supposed to authenticate tonight. I mean, what are the odds?"

Roxy chortled, evidently in agreement.

"Exactly. Molly and I need answers, and this pyramid is the first solid lead to come our way. That settles it—I can't let Rancourt take the pyramid. Not until I understand why it's important."

Chapter Ten

Melody Palantine leaned over the hotel room desk, planted both hands on the surface, and studied the locator screen. An exultant rush of relief and anticipation ignited her senses. The tracker psi-code she had succeeded in locking onto the Vortex key had been activated and was sending a strong signal.

That meant that Pandora's box had been opened and the pyramid was now resonating with another Vortex crystal. According to the readout on the screen, both stones were now at Leona Griffin's address.

Success.

Leona had not only made it out of the chaos of the FBPI raid, she had somehow managed to steal the box. That was amazing. It was also another unexpected twist in an evening full of them.

But at least one thing had gone right tonight.

For a devastating time she had been on the verge of succumbing to rage and despair. The beautiful, intricate spiderweb she had woven had been threatened by a couple of unforeseen events. It had been beyond infuriating. She had spent days on the elaborate strategy.

But the end goal had been achieved after all. She now had proof that Leona Griffin was the key to Vortex.

The next step was to lure her to Lost Creek. That shouldn't be too difficult. She would come up with a plan in the morning. She was good with plans.

Yes, things were finally back on the right track.

It just went to show that she truly did have an incredible talent for manipulating events. She should never have doubted her own abilities or her own power.

She lifted her palms off the desk, straightened, and shrugged out of her calf-length trench coat. Tossing the garment over the foot of the bed, she snagged the plastic liner out of the trash can and went down the hall to the bathroom.

The sight of the bloodstained caterer's uniform in the full-length mirror ignited another brief flash of rage. The last thing she had wanted to do at the reception was kill the woman. Dead bodies were always a potential problem. They attracted attention and raised questions. On the rare occasions when it was necessary to remove an individual who had become a problem, she almost always found a way to use someone else to do the job. But tonight she'd had no choice. The silly fool had tried to blackmail her.

Fortunately, that potential disaster had been handled. She had retrieved the pendant. The authorities would assume the dead woman had been involved in an artifact theft that had gone awry. No honor among thieves, et cetera, et cetera. Nevertheless, it was unnerving when an unanticipated event interfered in one of her elegantly designed strategies.

She peeled off the bloody shirt and trousers and stuffed them into a garbage bag. In the morning she would decide how to get rid of them. Yet another unscheduled twist in her grand strategy. She could have avoided the blood spatter problem if she had been able to use a mag-rez, but that had not been an option. She'd been obliged to use the only weapon available—a knife.

So messy. She hated messy.

If she were home in Frequency, she could have used her secret hole-in-the-wall to dispose of the bag of bloodstained clothing in the Underworld, where it would never be found. But this was Illusion Town, and she was in unfamiliar territory.

She showered and got into her pajamas and the robe with the hotel's logo on it. The extortion attempt had been a serious inconvenience, and Griffin's refusal to open Pandora's box for the audience had been deeply alarming. But the FBPI raid had been the last straw. She had barely managed to escape undetected. It had been a close call, and in the end it had required her to use her talent for hypnosis to make the Bureau agent look away.

Really, the entire evening had been hard on the nerves. She needed to center herself and regain her focus.

She took the newly purchased self-help book out of her suitcase. *Achieving Inner Resonance: A Guide to Finding Your Focus and Channeling Your True Potential* was getting five-star ratings all over the rez-net. She had some serious reservations about the author's techniques but she was determined to give the program a fair chance.

She turned to chapter six, "Opportunity Is a Flower That Blossoms in the Shadows."

She paused, doubts welling up immediately. In her experience, events that were concealed in the shadows usually brought disaster. Even a tiny glitch could destroy the most carefully constructed strategy. But according to the book, that was precisely the sort of rigid mindset that made it impossible to perceive opportunity concealed in the shadows.

She read the short chapter. When she had committed the new affirmation to memory, she set the book aside, de-rezzed the lights, and opened the blinds.

The hotel, one of a long line of glittering hotel-casino towers, was in the Amber Zone. She had requested a room that faced the glowing ruins. The Dead City gave her a visual focus, which, according to the book, made it easier to achieve inner focus.

I will put aside negative thoughts and focus on the positive aspects that will allow me to move forward. I will see the flower of opportunity that blossoms in the shadows.

The problem was that she had let the roller-coaster twists and turns of events tonight rattle her. Time to focus on the positive. The bones of the strategy were still in place. That was the important thing.

It was obvious now that, in the chaos of the raid, Leona Griffin had managed to steal the artifact. Although she had refused to open the box onstage, she had eventually done so, and the pyramid had resonated with another yellow crystal—almost certainly the one that Leona wore. She had recognized the significance of the pyramid. There was no other reason she would have risked her career—not to mention her life—by stealing such a high-profile artifact from a powerful organization like the Antiquarian Society.

No ordinary para-archaeologist could have pulled off such a daring heist and escaped the FBPI the way Leona had tonight. She had to be a high-level talent, maybe even a true triple. What's more, she was clearly stable.

"Like me," Melody whispered to the shadows.

She had been hiding her own multi-talent status since she had come into her psychic senses in her teens. The urge to lie low had been instinctive. A survival mechanism. No one trusted triples. They were assumed to be dangerous and, most likely, insane. But she was as stable as her notorious ancestor, Vincent Lee Vance.

Vance had failed in his quest to take control of the colonies, but she was going to succeed. She had inherited his talent and she was going to fulfill his unfinished destiny.

The key to the golden future she envisioned was Vortex, a machine that was capable of enhancing human paranormal talent. It was fundamentally Old World tech, and unfortunately there were still some flaws in the design—the version she had been working with currently produced highly unstable human monsters who either self-destructed or had to be destroyed. But she was convinced the basic theory was correct. Vincent Lee Vance had been living proof of that.

But now there had been another unexpected development, and the result was that she was at a possible turning point in the project. She had found the original version of the machine, the very one that Vance had used to transform himself into a powerful and *stable* multi-talent. There were answers to be had from the device, but she could not open it. She needed Leona Griffin to unlock Vortex.

Events had gotten chaotic for a while tonight, but all was well now. She could move forward with her plan.

Maybe the author of *Achieving Inner Resonance: A Guide to Finding Your Focus and Channeling Your True Potential* was right. It was just a matter of thinking positive.

CHAPTER ELEVEN

"You were *fired*?" Charlotte Griffin met Leona's eyes in the dressing room mirror. "I can't believe that. You're the university's star para-archaeologist."

"Turned out to be a temporary position, Mom," Leona said. "You know what they say about glory. Fades fast."

She had known that breaking the news to the family would not be easy. She was still reeling from the shock herself. Her day had started off on a depressing note when she had discovered that Roxy had disappeared at some point during the early-morning hours. There was no way to know if she would ever return.

The departure of the dust bunny had been followed by the devastating interview with the head of the para-archaeology department. Morton Bullinger had been weakly apologetic but he had claimed there was nothing he could do. The board of directors was in full damage-control panic mode, with the goal of severing any and all links to the Antiquarian Society. The FBPI raid had changed everything.

She had been given a cardboard box and thirty minutes to clean out her desk. A security guard had been sent to hustle her out of the building via the parking garage exit.

The doors of most of the offices that lined the hallway had been ajar. She had been aware of her colleagues watching her covertly as she did the academic perp walk. Some, like Drayton and Grant, who had shared the trauma of the kidnapping with her, had been sympathetic. Margery Bean, a friend, had cried. She had promised to call soon.

Others had been privately relieved that they were not the unfortunate individual being marched out of the building. One in particular was no doubt exultant: Leona was no longer standing in Matt Fullerton's way. He now had a clear path to tenured status.

The door at the end of the hall had been firmly closed. She had paused in front of it and reached for the door handle. The security guard had tried to stop her but he had changed his mind when he saw her mag-steel smile.

Matt Fullerton had been seated at his desk. He had looked up, first startled and then wary.

She kept her smile in place. "We had an arrangement, Matt, remember? We made a deal."

"What the fuck are you talking about?" He leaped to his feet. "This wasn't my fault. You can't blame me. I had nothing to do with—"

She had shut the door and continued on to the parking garage with her box and the escort. She had told herself that she had picked up a panicky vibe in Matt's energy field. As revenge went, making him nervous was not very satisfying, but she was realistic enough to know it was all she was going to get. It was time to move on. Her academic career was in smoking ruins but she had a new agenda. She had to find a way to maintain possession of the pyramid crystal until she learned its secrets, and she had to relaunch her career. Priorities.

This afternoon she would deal with the problem of persuading Oliver Rancourt to let her keep the yellow stone. The glimmer of a plan was taking shape in her mind, but Rancourt would not be easy to convince. She was sure he was as obsessed with the pyramid as she was. The question was, why?

But first things first. Her sister was getting married, and at the moment that was the number one priority. She and the rest of the family— Molly and the moms, Charlotte and Eugenie—were gathered in one of the spacious, elegantly furnished dressings rooms at the Amery Ames Wedding Salon.

She had waited to drop the news of her firing until the sales consultant had disappeared on a mission to find earrings to go with Charlotte's mother-of-the-bride gown.

Eugenie had already chosen her outfit—a stunning dark blue tuxedo that set off her mane of silver-blond hair. She had put up some token resistance but Charlotte had warned her that under no circumstances could a mother of the bride show up at her daughter's wedding in jeans, boots, and a lot of studded leather—Eugenie's go-to look.

Molly's crystal-beaded wedding gown, veil, and shoes had been selected at a previous appointment and were currently displayed on one side of the dressing room. Her dust bunny pal, Newton, had been packed off to spend the morning with the groom, Joshua Knight. Everyone had agreed that allowing Newton into the bridal salon would have been to invite disaster. No dust bunny would have been able to resist all the glitter and glamour. Gossamer veils, frothy fascinators, elbow-length gloves, and sparkling jewelry were artfully scattered across every available surface. It would have made for a dust bunny circus.

She had known Molly and the moms would be furious on her behalf.

That's what family was for. She took comfort from their sympathy, and under other circumstances she would have been happy to wallow in it for a time. But today she wanted to limit the drama as much as possible. This was supposed to be all about Molly and her upcoming Covenant Marriage wedding.

She and Molly were not biologically related but they had been sisters in all but blood from the beginning. Left on the front steps of the Inskip School for Orphan Girls when they were infants, they had spent the first six and a half years of their lives together in the orphanage before Molly had been kidnapped. That event had brought Charlotte and Eugenie Griffin, proprietors of Griffin Investigations (*Want answers? We'll get them for you. Call now. No waiting.*) into their lives. Charlotte and Eugenie had wound up adopting the girls, and that had proved to be a new beginning for all of them.

"They can't fire you," Eugenie snapped. She had been lounging in one of the plush chairs, her jean-clad legs extended out in front of her. Now she pushed herself to her feet, maternal outrage charging the atmosphere around her. "You're one of the heroes of the Hollister Expedition disaster. You kept your head and kept your team alive until you were rescued."

"The moms are right," Molly said, equally outraged. "You've brought nothing but good publicity to the Department of Para-Archaeology and the university. What possible reason could they have for letting you go?"

"I think the explanation involves covering several asses on the university's board of directors and the endowment fund," Leona said. "They're terrified of the potential fallout from the FBPI raid on the Society last night. If the media follows the money, it will discover that the university took huge donations from a secretive organization that just saw a whole bunch of its members arrested on charges of illegal artifact dealings."

Eugenie's jaw tightened. "If they think they can get away with blaming you for any part of that mess, they had better forget it."

"Damn right," Charlotte said, her eyes going cold. "This is Illusion Town. We've got connections."

"And Joshua is friends with the Guild boss, Gabriel Jones," Molly added. "Those sneaky, spineless creeps at the university will melt faster than chocolate in summer when they find themselves facing a few casino enforcers and some ghost hunters."

"Thanks, but believe it or not, figuring out my future career path is only number two on my to-do list." Leona braced herself to deliver the next bombshell. "There's one more thing I need to tell you about last night."

She gave them a brisk summary of her adventure with the mysterious Oliver Rancourt and the discovery of the yellow crystal inside the artifact known as Pandora's box.

There was a moment of stunned silence. The Griffin women looked at each other.

Leona cleared her throat. "I assume you see the problem."

"Oh, yeah." Molly touched her own yellow crystal pendant. "What are the odds that a rare stone like the one you and I wear just happened to turn up in one of the artifacts that you were supposed to authenticate at the reception?"

"That question occurred to me late last night after I had time to think," Leona said.

"Griffin Investigations doesn't believe in coincidences," Eugenie stated.

Charlotte took a deep breath. "I think I speak for all of us when I say we need a plan. We can't let Rancourt disappear with the crystal."

"We need background on Oliver Rancourt and this Foundation he claims to be associated with," Eugenie said. She took out her phone. "I'll get started on it right away."

Leona checked the time. "We've got about an hour before I'm scheduled to meet with him."

"Let's finish up here and go back to the office," Charlotte said, reaching for the zipper of her gown. "We need privacy."

She was interrupted by a muffled shriek of alarm from the other side of the dressing room door.

"Somebody stop them," a sales consultant shouted. "No, whatever you do, don't open that door."

It was too late. The door had been opened. Newton and Roxy raced into the room, chortling gleefully. They both stopped short at the sight of the tables piled high with sparkling accessories. Their bright blue eyes got brighter.

"*Newton.*" Molly leaped to her feet, seized Newton, and tucked him under her arm. "What are you doing here? You're supposed to be with Joshua."

"Roxy." Overjoyed, Leona leaned down and scooped up Roxy. "You came back. I was afraid you were gone for good."

"Oh, dear," the sales associate said, wringing her hands. "I'm afraid we can't allow animals in the salon."

Charlotte gave her a reassuring smile. "Don't worry. These are licensed emotional support dust bunnies."

CHAPTER TWELVE

Griffin Investigations was located on the second floor of a Colonial-era building in the Dark Zone, not far from the Dead City Wall. Leona and the others, including the dust bunnies, crowded into Charlotte's office.

The escape from the wedding salon had not been without incident. Somehow Roxy had acquired a souvenir. Charlotte had told the sales consultant to put the sparkly blue fascinator decorated with fluttering blue ribbons and a blue crystal butterfly on the bill. It had been evident that Roxy was not about to relinquish it.

Eugenie brought in a pot of strong coffee and poured it for the humans. She opened a couple of cans of Hot Quartz Cola for Roxy and Newton and then angled herself on the corner of Charlotte's desk. She took out her phone.

"Here's what I've got so far," she said. "Overall, the Rancourt family appears to be respectable and financially secure, but they have always kept a low profile."

Family was everything on Harmony, thanks to the First Generation colonists. After the closing of the Curtain, they had faced the knowledge that they had been cut off from the home world, possibly forever. With their high-tech machines crumbling around them, they had set out to establish the foundation of a society that would be able to hold itself together through the hard times they knew were coming. The experts—philosophers, scientists, psychiatrists, and religious leaders—had made the decision to shore up the family unit as the basic building block of the culture. They had reinforced the structure with every means at their disposal—the Constitution and the law as well as powerful social norms. The Covenant Marriage was the cornerstone. It was almost as indestructible as green quartz. Almost.

For those who were not ready to take the big step with a CM, there existed the far more casual Marriage of Convenience. Considered tacky and tawdry by many, the MC was little more than fancy packaging for an affair. Dissolving an MC required nothing more than filing the paperwork at the nearest courthouse. But a Covenant Marriage was supposed to be for life.

The results of the work of the First Generation were indisputable. The colonies had been pushed to the brink but they had stuck together and survived the tough challenges they had faced.

Now, after two hundred years, the descendants of the First Generation were thriving, but a lot of the old laws were still on the books and some of the rigid social and cultural attitudes continued to hold sway. A Covenant Marriage divorce was not only difficult to obtain—there were few legal grounds—it was hideously expensive.

But the real threat was the humiliation, scandal, and, not infrequently, financial disaster that inevitably ensued. Careers, friendships, and social connections were destroyed. So were the prospects for a second Covenant Marriage.

As insurance against the disaster of an unhappy CM, most people relied on matchmaking agencies—families insisted on it. But no system was perfect. In the end, two people who decided they simply could not live together generally opted to stay married but lead separate lives. The other option for getting out of a marriage while avoiding the legal, financial, and social perils was, of course, the convenient death of one of the two people involved. When a spouse died under suspicious circumstances, it was axiomatic that the first suspect was the surviving spouse.

"What else have you got on Rancourt?" Molly asked.

"Not that it's germane to the immediate problem," Eugenie said, "but he is not currently registered with a matchmaking agency."

Out of nowhere, Leona got a little ping of excitement. "Really? That's interesting."

Charlotte pinned her with a severe look. "Why?"

Leona waved one hand in a vague way. "Just another data point." She looked at Eugenie. "Go on."

"Evidently the Rancourt family's association with the Foundation for the Study of Atypical Phenomena dates back to the Old World. Here on Harmony the organization has a reputation for cutting-edge paranormal R and D. It takes mostly government contracts and much of its work is highly classified." Eugenie scrolled rapidly. "The Rancourt Museum is legit but it is not open to the public. Its primary objective is to support the research of the Foundation. Security is very tight."

"I'd really like to take a look at that collection," Leona said.

Eugenie lowered her phone and fixed her with a mom stare. "Speaking of interesting data points, I told you that Rancourt was not registered with a matchmaking agency. That much was true. What I didn't know until I talked to one of my contacts was that Oliver Rancourt was married in a Covenant Marriage ceremony."

Leona felt as if she had fallen into a very deep well. "I see." Then she rallied. "He *was* married? Widowed?"

Molly asked the question that had to be asked. "Divorced?"

"Neither," Eugenie said.

"Then, what——?" Leona asked.

"The marriage was annulled," Eugenie said quietly.

They all took a beat to absorb that news. Annulments happened but they were extremely rare.

"What were the grounds?" Charlotte asked.

"Unknown," Eugenie said. "The records were sealed by the court. That's standard practice because, legally speaking, the marriage was declared null and void. Technically, it never existed."

"Except, of course, it did," Molly pointed out.

Charlotte pursed her lips. "Annulments are difficult to get. There are very few grounds. Bigamy, age-of-consent issues, fraud, or failure to declare a complete para-psych profile."

Leona remembered Oliver's powerful energy field and the way he had slipped through the crowd as if he were invisible. "Probably the last one in Rancourt's case—failure to declare a complete para-psych profile. I got the impression he is a very high-grade talent."

Eugenie raised her brows. "There is one more reason for an annulment—failure to consummate the marriage."

Leona choked on the coffee she had just swallowed. *Did not even think of that possibility.*

She lowered the mug and considered the unmistakably sexual vibe she had picked up during her time with Oliver. She had been aware of a low, smoldering heat in the atmosphere between them that had thrilled her senses.

"Anything is possible, I suppose," she said. "But I doubt that failure to consummate the marriage was grounds for the annulment in Rancourt's case."

She did not realize she had sounded far too sure of herself until it dawned on her that the others were watching her with very intent expressions.

"Just idle speculation," she said quickly.

"Right," Charlotte said. "Idle speculation."

Molly smiled a superior, knowing smile, the sort of smile only a sister can pull off effectively. "It occurs to me that neither rule number one nor rule number two of the free spirit sisterhood was designed to cover annulments. We never even contemplated that option when we made the rules."

Leona was annoyed by the flush she knew was heating her face. She and Molly had established the rules for dating shortly after they had accepted the fact that they would probably never marry. Their status as orphans combined with the mystery of their births were serious impediments, but the real issue was their para-psych profiles. It was obvious that no matchmaking agency would take them on as clients, not if they were honest on the registration questionnaires.

The moms had pressured both of them to register with an agency and to lie when it came to questions about their profiles. *Everyone lies on those damned questionnaires,* Eugenie had assured them. *There's plenty of time to discuss that side of things in private with the person they select for you. Or not. Everyone is entitled to their secrets.*

The moms meant well, Leona thought. But early on, she and Molly had decided they would not marry unless they found potential spouses who could deal with the mysteries of their birth and their profiles. They knew the odds were stacked against them, so they had determined to live by their own rules.

Rule number one: Never date a married person or one who is registered with an agency.

Rule number two: No sleepovers. They were too risky. They had the power to turn a simple dating relationship into something more; the power to make a woman dream. A free spirit had to maintain some emotional distance for the sake of protecting her heart.

Leona retreated into her logical, academic place. "The rules do not apply to this situation. I am not contemplating an affair with Oliver Rancourt. In case you weren't paying attention, I'm pursuing a viable lead on the yellow crystals."

Molly's smile got a little more superior, a little more knowing. "Right. That certainly clarifies things. But promise me that when you find out for sure whether or not failure to consummate the marriage was the grounds for the annulment, you'll let me know."

Leona glared at her and then decided to rise above the taunt. "I think it's far more likely that the grounds were his para-psych profile. Whatever he is, he's strong." She made a show of checking her watch and got to her feet. "I should leave. I'm supposed to meet Rancourt early this afternoon. Before I go, is there anything new on the fallout from the FBPI raid?"

Eugenie glanced at her phone and shook her head. "Nope. Still no mention of the expert from Hollister University who was supposed to authenticate the membership submissions."

"What about the dead woman?"

"They have a name," Eugenie said. "Astrid Todd. She was new in town. Living at a low-rent motel in the Shadow Zone."

"What about the Vance cult pendant she was wearing?"

Eugenie shook her head. "No mention of it."

"The Bureau is probably keeping that piece of evidence out of the media," Charlotte said, "because it's something only the killer would know. That's common practice in a murder investigation."

"One more thing," Eugenie said. "I think I can guess what sort of talent Rancourt is."

She gave them her theory. There was a moment of silence.

Charlotte picked up a pen and tapped it lightly against the desktop. "That probably explains the annulment."

CHAPTER THIRTEEN

Oliver watched Leona cross the street and stride briskly toward the sidewalk café where he was waiting. This afternoon she was crisp and professional in a tailored suit with sharp shoulders, a nipped-in waist, and a knee-length skirt, which she paired with low heels. Her hair was once again in a severe bun. There was a messenger bag slung across her trim frame, a nod to her academic status. He had one like it, except larger.

The only thing that ruined the effect of woman-on-a-mission was the dust bunny tucked under her arm—a dust bunny wearing an outrageously frilly little blue hat.

He smiled, enjoying the daytime metamorphosis, and mentally cataloged the stages he had witnessed in the short time he had known Leona. Last night she had first appeared mysterious and aloof in the evening gown, her hair in an elegant knot. When he had found her hovering over a dead woman, her hands and dress stained red with blood, she had looked so fierce and determined that he had actually wondered for a beat if she was the murderer. But in the next second he realized that she had been trying to help the victim.

She had been badly rattled by the blood and gore but during the escape she had stripped to her underwear, grabbed a flamer, and slipped into the role of gutsy comrade in arms. Later, on the walk back to her apartment, she had looked incredibly sexy wearing his evening jacket and high heels, her hair tumbling free of the pins.

So many fascinating aspects to the woman. No question about it, she was definitely dangerous.

His senses stirred when he realized she had spotted him and was heading directly toward him. He was using a little talent, just enough to make sure he blended in with the crowd seated at the umbrella-shaded tables, but her eyes met his immediately.

He probably ought to be worried, not thrilled. He wasn't used to people seeing him—not the way Leona did. But she was different. Fascinating.

When she arrived at the table, he saw the steely expression in her eyes and knew something had shifted in their relationship—probably her agenda. He was pretty sure she was no longer willing to hand over the pyramid crystal in exchange for his promise to allow her to study it at a later time. She looked ready to put up a fight. He wondered what had happened to make her decide to dig in her heels.

"Sorry I'm late," she said, taking the chair across from him. "It's been a difficult day. Say hello to Roxy."

"Hello, Roxy," he said. "Nice to see you again." Roxy wriggled out of the crook of Leona's arm, bounced up onto the table, and chortled a greeting. He started to pat her on the head but stopped when he realized the silly hat was in the way.

"What's with the fancy headgear?" he asked.

"It's a fascinator," Leona said, sounding somewhat defensive. "You know, the kind of hat women often wear to weddings and summer garden parties."

"I see." He rezzed a little energy, just enough to get the waiter's attention. "Can I ask how Roxy ended up with a fascinator?"

"It's a souvenir," Leona said. Very cool and very firm now. "I told you, I had an appointment with my sister and my moms at a wedding salon. There were a lot of accessories lying around the dressing room and—"

"And Roxy stole a hat."

Leona narrowed her eyes. "She did not steal it. The moms had it added to the bill. It belongs to Roxy now. We figured out how to attach it to a stretchy headband so it would stay on, and my sister tuned the blue crystal butterfly in case it gets lost. Now, about the pyramid crystal."

"We can talk about it later."

The waiter appeared at the table with another cup and a pot of coffee. He glanced at Roxy. "I'm not sure it's legal to have a dust bunny at the table."

"She's an emotional support dust bunny," Leona said.

"But you might want to keep an eye on the silverware," Oliver added in low tones.

Leona shot him a quelling look and turned back to the waiter. "He's joking, of course. This dust bunny is licensed."

Roxy blinked her big blue eyes at the waiter, who, predictably, melted.

"Well, okay, I guess," he said. He turned back to the humans. "Can I get anything else for you?"

"We'll take one of those," Leona said, nodding at a counter that displayed a row of tiered serving trays filled with small sandwiches and an assortment of cookies and sweets. "I haven't had anything to eat since breakfast."

"Certainly," the waiter said.

He poured the coffee, plunked a tower of treats in the center of the table, and vanished.

Roxy studied the goodies on the various tiers the way small children study the packages under the Christmas tree. With great deliberation, she selected a lemon square.

Leona took a tiny sandwich and ate half of it in one bite. Oliver waited until she was munching before he spoke.

"You have a license for the dust bunny?" he said.

"About the pyramid crystal."

"First, let's discuss your difficult day," he said.

She brushed off her fingers and reached for another sandwich. "What about it?"

"I'd like a few details," he prompted.

"I got fired this morning."

"Shit."

"That's what I said." She took a bite of the second sandwich. "In hindsight, I suppose it shouldn't have been such a shock. The raid at the mansion is making big waves in the antiquities world. So far my name has not come up in any of the media coverage, but the university figures it's only a matter of time before word leaks out that a member of the Department of Para-Archaeology was on the scene. After that, it won't be long before some reporter discovers that the university received some extremely sizable donations from the Antiquarian Society. The decision to sever all connections with the organization was made early this morning in an emergency board meeting. I'm a connection."

"That is not right." He reached for one of the sandwiches. "I'm sorry to hear that."

"It isn't your fault. The university authorities are responsible for sending me into the line of fire. Let's focus here. About the crystal."

"Right." He ate half the sandwich. "Speaking of my pyramid, where is it?"

"Safe." She rezzed up a bright, shiny smile that was probably meant to be reassuring. "You didn't expect me to carry it through the streets of Illusion Town, did you?"

"Please don't tell me you left it in your apartment."

"Of course not."

Roxy selected a scone.

"Good choice," Oliver said. He did the same. "Where is the pyramid, Leona?"

She apparently concluded he was serious. She patted her messenger bag. "In here."

"In other words, you did carry it through the streets of Illusion Town."

"There's also a flamer inside my bag. The moms gave one to my sister and one to me when we moved out into our own apartments. Griffin women can take care of themselves."

"I don't doubt that." He slathered clotted cream on the scone. "All right, what's the ransom demand?"

"Information, Mr. Rancourt," she said. She was no longer smiling. "That is what I want."

"About?"

"I want to know everything you can tell me about the pyramid."

He considered the terms while he finished eating the scone and then picked up his coffee cup. "Why is the crystal so important to you?"

"Long story." She glanced around and then leaned forward and lowered her voice. "I'd rather not go into the details in a public place like this. Why are you so interested in the stone?"

"Long story, and I agree, this isn't the place for it. Let's find a more private location."

She eyed him with cool, calculating suspicion. "My parents did some background research on you."

"And?"

"As far as they can tell, you're who you claim to be: the director of the extremely private Rancourt Museum, which specializes in artifacts that have an Old World paranormal provenance."

He got a ping of intuition and suddenly knew her mothers had done more than just verify his employment status.

"I told you about my day job last night," he reminded her.

"They also checked out your ability to make yourself a ghost in a crowd. They think you're an illusion talent. Is that true?"

He told himself he shouldn't be surprised. He *wasn't* surprised, damn it. She had seen what he could do with his talent. He forced himself to lift one shoulder in an unconcerned shrug and drank some coffee.

"Runs in the family," he said, lowering the cup. "Usually shows up at least once in each generation. I'm the one who got stuck with it this time around."

Leona peered at him as if he were an unusual artifact. "How strong?"

He realized he was getting irritated. "That's a very personal question. I would like to point out that this is a business meeting. I'm not filling out a matchmaking agency questionnaire."

"Thought so." She nodded in a way that told him he had confirmed her conclusions about his talent. "You're strong. I assume that is the reason your marriage was annulled."

How in green hell had they veered off into the minefield subjects of his para-psych profile and the annulment? They were the last things he wanted to discuss. Neither topic was any of her business. There was something seriously wrong with the power dynamic in this relationship. He had protected her last night. She owed him, damn it. She had no right to sit there nibbling little tea sandwiches while she asked him extremely personal questions.

"Are you finished with your coffee?" he asked. "Let's get out of here."

She signaled the waiter before he could act. When the guy arrived at the table, she rezzed up a charming smile.

"We'll need a box for the rest of the items on the tea tray," she said. "The dust bunny and I are both still hungry."

So am I, Oliver thought. *And not just for scones and tea sandwiches.* No question about it, there was something seriously out of balance here. For some weird, inexplicable reason he was suddenly spoiling for a fight.

That made no sense. He never lost his temper. Okay, almost never. It took him another beat to figure out why he was overreacting to the extremely annoying woman on the other side of the table.

He wanted an excuse to get closer to her, to put his hands on her.

Chapter Fourteen

It was a short walk to a nearby park. Leona took the opportunity to analyze the mix of emotions that had burned in Oliver's eyes when she asked him about his talent and the annulment. It was obvious that he had some issues with his unusual paranormal profile. It had apparently affected his life in significant ways.

She understood. She had a few problems in that department herself. But she could not afford to let sympathy weaken her resolve. She was a woman on a mission.

They found a picnic table and sat down across from each other. She set the restaurant box containing the leftovers from the tea tray on the table and opened it. After a moment's consideration, Roxy chose the last lemon bar, chortled, and bustled off to explore the nearby water feature, a large pond.

Oliver used both hands to remove his black-framed glasses with a cool, deliberate motion. He dropped them into his shirt pocket and replaced them with a pair of sunglasses.

He angled his head in Roxy's direction. "Think the dust bunny will stick around?"

Maybe changing the subject was his way of trying to de-escalate the tension between them, Leona thought. If so, he got a couple of bonus points. She could de-escalate, too.

"I don't know," she said. "I hope so."

She heard some excited chortling and looked at the big pond. Roxy was perched on the rim. She was not alone. Two children, a boy and a girl who appeared to be about eight or nine years old, were in the process of placing a remote-controlled miniature boat in the water.

Leona suppressed an uneasy ping. It was just two kids, a dust bunny, and a toy boat. What could possibly go wrong?

She turned back to the restaurant box and chose one of the few remaining sandwiches.

Oliver helped himself to the last scone. "Roxy makes a handy little partner in crime."

"If that was meant to be amusing, it landed badly."

"That happens a lot with my jokes," he admitted.

She could no longer get a read on his eyes because of the dark glasses, but she was very aware of his energy field. The effect on her senses was as strong as it had been last night. That was both unsettling and intriguing. It stirred things inside her that had not been stirred in previous encounters with the male of the species.

Late last night as she lay awake in bed, she had told herself that her reaction to Oliver was due to the ambient energy in the atmosphere, first in the artifact-filled gallery and later in the psi-flooded tunnels. Everyone got a little buzz in the Underworld. Then, too, there was all that adrenaline pumping through her bloodstream. It made for a potent bio-cocktail.

But now they were outdoors in a public park, not in the tunnels, and no one was chasing them. Nevertheless, the frissons of deep awareness—of *recognition*—were as strong as they had been during the night.

Focus, woman. Your life is a hot mess at the moment. You can't afford to get distracted.

"We're here to exchange information," she said, determined to take charge of the conversation. "You go first. Tell me about the yellow crystal."

He munched, swallowed, and evidently made a decision.

"The most important data I have on that pyramid is what I learned last night," he said.

"What is that?"

"It's hot, it's tuned, and you can resonate with it."

She paused in mid-chew. "Sounds like I might be useful to you."

"Oh, yeah."

She thought about that while she swallowed the last of the sandwich.

"Look, I'm a professional para-archaeologist," she said. "My ability to resonate with certain crystals is a side effect of my core talent. I can't tune them like my sister does, but I can usually sense the energy locked inside."

"And unlock it?"

"Sometimes," she said smoothly. "I happen to have a crystal that appears to be the same kind of stone as the pyramid, so yes, I want to know more about both."

"Here's what I think. You know more than you're letting on. I assume you're not going to tell me that it was just an amazing coincidence the pyramid crystal turned up in Pandora's box on the very night you were scheduled to not only authenticate the box but open it for the Society?"

She flushed, Molly's words ringing in her ears. *What are the odds that a rare stone like the one you and I wear just happened to turn up in one of the artifacts that you were supposed to authenticate at the reception?*

"No, I don't think it was a coincidence," she said. "But I swear I have no idea what was going on last night, and neither does anyone else in my family."

That was nothing less than the truth.

He nodded, reluctantly accepting her denial. "Okay."

She narrowed her eyes. "I realize you don't trust me. The feeling is mutual."

"Because I'm an illusion talent? I get it. A lot of people have a problem with my kind of psychic vibe. They figure we're all con artists, magicians, or crooks."

"No," she shot back, annoyed. "My lack of trust has nothing to do with your talent. I'm being cautious because it's clear you're trying to tell me as little as possible about the pyramid. You're keeping secrets."

His mouth became a hard line. "What would you say if I told you it was for your own good?"

She rezzed up a cold smile. "I would say that's ghost shit."

"Figured you would." He folded his arms on the table. "I'm telling you the truth. Pandora's box belongs to the Rancourt Museum. It disappeared a few days ago. I contacted one of my connections in the artifact gray market."

"I'm not surprised to hear you dabble in that market."

"Name me a museum that doesn't."

She winced. "Fair point."

"I picked up the rumor that the box was going to be submitted by an anonymous collector who was applying for membership in the Antiquarian Society. I knew the FBPI had a task force investigating the Society and that it was getting ready to conduct a raid. I offered to assist the Bureau in a coordinated action. I knew the box would be one of the objects on that stage. I was as surprised as you were when it turned out the pyramid was inside."

She raised her chin. "Now you're telling me that it really was all a coincidence?"

"No," he said, "I don't think it was a coincidence, but like you, I don't know what is going on."

"Sounds like we both have questions and we both want answers," she said.

"Yes, it does. You said your sister found the crystals when she was a kid?"

"That's right."

"Tell me more about that."

She had known he would want details, so she had prepped for the question on the way to the café. She had a version of the truth ready to go.

"Molly and I were left on the doorstep of an orphanage. That's where we spent the first six and a half years of our lives. Then one day, when we were playing in the garden, Molly was grabbed by a deranged man named Nigel Willard. He was a chemist who evidently wanted to run some bizarre experiments on my sister. He took her down into the tunnels, where he had a lab. Thankfully Charlotte and Eugenie Griffin were able to rescue her before he could hurt her. While she was held prisoner, she saw some yellow crystals on a table and took two of them."

"Why?"

"She was just a little kid." Leona shrugged. "She was attracted to them. We didn't know it then, but she was a budding crystal talent."

"Are you and Molly biological sisters?"

"No, but we are sisters in every way that counts." She fixed him with her chilliest glare, daring him to deny the bond. "And we are the daughters of Eugenie and Charlotte Griffin."

"I understand," he said.

Maybe he did, she thought. Orphans and children born outside of marriage were protected by the law. They were cared for and usually adopted at some point. But their lack of close blood relatives and a respectable family tree inevitably affected their status in society—in subtle ways when it came to careers and social connections, and in not-so-subtle ways when it came to marriage.

"Can I ask how you and your sister wound up in an orphanage?" he said.

"The usual way," she said, once again prepared to skate on the surface of the facts. "We were abandoned as infants. We found out later that our birth mothers died soon after they left us at the Inskip School. There is no record that either of them was married and no next of kin. No one was able to identify our fathers."

His jaw tightened. "Tough road."

"Molly and I got lucky."

"Because the Griffins adopted you?"

"Yes. My turn. Why are you obsessed with the yellow crystal?"

"I am not *obsessed* with it."

"I disagree, but that's not important. Tell me more about it."

He gave the question a moment's thought and then he evidently made yet another decision.

"Ever heard of a Vortex machine?" he asked.

CHAPTER FIFTEEN

"What is a Vortex machine?" Leona asked.

"It would be more accurate to say Vortex machines—plural," Oliver said. "There have been several attempts to perfect the basic technology over the years. The first versions were introduced back on the Old World in the twentieth century as part of a secret government research program called the Bluestone Project. There were more upgrades in the twenty-first century. Someone among the First Gen colonists evidently managed to smuggle at least one through the Curtain."

"What are the machines designed to do?"

"Enhance human psychic talents."

She took a deep breath. "That kind of experimentation is seriously illegal."

Everyone knew that research carried out with the goal of enhancing the psychic senses was strictly prohibited because it was incredibly dangerous. The historical records were replete with cautionary tales of experiments that had invariably resulted in death or insanity. Humans were still adapting to the unpredictable effects of the paranormal environment on Harmony. Using technology or chemistry to speed up the process was unquestionably risky.

So yes, she repeated the common wisdom without any hesitation because she had practiced it since childhood. But inside she went ice-cold. She and Molly were the products of just such an illegal experiment.

"There are credible rumors that an individual or maybe a clandestine organization is attempting to engineer a new version of Vortex here on Harmony," Oliver continued.

"Did the old Vortex machines work?" she asked cautiously.

"Depends on your perspective."

She frowned. "What does that mean?"

"Evidently at least some of the various versions of Vortex have had some limited success. There has always been a theory that Vincent Lee Vance used a Vortex to turn himself into a triple."

She wasn't just cold now. It was getting hard to breathe. She stayed very still, desperately trying not to show any reaction. Thankfully, Oliver did not seem to notice that she was fighting off an anxiety attack. She had to make sure he remained oblivious. She had to protect the Griffin Family Secret.

"So, the Vortex technology worked," she said, leaning in to her detached academic voice. Just one professional chatting with another. "At least some of the time?"

"Yes, but according to the records in the Foundation archives, inevitably the test subjects proved unstable. If the process did not kill them outright, they deteriorated and went insane within weeks—sometimes days. If they did not take their own lives, they were tracked down and killed."

"Killed?" She stopped breathing altogether for a few horrible seconds. "They weren't locked up in a para-psych ward?"

"This was back on the Old World, remember? They didn't have hospitals or prisons designed to house people with dangerous talents. They didn't have the medications to treat para-psych instability, either. Society and the scientific community as a whole didn't take the paranormal seriously. Law enforcement wasn't equipped to deal with the monsters because they didn't believe they existed."

Monsters like Molly and me, Leona thought. Back on the Old World they would have been tracked down and destroyed. Here on Harmony they would be considered candidates for a locked ward in a para-psych hospital.

She needed answers but she had to be careful. Oliver Rancourt was looking more dangerous by the minute.

"How are the yellow crystals connected to the Vortex technology?" she asked.

"We don't know for certain," he said. "But the theory is that the crystals, when tuned, served as a source of power for the machine that was smuggled through the Curtain two hundred years ago, the one Vance may have used."

She started to touch the crystal pendant she wore beneath her jacket and quickly lowered her hand. "Are you telling me that I might be wearing a stone connected to an Old World device that was used to create monsters?"

"It was meant to enhance human psychic talents," Oliver said. "The monsters were what you might call unintended side effects."

A dose of fight-or-flight adrenaline rezzed her nerves. *Don't panic,* she thought. He was fishing in the dark, trying to find out how much she knew. *You know nothing.*

"I'm afraid I can't tell you anything about the yellow crystal I'm wearing except that it has sentimental value to me," she said.

"You said your sister found the two stones you wear in the location where she was held captive. Were there more of the crystals?"

"Yes, there was a small pile of them, she said. I'm sure the FBPI confiscated them as evidence when they investigated the scene. They found the kidnapper, Nigel Willard, but he was dead. That's about all I can tell you. Remember, Molly and I were just little girls at the time."

No need to mention that Eugenie and Charlotte had found Willard's journal when they rescued Molly. They had taken possession of it without bothering to mention it to the Bureau. The journal containing the Griffin Family Secret was stored in a concealed safe in the Underworld. It did not answer all the questions that she and Molly had about their past, but it answered more than enough to convince them that the contents had to be kept secret.

Oliver looked thoughtful. "I'll check the FBPI files and see if there's a record of the crystals being taken into evidence."

"You can do that? Check the FBPI files? Doesn't that require some sort of special clearance or something?"

"It requires connections. I've got a few."

"How convenient."

"Sometimes," Oliver said. Sunlight glinted ominously on his dark glasses. "Let's see what we've got. First, we have agreed it probably wasn't a coincidence that the pyramid crystal showed up inside Pandora's box last night."

"Agreed," she said reluctantly.

"Second, I assume you noticed that the news reports about the raid did not mention that the dead woman was wearing a pendant indicating she was a member of a Vance return cult."

"Yes, but one of my moms reminded me that law enforcement often holds back an important piece of evidence, something only the real killer might know about."

"That's true," Oliver said. "But that is not what happened in this case."

She swallowed hard. "You're sure?"

"I told you, I have connections. There was no Vance cult pendant on the body when it was found."

She tried to process that information but came up with nothing. "What do you think happened to it?"

"I think the killer went back after we left and grabbed it."

"Why take the risk of getting caught at the scene? There was a raid in progress. The FBPI was swarming through the mansion."

"There's only one reason why the killer would have taken the chance," Oliver said.

"The pendant was evidence that might have provided law enforcement with a lead."

"Yes. And speaking of coincidences, I did a quick background check on the dead woman after she was ID'd by the authorities this morning. Her name is Astrid Todd. Turns out that before she moved to Illusion Town a few weeks ago, she lived in a little community in the Mirage Mountains called Lost Creek."

"Never heard of it."

"I'm headed there today."

"Why?"

"That's where the coincidence thing comes in again," Oliver said. "I already had plans to drive to Lost Creek today. I made those arrangements before the reception. Before I knew Astrid Todd existed. Before she was murdered. Before the pyramid crystal popped up inside Pandora's box."

Leona got a frisson of knowing. "I think I see where you're going here."

"I'm going to Lost Creek. Want to come with me?" he asked, as if he had read her mind.

She stared at him. "You're *inviting* me?"

He smiled a slow, satisfied smile. "Don't tell me you weren't already thinking of heading there yourself."

"Why would I want to drive all the way to Lost Creek?" she asked, working very hard to sound innocent.

"You're as curious about the coincidences piling up around us as I am."

"Well, yes," she allowed.

"I can give you another one. There's an old legend that claims Vance's original headquarters was located in or around Lost Creek."

She absorbed that information and got another intuitive ping.

"I've never heard that," she said slowly. But it wasn't like she was an authority on Vance or the history of the rebellion that had nearly destroyed the colonies a hundred years earlier. Oliver, however, appeared to be very certain of what he was talking about.

He shrugged. "It's just one of a few dozen Vance myths that circulate on the rez-net. But, like I said, it's another interesting coincidence."

"Why were you originally planning to go to Lost Creek?" she asked.

"A collector obsessed with Vance memorabilia lives in the Lost Creek area. He contacted me a few days ago. Said he recently came across a file on the Bluestone Project."

"The Old World government program that produced the first Vortex machine?" she asked.

"Right. He claims the file is authentic. He'd heard I might be interested in it. He offered to sell it to the museum. We set up an appointment for me to view the document."

She blew out a breath. "You're right about the coincidences. They certainly are coming in hot."

"What do you say? Want to come with me? There's no point driving two separate cars to the Mirage Mountains. We'll take mine. We can talk on the way. Make plans for how we want to deal with our inquiries in Lost Creek."

"You really think there's something important to find there, don't you?"

"Yes," he said, "I do."

"It's an interesting idea," she allowed.

He checked his watch. "If we leave within the hour, we can be there early this evening. I've got reservations at the local inn."

Her heart rate picked up as understanding struck. She smiled slowly.

"This isn't about doing me any favors, is it?" she said. "You think I might be useful."

"And you think you might be able to use me," he said. "Our agendas are aligned, at least for the moment. We've both got questions about the pyramid crystal and all those coincidences. We are more likely to get answers if we coordinate and work together."

"Partners as long as the partnership is mutually beneficial," she said, tasting the concept.

"Exactly."

"All right. We have a deal."

He did not even try to hide his satisfaction. It was irritating that he had known she would not be able to resist his offer, but she refused to let that stand in the way. This was too important. It was about the past—Molly's and her own. There might be answers in Lost Creek.

She slipped off the bench and stood. "I need to go home and pack. Where shall I meet you?"

"I'll pick you up at your apartment in the DZ."

"I took public transportation to get here today. It will take me a while to get home."

"I'll drive you."

She raised her brows. "You really are in a hurry to get to Lost Creek, aren't you?"

"Yes," he said. "I've got that feeling you sometimes get in our work."

"The feeling that this is important."

"That one."

Shrieks of excitement and a lot of chortling interrupted her thoughts. She turned toward the large pond and saw that the two kids had launched the remote-controlled boat. The vessel was heading out across the pond, picking up speed.

Roxy was on board.

CHAPTER SIXTEEN

"This doesn't look good," Leona said.

She leaped to her feet and started toward the pond.

"I dunno." Oliver rose and fell into step beside her. "Looks like fun."

"Faster," the boy shouted. "Make it go faster."

"You know what Dad said," the girl warned. "If we crash it, we won't get another one."

"It's supposed to go fast. Here, give me the remote."

The boy grabbed the control box and rezzed one of the buttons. Out on the pond the boat picked up speed. Roxy was chortling madly now, clearly thrilled. The blue ribbons of the fascinator streamed out behind her like a banner. Her fur was plastered back by the breeze.

"Slow it down," the girl said. "It's going to hit the other side of the pond."

"Okay, okay." The boy did something to one of the controls. "It's stuck. It won't move."

"It's going to crash," the girl yelped. "Do something."

Leona watched, stunned. If the speeding boat smashed into the stone rim on the opposite side of the pond, Roxy would be injured, maybe even killed.

"Roxy," she shouted, "jump. *Jump!*"

The boy holding the control box had frozen.

"Dad is going to be so mad," the girl whispered.

"Roxy, jump," Leona called.

"Let me see that," Oliver said. He plucked the control box from the boy's unresisting hands and experimented with the buttons. "You're right. The throttle is stuck and the controls are not responding."

"The dust bunny is gonna crash into the wall along with the boat," the boy said, horrified. "And it's gonna be my fault."

"Roxy," Leona yelled again. "Jump. Please, jump."

Roxy chortled, rezzed on dust bunny adrenaline. She was evidently oblivious to the danger.

The whine of the yacht's little motor ceased abruptly. The vessel stopped with a jerky movement. Unprepared for the sudden deceleration, Roxy went overboard into the water. She surfaced immediately, still chortling. The fascinator was waterlogged but it was still approximately in place.

She swam to the edge of the pond and vaulted up out of the water, onto the stone rim. She gave herself a shake to fluff out her fur, and then bustled toward Leona.

"Thank heavens," Leona whispered.

She looked at Oliver. So did the youngsters.

"How did you stop it, sir?" the boy asked, impressed.

Oliver opened one hand and displayed the small amber batteries he had removed from the control box.

"Oh, yeah," the boy said. He looked at Oliver, eyes widening in admiration. "I should have thought of that."

Leona winced, chagrined. "I should have thought of it, too."

"In my experience, simple plans work best," Oliver said.

CHAPTER SEVENTEEN

Leona waited to call Charlotte and Eugenie until she was in her bedroom, throwing clothes and travel gear into a small suitcase. Her messenger bag with the pyramid crystal tucked inside was on the bed next to the open suitcase.

She put the phone on speaker, set it on the bedside table, and opened a drawer to grab some underwear.

"Good news," she said, setting the panties in the suitcase. "We've got a lead on the pyramid crystal."

"We?" Charlotte said.

"Oliver Rancourt traced the murdered woman to a town called Lost Creek in the Mirage Mountains. We are driving there this afternoon to see what we can find in the way of answers."

There was a short, sharp beat of silence.

"Let me get this straight," Eugenie said. "Are you telling us that you and Rancourt are working together on this project?"

"As he pointed out, our agendas are aligned," Leona said, trying to sound assured and determined. Professional.

"You hardly know the man," Charlotte said.

"I'm not dating him," Leona said. "We're temporary colleagues. He was already planning to go to Lost Creek to view an Old World document he wants to acquire for his museum. The only difference is that I'm going with him. Let's face it, it's not like I've got anything more pressing to do. I'm currently unemployed, remember?"

"Don't remind us," Eugenie said. "How is Rancourt going to explain your presence?"

"Relax, Mom. I'm going as his consultant, not his girlfriend. The plan is to tell the collector and anyone else who asks that I was hired to authenticate the document. There is absolutely nothing to worry about."

"A woman was murdered last night," Charlotte said.

"The FBPI and the cops are on that case," Leona said quickly. "Oliver and I are not involved. Our interest is in the pyramid crystal. We're not trying to solve a murder. Look, I've got to run. Long drive ahead. Oh, by the way, according to the maps, our mobile phones won't work once we're in the Mirage Mountains—too much energy in the area—but there's a landline at the inn where we'll be staying. I'll give you the number."

She read it off the screen of her phone.

"Got it," Eugenie said. "Listen, I know this trip is important to you, but I agree with Charlotte. I'm not at all sure this is a good idea."

"It's the only lead we've got," Leona said. "And I repeat, it's just a research trip. I do those all the time down in the tunnels."

"This is different," Charlotte insisted.

"Not really," Leona said. "And there's something else to consider. I'm thinking of setting myself up as a private antiquities consultant. Rancourt has agreed to let me list his museum as a client in any promo I decide to do. That will make for a good launch for my business."

"I seem to recall an old legend about Lost Creek," Charlotte said slowly. "Something to do with Vincent Lee Vance."

"Rancourt mentioned that." Leona reminded herself that the nights would probably be chilly in the mountains. She went back to the drawer to pick up her flannel pajamas. "Evidently the collector we're going to see specializes in Vincent Lee Vance and Era of Discord materials."

She turned to carry the pajamas to the suitcase but paused at the sight of the dainty pink vibrator in the drawer. Why was she even thinking about packing it? She definitely would not need it. This was a business trip, not a romantic getaway.

She shut the drawer very firmly and dropped the pajamas into the suitcase.

"I did a little more research on Rancourt," Eugenie said. "On the plus side, there's no indication that he's a serial killer."

"Good to know," Leona said. "A woman can't be too careful."

She studied the contents of the suitcase, wondering what she had forgotten. There was always something. She was accustomed to packing for an expedition into the Underworld—she had a checklist—but a road trip to the Mirage Mountains with a man who was very much a stranger was an entirely different matter.

"He's got a couple of advanced degrees—one in the history of the Era of Discord and another in para-archaeology. He is one of a handful of experts who specialize in Old World antiquities with a paranormal provenance. He's been involved with the Rancourt Museum for his entire career. On the surface he looks a little boring."

"I told you, he's harmless," Leona said. Mentally she crossed her fingers behind her back. Whatever else he was, Oliver Rancourt was not boring.

"He sounds like he may be the obsessive type when it comes to his work," Eugenie warned.

"Never met a museum director or a collector who wasn't," Leona said. "It's the nature of the beast. Some people would say I'm a little obsessive myself, when it comes to artifacts."

"True," Charlotte muttered.

Leona closed the suitcase and hoisted it off the bed. "Is that all you've got on him?"

"Yes," Eugenie said, "but keep in mind that there's an old saying about illusion talents. *They make very good criminals because you never see them coming.*"

"I will keep that in mind."

She stopped at the window and looked down. Oliver's sleek gray Slider was illegally parked in the narrow lane below. Roxy was perched on one gleaming fender. The fascinator, now limp and bedraggled but dry, was still on top of her furry head. The blue crystal butterfly sparkled in the sun.

Oliver lounged casually against the fender, his arms crossed, dark glasses concealing his eyes. She was too far away to pick up the vibe of his aura, and yet, just looking at him through the second-floor window, she was aware of his quiet, centered power.

Nope, not boring.

"Leona, please be careful," Charlotte said.

"Griffin women can take care of themselves."

"That reminds me," Eugenie said. "Don't forget to pack your flamer."

"It's in my messenger bag." She turned away from the window and grabbed the handle of the suitcase. "Don't worry, I know what I'm doing."

"That's what you said when you joined the Hollister Expedition," Charlotte pointed out.

Leona felt as if the breath had been knocked out of her. *Maybe if I had been paying more attention.*

"Everything turned out okay," she managed.

"No, everything did not turn out okay," Charlotte said. "You got kidnapped and very nearly killed. And that's not all that's happened recently. Your latest relationship just ended badly."

"They all end badly. I'm used to it."

Charlotte ignored her. "Last night you stumbled over a dead body and you almost got swept up in an FBPI raid. You were chased through the tunnels by a couple of very dangerous people. This morning you were fired from your job. This afternoon you're taking off with a man you barely know for a destination associated with the megalomaniac who tried to destroy the colonies. In case you haven't noticed, your life is turning into a mag-lev train wreck."

"She's got a point," Eugenie said. "You should probably be talking to a therapist, not going on a road trip with a stranger."

"A stranger who, you have assured me, is not a serial killer," Leona said.

"*Probably* not a serial killer," Charlotte clarified.

"I understand your concerns," Leona said. She pulled herself together, marshaling her arguments. She could do this. "But I have two very good reasons for the road trip to the Mirage Mountains. The first is that, if things go well, I can use it to start a résumé as a private consultant in the antiquities world."

"What's the other reason?" Eugenie said. "And please don't tell me it's because you've always wanted to visit the Mirage Mountains."

"Here's what I haven't had a chance to tell you," Leona said. "The other reason I'm taking this job is that Rancourt is convinced there's a connection between the yellow crystals and something he calls a Vortex machine."

A short, resounding silence greeted that statement.

"What," Eugenie asked, "is a Vortex machine?"

"Old World tech designed to enhance paranormal talents," Leona said.

"Oh, shit," Eugenie whispered.

"It may be a Vortex machine that was used to create Molly and me," Leona added.

"You were not created by a machine," Charlotte said, very fierce now. "You and Molly were born, just like everyone else."

"I know, but a Vortex machine may have been what was used to irradiate our birth mothers," Leona said. "Now do you understand why I have to follow up on the Lost Creek lead? I'm well aware that Rancourt is using me, but I'm using him. We both want answers. We need to work together, at least in the immediate future."

There was another poignant silence on the other end of the connection.

Eugenie sighed. "Well, at least we're pretty sure Rancourt is not a serial killer."

"There's that," Charlotte agreed.

"Right," Leona said. "Look on the positive side. *Opportunity is a flower that blossoms in the shadows.*"

"What in green hell does that mean?" Charlotte asked.

"I have no idea," Leona said. "I'm only halfway through chapter six. I had to go back and reread chapter four. Goodbye. Love you both."

"Love you," Charlotte said.

"Love you," Eugenie said. "Be careful."

"I will."

Leona ended the call before Charlotte and Eugenie could come up with any more arguments, and headed for the door of the bedroom with her suitcase and the messenger bag.

She stopped on the threshold and looked back at the copy of *Achieving Inner Resonance: A Guide to Finding Your Focus and Channeling Your True Potential.* Charlotte was right—her life was a train wreck. She needed to regain her focus.

She went to the bedside table, picked up the book, and dropped it inside the messenger bag.

Outside in the hall, she rezzed the lock and went downstairs. When she opened the lobby door and stepped out onto the narrow sidewalk, Oliver unfolded his arms, straightened, and came forward to take the suitcase. He held out a hand for the messenger bag. She tightened her grip on it.

"I'll hang on to this," she said.

He raised his brows. "The pyramid is still inside, I presume?"

"Yep."

He gave her a quick once-over, frowning a little, and then turned away to open the trunk.

"Everything okay?" he asked.

She thought about the mystery of his annulment, his obsession with the machine he called Vortex, his connection to a museum she had never heard of, and the fact that he had been able to steal an extremely valuable artifact from an organization that hired armed goons for security. Then she recalled Eugenie's warning about illusion talents: *They make very good criminals because you never see them coming.*

Yes, her agenda was aligned with Oliver's—for now. But that could change at any moment. If he decided she was no longer useful . . .

Okay, he probably wasn't a serial killer, but that didn't mean he wasn't dangerous.

Think positive.

"Everything's great," she said. "I spent some time on the phone talking to my moms. The good news is that you evidently passed the serial killer test. They're pretty sure you're not one."

"Good to know. A man likes to make a good impression on the parents." He opened the trunk. "What else are they worried about?"

She scooped up Roxy and slipped into the front seat. "They're afraid you are using me for unknown and possibly nefarious reasons."

"I see." He stashed the suitcase in the trunk, closed the lid, and walked back to the passenger door. He looked down at her through the open window, sunlight glinting on his dark glasses. "Were you able to reassure them?"

"Of course. I told them I was using you and that we had an understanding."

"So what we have here is a use-use relationship?"

She thought of the advice in chapter one of *Achieving Inner Resonance*: *Negative words generate negative outcomes. Build a positive vocabulary if you want to ensure a positive outcome.*

She rezzed up a bright smile. "Why don't we think of our association as a win-win relationship?"

"That works only if we both get what we want in Lost Creek."

CHAPTER EIGHTEEN

The manager of the Lost Creek Inn had introduced herself as Edith Fenwick. She was a robust middle-aged woman with a haircut that was several years out of style. She wore a plaid flannel shirt and jeans designed for comfort, not fashion. Roxy charmed her immediately.

"Aren't you just the cutest thing?" Edith chuckled. "I love that adorable little hat. I don't generally allow animals in the rooms but I think I can make an exception for an emotional support dust bunny."

"Thank you," Leona said.

Roxy was perched on the front desk, admiring a bowl of wrapped candies. She blinked her bright blue eyes a couple of times. Edith got the message. She picked up a foil-wrapped chocolate and offered it. Roxy took it with perfect manners and set about unwrapping it as if it were an impossibly expensive gift of gold amber.

Edith smiled and turned back to Leona and Oliver. "You two got lucky," she said. "You made it into town ahead of the big storm. It's due to hit later tonight. Now, will that be one room or two?"

"Two, please," Leona said before Oliver could reply.

He gave her a not-so-subtle *I'm in charge here* look and switched his attention to Edith. "We're in town on business," he said, adjusting his black-framed glasses. "I'm the director of the Rancourt Museum. Dr. Griffin is a consultant who specializes in authenticating objects with a paranormal provenance. We're here to examine an Old World journal in the collection of a local resident. Norton Thacker. Perhaps you know him?"

Edith snorted. "Everybody knows Thacker. Lives in the big house up in the woods. He's what folks like to call eccentric."

"Eccentric?" Oliver repeated.

"That's the polite term for it, I guess. If you ask me, the right word is *hoarder.*"

"I see," Oliver said. "I'm looking forward to viewing a document he wants to sell. I hope we haven't made this long trip for nothing."

Leona resisted the urge to lift her eyes to the ceiling. Somewhere between parking the car in the small lot in front of the inn and walking into the rustic lobby, Oliver had gone through a transformation. He was no longer the quietly competent, possibly dangerous man she had sat beside during the long drive from Illusion Town. Instead, with the aid of the glasses, a dark jacket and trousers, a button-down shirt, and a worn leather messenger bag, he was back in his nothing-to-see-here antiquities-expert persona.

"So, you two work for a museum?" Edith asked.

"To be clear," Oliver said, "I am the director of the museum. Dr. Griffin is currently employed by me."

"I'm an independent consultant," Leona said crisply.

"Yeah, well, whatever." Edith shrugged. "Makes a change. We don't get a lot of academic types here. Most of my guests are folks who take a wrong turn fifty miles back on the highway and get stuck here overnight. They don't hang around long."

"What about the other guests?" Leona asked. "The ones who come here on purpose?"

"You mean the Vance tourists." Edith snorted again. "We get a few of those, all right. Mostly in the summer, though, not this time of year."

"What's the definition of a Vance tourist?" Oliver asked.

Edith handed him a pen to sign the register. "There's an old story that claims Vincent Lee Vance used Lost Creek as his base of operations when he was firing up the rebellion."

Oliver made an illegible scrawl on the page. "It's not completely outside the realm of possibility. For decades historians have speculated that Vance recruited his early followers from somewhere in the Mirage Mountains."

"I've heard that," Edith said. "But as far as I know, the Vance tourists haven't ever found any proof that Lost Creek was his headquarters." She winked. "Except for the ghost, of course."

Leona smiled. "You've got a resident ghost here in Lost Creek?"

"They say Vance stayed right here in this inn. The tourists like to think he still haunts the place." Edith raised her brows in a sly manner. "I don't mind admitting I've made some money off that story. No harm in it. But to tell you the truth, I've operated this inn for over thirty years and I've never seen a ghost."

"Not surprising, since ghosts don't exist," Leona said.

"Do me a favor. Don't tell the Vance tourists." Edith leaned against the counter. "So, you're planning to buy some old document from Thacker, hmm? Word of advice. Be really careful when you go inside that old house."

"Why?" Leona asked.

"The place is crammed with junk. Folks around here figure he'll either get crushed when some of the stuff collapses on him or else the house will catch fire. Talk about a tinderbox."

"Serious collectors tend to become obsessed," Leona said.

"There's obsessed and then there's batshit crazy. My advice is to take a real close look at whatever Thacker wants to sell to you."

"Are you saying he might attempt to defraud us?" Oliver asked, gravely disapproving now.

"It's a lot more likely that he's the one who got taken," Edith said. "He'd buy an old chipped mug if you told him Vance drank a cup of coffee out of it."

"Does he come into town often?" Oliver asked.

"I don't think anyone has seen him outside of that creepy old house of his in years," Edith said. "If it weren't for Hester Harp, we'd have figured Thacker died a decade ago."

"Who is Hester Harp?" Leona asked.

"His housekeeper. She's the one who does his grocery shopping, picks up his mail, and pays his bills. The man would probably starve to death without her." Edith plucked two keys out of a drawer and handed them across the counter. "Here you go, rooms two-oh-three and two-oh-four on the second floor. Take a right at the top of the stairs. Breakfast is served from seven to eight. Coffee is on all day."

"Thanks," Oliver said.

"Any restaurant suggestions?" Leona asked. "We haven't had dinner."

"Can't do any better than the diner across the street," Edith said. "It's the only restaurant in town. Closes at eight."

"Good to know," Leona said.

Oliver picked up his suitcase and reached for hers.

"That's all right," she said. "I've got it."

"I'll take it," Oliver said.

Really? They were going to argue over who carried her suitcase? She thought about explaining that when she went into the Underworld, she always handled her own gear, but this did not seem to be the right moment for that conversation.

"Thank you," she managed, aware that she sounded grudgingly polite.

Oliver was already heading for the stairs. "You're welcome."

Stifling a sigh, she scooped Roxy off the counter and hurried after Oliver. The sight of the small amber-and-steel sculpture on a nearby table stopped her. It was a beautifully realized specter-cat. The artist had captured the power and elegance of the creature. The cat's amber eyes reminded her of Oliver—intelligent and dangerous. Everything about the predator was infused with control.

There was a small price tag attached. Curious, she picked up the cat and turned it over. The name *Stark* was engraved on the bottom.

She put the cat down. "I see this piece is for sale."

"Yep." Edith smiled. "Local artist. We don't have any fancy galleries in town so I let him put some of his work on display here at the inn. I sell a few pieces for him every season."

"I see," Leona said. She realized Oliver was already on the second-floor landing. "I'll take another look later."

"No rush," Edith said. "Not like we're overrun with outsiders looking to buy souvenirs right now."

"It's not a souvenir, it's a work of art."

"Whatever."

Leona abandoned the discussion and hurried up the stairs. She joined Oliver at the top and they started down the hall. The old floorboards squeaked and groaned beneath their feet.

"This inn definitely dates from Vance's time," she observed. "You can tell from the architecture."

"That doesn't mean he slept here."

"I know, but it's possible that he did," Leona said. "You can't blame the locals for leaning into the Vance ghost story. There's not much else here they can use to promote this town. It's not exactly a vacation paradise."

"No, it isn't."

"Actually, it's amazing anyone can even find this place. If we hadn't had those old-fashioned paper road maps, we'd still be driving around looking for the right turnoff."

"Something tells me the locals don't want to encourage tourism," Oliver said. "Fenwick was right about that oncoming storm, by the way. I can feel the energy building in the atmosphere."

"So can I."

She stopped in front of room 203 and used the old-fashioned key to rez the simple amber lock.

The door swung open on a small, narrow, gloom-filled room crowded with heavy vintage furniture. The one window looked out on the thick woods that surrounded the town.

"Well, at least the bed doesn't date from Vance's time," Leona said. "No minibar, but hey, there's a rez-screen."

Oliver set her suitcase on the small luggage rack and studied the vintage rez-screen set. "I'm amazed there's any reception in these mountains."

Leona picked up the small brochure on top of the rez-screen. "According to this, there's a local station. Channel one is available from noon until eight p.m."

"So probably not much in the way of late-night adult entertainment," Oliver said.

"Disappointed?"

"I'll manage." He headed for the door. "Give me a couple of minutes to dump my bag in my room. Then we can head out and get a drink and something to eat."

"Sounds like a plan."

"I'm good when it comes to plans."

She thought about how he had grabbed the artifact at the reception, whisked her away from the scene of the FBPI, and then saved Roxy from the remote-controlled boat.

"I've noticed," she said.

Chapter Nineteen

The storm struck during dinner. Leona was eating pizza with Oliver and Roxy in the Lost Creek Diner when the rain started. Night had fallen but they had a clear view of the inn across the narrow street. She watched a vehicle pull into the parking lot.

"Looks like we aren't going to be the only guests at the haunted inn after all," she said.

Oliver studied the man and woman who emerged from the car. "I wonder if they are Vance tourists or if they fall into the wrong-turn-fifty-miles-back-on-the-highway category."

She studied the couple hurrying through the rain to the front steps of the inn. The two people were in their early thirties, casually but fashionably dressed. "I bet they're in the wrong-turn crowd."

"What makes you think that?" Oliver asked.

"Something about their attitude and their clothes. Also, Edith Fenwick said the Vance tourists usually show up in summer, not this time of year. Those two definitely took a wrong turn."

"Whoever they are, they're lucky they got here before the worst of the storm hit."

"Very lucky."

She was in the process of taking another bite of her pizza when a pickup truck parked in front of the diner. A man in a windbreaker, jeans, boots, and a cap climbed out of the front seat and jogged through the rain to the front door. When he walked inside, the handful of locals greeted him with easy familiarity.

The waitress smiled and came out from behind the counter. "There you are, Burt. I was getting a little worried about you."

"You know better than that, babe." Burt gave her a quick kiss and started to unfasten the windbreaker. "I've been living in these mountains my whole life. This ain't the worst storm we've had, not by a long shot."

"I know," the waitress said. She went back behind the counter. "But it's getting bad out there."

"Hey, Burt, how's the road looking?" a thickset man at the dining counter asked.

"Not good," Burt said. He strolled toward the counter. The route took him past the booth where Leona and Oliver sat with Roxy. "If the rain keeps up like this for the next few hours, the creek will flood and take out the bridge. That's what usually happens every time we get a big storm."

The bartender snorted. "One of the reasons we like living here, right? The storms help keep most of the tourists out of our little town."

"Those folks who checked into Edith's place today are gonna be sorry," the thickset man said. "Might find themselves stuck here for a few days. Road repairs take a while up here in the mountains."

Burt chuckled. "That's a fact."

Leona rolled her eyes at Oliver. He shrugged and ate another bite of pizza. Roxy, too, focused on the food.

Burt reached their table and stopped as if he had just noticed them. He eyed Roxy, who ignored him.

"That's a dust bunny, isn't it?" Burt said.

"Yes," Leona said. She put a protective hand on Roxy, who stopped eating pizza and fixed Burt with a steady gaze.

"What's that silly thing on her head?" Burt asked.

"It's a hat," Leona said politely.

Oliver watched Burt with his specter-cat eyes. An ominous vibe whispered in the atmosphere.

"We don't get a lot of dust bunnies around here," Burt continued. "Didn't know they made good pets."

"They don't," Leona said. She went for a light, chatty tone in an attempt to lower the rising temperature. "But they do make very good companions."

"They say that by the time you see the teeth, it's too late."

"There's no need to worry about Roxy. She doesn't bite. She's a licensed emotional support dust bunny."

On the other side of the table Oliver smiled his faint, edgy little smile.

"I'm not worried about the dust bunny," Burt said. He finished unzipping the windbreaker, let the edges fall open, and rested one meaty hand on a holstered mag-rez. "When you live in the mountains, you learn real quick how to take care of critters that bite."

Leona went cold.

Roxy rumbled softly. Alarmed, Leona plucked her off the table and tucked her under one arm, silently willing her not to go into attack mode.

Oliver did not growl but the cold fire in his eyes was alarming. The last thing they needed was a confrontation in the local diner.

Evidently oblivious to the charged atmosphere, Burt laughed and continued on his way to the dining counter. He sat down and started talking to Thickset Guy and the bartender. The waitress threw Leona an uneasy look, sending the ancient woman-to-woman appeal. Leona got the message.

She looked at Oliver. "I vote we get a box for the rest of the pizza and take it back to the inn to eat."

"Works for me."

Leona signaled the waitress, who rushed over with a pizza box and the bill.

Burt, the bartender, and Thickset Guy chuckled when Leona and Oliver paid the tab and headed for the door with Roxy. The waitress looked grateful.

Outside on the steps, Oliver raised an umbrella. "This town definitely isn't interested in developing the tourist business."

Leona clutched the box of unfinished pizza in one hand. She kept Roxy secured under her arm.

"You saw it, too, didn't you?" she said.

"Oh, yeah," Oliver said. "I saw it."

When Burt had opened his windbreaker to show off the mag-rez pistol, the top two buttons of his shirt had been undone. A pendant on a steel chain had been nestled in his chest hair—a pendant inscribed with a familiar phrase and a colorless crystal.

"It's just like the one Astrid Todd was wearing when I found her body," Leona said. "What is going on in this town?"

"I don't know," Oliver said. "But I think we can once again rule out coincidence."

CHAPTER TWENTY

Leona rezzed the lock on the door of room number 203 and led the way inside. She set the unfinished pizza on the small table near the window and released Roxy, who bounced up onto the room's one and only chair and then hopped to the table.

"I wonder how the honeymooners are doing," Leona said. "I'll bet they never expected to spend the wedding night from hell here in Lost Creek."

Oliver stopped in the doorway. "What makes you so sure the other two guests are honeymooners?"

"Pure speculation. But what if I'm right? Think about it. A couple takes a wrong turn and ends up in a remote mountain town that has a very weird vibe. Night is falling fast. They check into an almost-empty inn that is rumored to be haunted. There is an ominous feeling about the small town. A storm strikes. Doesn't that sound like the setup to a honeymoon from hell?"

"Or the plot of a Gothic novel."

"Or that."

"Or us," Oliver said, "except that we didn't take a wrong turn. We're here on purpose. Hang on, I'll be right back. I'm going to pick up a few things in my room."

He disappeared into room 204. When he returned he was carrying his messenger bag, a glass, and a bottle of whiskey.

She watched, intrigued, as he closed and locked the door. "Where did you get the booze?"

"I packed it."

"Very wise of you." She glanced at *Achieving Inner Resonance* on the nightstand. "I packed a self-help book. In hindsight, that may have been a mistake."

"Don't worry, there's plenty of whiskey for both of us."

"I'll get the glass in the bathroom."

She emerged a moment later, glass in hand, and found Oliver ensconced in the room's one and only chair. Roxy was eating a slice of pizza.

She sat down on the edge of the bed.

"I've been thinking about your theory that the other guests are honeymooners," Oliver said, pouring two glasses of whiskey. "Sounds like you're the romantic type."

"Me?" She picked up the glass and took a fortifying swallow. The whiskey burned, quite pleasantly, all the way down. "Nope, not in the least. Just ask anyone who knows me. They'll tell you I'm an overachiever. Very goal-oriented. Driven. To a fault, according to some." She hesitated, remembering the scene in the lab with Matt. "I've been told I've got ice in my veins. But no one has ever indicated that I'm the romantic type."

Oliver's brows rose. "Who told you that you have ice in your veins?"

"Matt Fullerton, my most recent ex. To be honest, he wasn't the first man to make that observation."

"Got a lot of exes?"

"A few. What about you?" She regretted the question instantly. His annulment had to be a painful subject. "Sorry. I didn't mean to go there. Your personal history is absolutely none of my business."

"True," he agreed.

She knew she should take the conversational off-ramp and change the subject, but curiosity got the better of her. As usual.

"Were you matched?" she asked.

"Yes." He gave her a thin smile. "We were an almost-perfect couple. Just ask the matchmaker."

"Think you'll register with a matchmaking agency again?" she asked.

"I doubt I could find one that would take me on as a client, not after the disaster. Theoretically the grounds for the annulment are confidential, but rumors travel in the matchmaking business. And why would I take the risk anyway? Things did not go well the first time. There's no reason to think they would be any better the next time. If I try again there will be a Marriage of Convenience first. Then, if things are working, maybe take the leap to a CM."

"I understand," she said. She gave him a tentative smile. "I guess we have something in common. I don't have any plans to register with an agency, either."

"Is that right?"

He looked and sounded skeptical.

"Years ago I made the decision to dedicate myself to my career," she said, employing her most sincere voice. "When it comes to relationships, I'm a free spirit."

"Yeah?" He turned the whiskey glass in his hands. "How does your family feel about that?"

"My sister, Molly, understands. She was a free spirit, too, until things changed. But, as you can imagine, the moms are not happy about my decision. They keep pushing me to register."

"Take it from me, the matchmaking agencies don't always get it right."

"Do you know where they got it wrong in your case?"

"Sure. My fault. They were working with bad data. I lied on the questionnaire."

"You mean you finessed the para-psych profile sections."

"Finessed, lied, whatever. In my own defense, all I can tell you is that I was following my mother's advice. She said it was a conversation I could have later, in private, with the person who looked like a good match."

Leona studied him over the rim of the glass. "Did you have that conversation with your match?"

"Yes. And she assured me that she was okay with my talent. But she changed her mind."

"After the marriage."

"Yes," he said. "After the marriage."

She thought about that for a moment, tasting the whiskey. "Doesn't sound like she had grounds for the annulment, in that case. I mean, if she knew the truth before the marriage—"

Oliver looked bleakly amused by her naïveté. "See, that's where things get interesting, legally speaking. All she had to do was claim I had not been entirely candid on the questionnaire. Which was true."

"So she claimed fraud and you didn't defend yourself."

"Why would I want to force her to stay in the marriage? She was terrified of me."

"Terrified?" Leona frowned. "That seems a little over-the-top."

"I guess you had to be there."

"I understand. Still, it's a very sad story."

"But it's over." He drank some whiskey and lowered the glass. "I can't help noticing that you seem to be okay with my talent."

She waved that off. "We're not dating."

"If we were dating?"

"I'd still be okay with it," she said.

"You don't know that. You've never witnessed my talent at full rez."

She shrugged. "Fine. Show me."

He shook his head. "It doesn't work like that."

"Relax, I know where you're coming from."

"What makes you so sure of that?"

She swirled the whiskey in her glass. "If you must know, I managed to scare the crap out of my most recent ex."

"Sounds interesting. With your talent?"

"Yep."

"Do I get details?" he asked, his eyes heating.

"It was a lab accident."

"Accidents happen."

She brightened. "They do, don't they? Can I have some more whiskey?"

CHAPTER TWENTY-ONE

The storm blew itself out shortly after ten o'clock. Oliver was still lounging in the chair but now his heels were stacked on the window-sill. Roxy had been perched on the sill, seemingly entranced by the storm and the night. She abruptly chortled.

He looked up from the Vortex file he had been studying. The rain had stopped. Energy-infused fog glowed on the other side of the window.

"Looks like the worst is over," he said. "It wasn't that bad. I doubt the bridge washed out. The gang back at the diner will be disappointed."

"I'm sure that was a threat meant to intimidate us into leaving," Leona said.

"I got the same impression."

He looked at her, aware of the quiet pleasure of her company. She was sitting on the bed, propped up against a stack of pillows, fully dressed except for her shoes. The files he had given her to read were stacked on the quilt beside her. Several tendrils of her hair had come free and there was a sexy, rumpled look about her that rezzed a pleasant fantasy. The vision involved him getting out of the chair, moving to the bed, and pulling her into his arms.

Roxy chortled again and tapped the glass with one of her paws.

"I think she wants out," Leona said.

Oliver swung his legs off the sill and got to his feet. "I'll open the window for her."

"No, wait. We're on the second floor. I'll take her downstairs."

"I don't think you need to worry. Those six paws probably make her a very good climber."

"Yes, she is, actually. You're right."

He opened the window. Damp, psi-heavy air flowed into the room. Roxy chortled farewell and dashed out onto the ledge. The ribbons of the fascinator fluttered behind her. She shimmied down a drainpipe and vanished into the radiant mist.

Leona got up and walked to the window. He looked at her, conscious of the deep sense of recognition that whispered through him. *I've been waiting for you all of my life, Leona Griffin.*

"There's certainly a lot of energy in these mountains," Leona observed.

So much for the crystalline moment of romantic intimacy. She was thinking about the local atmosphere, not him.

Suppressing a groan, he closed the window. "Yes, there is. I'd better get back to my room. It's late and we've got that appointment with Thacker in the morning. Breakfast at seven."

"I remember."

He did not want to leave. It had been very comfortable sitting here with Leona, going over paperwork, discussing the history of Vortex, the Bluestone Project, and the legends that swirled around Vincent Lee Vance. Maybe too comfortable. He could get used to not having to rez the low-level vibe he habitually generated when he was with people he did not know well—the vibe that made them see what they expected to see: a dull, harmless academic who belonged in a museum.

The effort would have been wasted on Leona. She saw through the camouflage and she was unfazed by what she saw. That raised a question that he knew was going to haunt him. What, exactly, did she see when she looked at him? Did she see the man who wanted to climb into bed with her?

And yes, he really needed to get out of here now before he did something stupid—like ask if he could stay for a while longer. The whole night, maybe.

He gathered up the files, stuffed them into the messenger bag, and headed for the door. "See you in the morning."

"Good night," she said.

She trailed after him to the door. He went out into the hall and stopped.

"You were lying when you said the reason you weren't planning to register with a matchmaking agency was that you were dedicated to your career," he said.

She folded her arms and propped one shoulder against the doorframe. "I am dedicated to my career."

"But that's not the reason you've never registered, is it?"

"I'm a free spirit, remember?"

He nodded. "Okay. I get it. None of my business."

He took the few steps to his room and rezzed the lock. When he opened the door, she spoke.

"I told you the truth," she said. "I love my work and I plan to live my life as a free spirit, but you're right. Those aren't the reasons I've never registered."

He waited, saying nothing.

"My reason is similar to yours," she said quietly. "A problematic parapsych profile. I guess I'm afraid of rejection."

"Figured as much," he said. "You're strong, aren't you?"

She blinked. "What makes you say that?"

He smiled. "The mysterious lab accident. In addition to your lock-smith abilities, you can activate Alien artifacts, can't you?"

She winced. "Some of them."

"Only some?"

"It's not the sort of talent you want to run a lot of experiments with. That would be a good way to accidentally murder someone. There's a reason there are strict laws regarding the handling of artifacts of un-known power."

"Sure. But just so you know, if you mentioned that aspect of your talent on a matchmaking agency questionnaire, I wouldn't reject you be-cause of it."

Her eyes heated. "Are you suggesting that you might ask me out on a real date, not just a date to tour your museum?"

"If I did, would you turn me down?"

"No," she said. "No, I wouldn't turn you down. Good night, Oliver."

She straightened and gently closed the door.

He went into his room and rezzed the lights. He was suddenly feeling remarkably cheerful—more cheerful than he had in a very long time.

CHAPTER TWENTY-TWO

Oliver was okay with her artifact talent. He hadn't even asked her for details.

Leona locked the door of her room, walked a few steps toward the bed, and stopped, trying to process what had just happened. She had taken a huge personal and professional risk when she had admitted that she could activate some Alien artifacts. Most people in the para-archaeology world were nervous around people with that particular talent. Some refused to join any Underworld teams that included a person who might accidentally rez an AUP.

And then there were obsessive collectors and assorted bad guys who would pay any price to obtain the services of someone like her.

But Oliver had guessed the truth and had as good as asked her out on a date. Maybe he wasn't worried about her talent because he was confident in his own powerful para-psych profile. He did not view her as a threat. He was no Matt Fullerton.

She pulled herself together and walked past the bed to the window. She stood there for a time, gazing out into the luminous fog, remembering the scene in the lab with Matt.

"... *You stole my research,*" *she said.* "*Did you really think I would be okay with that?*"

"*I did not steal your research,*" *Matt insisted.* "*We were a team.*"

"*In that case, why isn't my name on that paper you published in the* Journal of Para-Archaeology? *You never even told me you had submitted to the journal. We agreed to wait until the final results were in.*"

"*There's a team from the University of Cadence working on a similar project. I couldn't take the chance that they would publish first.*"

"*That is no excuse for taking full credit for the Mirror Chamber analysis. I'm the one who took the measurements and the readings from those artifacts and ran the resonance tests.*"

"*We were a team,*" *Matt insisted.*

"*Ghost shit. You used me. That's what our relationship has been about all along, isn't it?*" *she said.* "*You always intended to use me. I'm a better para-archaeologist than you will ever be and you know it. You needed me to assess those mirrors. You never would have been able to analyze them on your own. Admit it.*"

"*You're overreacting.*"

"*You're a lying, cheating fraud. Don't you dare tell me I'm overreacting. You want to know what overreacting looks like? Allow me to demonstrate.*"

She grabbed the small Alien mirror off the lab bench and rezzed her talent. The artifact exploded in a dazzling, senses-stunning display of paranormal fireworks that lit up the room. For a harrowing moment it seemed as if the entire lab would go up in flames ...

Okay, so she might have overreacted. She had gotten things under control very quickly, but she would never forget the panic and shock in Matt's eyes. He had stared at her as if she were a monster. Maybe he was right.

She knew in that moment that if—*when*—he told their colleagues what had happened in the lab, her career in the academic world would be finished. She had done the only thing she could think of. You had to fight fire with fire. But in the end, her tactics hadn't worked after all. She had lost her job and her once-promising future. Probably one of those karma things.

She was turning away from the window when she caught the shadowy movement at the corner of her eye. The hair on the back of her neck stirred. Her palms tingled. Her intuition kicked in, warning her to pay attention.

The shadow shifted in the fog. It occurred to her that she was silhouetted against the room lights, making a perfect target of herself. She moved quickly, de-rezzing the lamps before returning to the window.

The shadowy figure had gone very still now. She could not see the face or make out any details but her senses told her that she was being watched.

Curious to see what would happen, she closed the drapes, moved to the side of the window, and peered out through the narrow slit between the curtain and the wall. Down below the figure moved again, disappearing into the mist.

She waited awhile but the watcher did not return.

Abandoning the vigil, she turned on the bedside lamp and changed into the flannel pajamas. A short time later she crawled into bed and picked up *Achieving Inner Resonance*. She turned to chapter six and reread the mantra: *I will put aside negative thoughts and focus on the positive aspects that will allow me to move forward. I will see the flower of opportunity that blossoms in the shadows.*

For some reason, she was unable to concentrate. She put the book aside, de-rezzed the lamp, and lay still for a while, wondering if Oliver was in bed. Then she wondered if he had seen the figure in the fog. Maybe it had been a trick of the light.

Eugenie's old lecture on the subject came back to her. *Stop doubting yourself. If you don't trust your own senses, no one else will, either.*

She had seen someone out there in the fog.

CHAPTER TWENTY-THREE

She dreamed the old dream, the one that took her back to that fateful day at the orphanage.

"You need to push harder," she says. "I can't see the sign."

She was six and a half years old and she was learning that people often needed directions and instructions. She was good at giving both—not that everyone appreciated her help.

She and Molly were alone in the walled garden, playing on the swings. It was a rare treat. Usually they had to share the swings and slides with the other girls, but for some reason Ms. Inskip had sent them outside on their own that afternoon.

Her name was Leona No Middle Initial No Last Name. Molly's name was Molly No Middle Initial No Last Name. The Inskip School for Orphan Girls was the only world they had ever known, but they were sure of two things. One was that last names were important. The other was that there was a bigger, more exciting world beyond the school grounds waiting to be explored. They knew it was out there because the sign on the other side of the high walls offered proof.

"I'm pushing as hard as I can," Molly says.

"Do it again. I can see part of the sign now."

Her sister gives her another push. She soars higher. Now she can read the entire sign. GRIFFIN INVESTIGATIONS. WANT ANSWERS? WE'LL GET THEM FOR YOU. CALL NOW. NO WAITING.

There is a phone number. She and Molly have memorized it.

"Okay, I can see it," she says.

She waits for her sister to demand her turn on the swings. There are rules. Once you can see the sign you have to let the other person have a turn. But Molly doesn't say anything. That's not right. Why isn't Molly demanding her turn?

The swing slows down. She prepares to jump off and switch places. But when she looks back, she sees that Molly is no longer there . . .

A man's voice slithers into the dream, changing the script . . .

". . . You will be my Guardians. In exchange for your loyalty, I will give you power such as you have never known. Together we will establish a new civilization. Follow me into the glorious future . . ."

She came awake, aware that something or someone was tapping on the window. But that was impossible. Her room was on the second floor.

The voice came again . . .

". . . The future I will give you is one in which all power will be in the hands of those whose paranormal senses have evolved to the next level. I will use the greatest secret of the Old World to endow you with talents beyond anything you have dreamed of . . ."

She sat up suddenly, her pulse pounding.

The rez-screen was on, illuminating the room in a cold blue light. A video featuring an all-too-familiar figure from history was playing. Vincent Lee Vance, dramatically handsome, charismatic, and endowed with the mesmerizing voice of a prophet, held forth to a silent, unseen audience.

Dressed in the black-and-khaki uniform of the rebellion, Vance commanded the stage. His dark, gleaming shoulder-length hair was brushed straight back in a style that emphasized his sharp bird-of-prey profile.

There appeared to be a wall of solid rock in the background, but it was impossible to make out the rest of his surroundings because the lighting was strategically focused on him.

Historians had frequently pointed out that Vance had possessed a flair for the theatrical. Modern psychologists who had studied his rise and fall had concluded that he had the scary para-psych profile of a classic cult leader. There was no question but that his charisma was off the charts. Even in a grainy video it was hard to look away.

More tapping on the glass.

She scrambled out of bed and peeked through the curtains. Roxy was on the ledge. There was a small object clutched in two of her paws.

"Roxy."

She opened the window. Foggy night air flowed into the room. Roxy chortled, fluffed out, and tumbled inside. Ignoring the rez-screen, she bounded up onto the foot of the bed and graciously held out an unpolished, untuned crystal.

A *yellow* crystal.

Dread iced Leona's senses. She shut the window and went back to the bed to accept the crystal gift.

"Where have you been, or shouldn't I ask?" she whispered.

A couple of sharp raps on the door jolted her. She checked the time. Nearly one in the morning. She glanced at Roxy, who appeared unconcerned about the late-night caller.

"So, probably not the ghost of Vincent Lee Vance, right?"

She crossed the room on bare feet and peered through the peephole. Oliver stood in the hall. He was not wearing his glasses. His hair was tousled from sleep. He was dressed in a black T-shirt and the trousers he'd had on earlier. He was wearing shoes but he had not bothered to tie the laces.

She yanked open the door. "Did your rez-screen come on a few minutes ago?"

"Yes," he said.

The cold energy in his eyes was unnerving. No wonder he usually wore glasses, she thought.

He moved into the room and patted Roxy, who responded with a welcoming chortle. Leona closed the door and turned around. Oliver was studying the screen as if it were a mysterious artifact.

"Interesting," he said.

She realized she was very glad to see him. His presence eased some of the tension inside her. She was not alone in this very weird town. Belatedly it occurred to her that she was in her ancient flannel pajamas. After her restless sleep she probably had bed head. It should not have mattered. But it did.

Not that Oliver was paying any attention to her. He was focused on the rez-screen.

"Did you turn it on?" Oliver asked.

"No."

"I didn't turn mine on, either."

She opened her hand to show him the crystal. "Roxy had this when she returned a moment ago."

Oliver's eyes glittered. "Think we could get her to show us where she found it?"

"Maybe. I don't know." She glanced at the rez-screen. "I wonder if something went wrong at the local broadcasting station. A technical glitch, maybe. But how did they manage to rez the screens in our rooms?"

"Got a feeling this bit of unscheduled programming is designed to reinforce the rumor that Vance haunts the inn."

"It's not a ghost," she pointed out. "It's an old video clip from one of Vance's recruitment rallies."

"Yes, but you have to admit that playing it unexpectedly at one o'clock in the morning on a channel that went off the air hours ago makes for a dramatic presentation."

She shivered. "Yes, it does."

Footsteps and muffled, excited voices sounded out in the hall.

"I'm not getting a reading from that room," a woman said. "Try the next one. Hurry. There's no way to know how long the manifestation will last."

"Give me a minute to adjust the gauge," a man responded. "It's set too low. We need more sensitivity."

"That does it." The woman's voice quickened. "I'm picking up a cold spot in room two-oh-three. See if there's anyone inside."

"We're about to get company," Oliver said.

He ran his fingers through his hair and crossed the room. Leona was aware of a whisper of energy. By the time he reached the door, he had somehow camouflaged the specter-cat beneath the surface. Even without the aid of the black-framed glasses, he was once again Museum Guy.

He opened the door, startling the man on the other side, who had his hand raised to knock.

"Oh, sorry," the man said, taking a quick step back. "Didn't mean to alarm you."

The woman moved to stand behind him. "We heard the rez-screen so we assumed whoever was in here would be awake."

Leona recognized the couple as the two people who had checked into the inn earlier that evening while she and Oliver and Roxy had been eating pizza in the diner. They were no longer wearing their stylish country-casual attire. Instead, they were bundled up in bathrobes, slippers on their feet.

"We are awake," Oliver grumbled. "Do either of you have any idea what is going on here?"

"As a matter of fact, we think we do," the man said, waxing enthusiastic. "First, we should introduce ourselves. I'm Baxter Richey. This is Darla Price. We are paranormal investigators who specialize in hauntings and apparitions. We have a website, a podcast, and a video channel. The brand is Messages from the Other Side. Maybe you've heard of us?"

"No," Oliver said. "Are you telling us you're ghost hunters?"

"*Real* ghosts," Darla clarified quickly. "The supernatural kind. Spirits, phantoms, revenants. Not the Unstable Dissonance Energy Manifestations that appear in the Underworld."

"You can't be serious," Oliver said. "No one believes in that sort of nonsense."

"You'd be surprised," Baxter said, very earnest now. "A lot of people prefer to keep an open mind when it comes to ghosts. They want to know the truth. That's why Darla and I are in business."

"We've checked out a number of properties rumored to be haunted," Darla said, equally intense. "Most were dead ends, but we have identified a few genuine manifestations." She tapped the device she held in her right hand. "We got a strong reading in my room a few minutes ago when the rez-screen suddenly came on."

"We decided to walk the halls with the detector to see if we could pick up any more data," Baxter added. "We're getting a strong reading from this room. It's very exciting. Would you mind if we came in and took a closer look?"

"Well—" Oliver said.

Alarm jolted through Leona. "*Yes.* Yes, I would mind. I'm not exactly dressed to entertain guests. It's after one in the morning. I'd like to get some sleep."

"It would just take a few minutes," Baxter assured her.

"No, absolutely not," Leona said.

Darla's eyes widened. "We understand. Totally. Sorry about the intrusion. Baxter and I will see you at breakfast tomorrow morning."

"Sure," Leona said. "Now, if you wouldn't mind—"

"Okay, sorry to bother you," Baxter said. He paused. "Take notes, would you? Jot down anything that strikes you about the energy around the rez-screen—or anywhere in your room, for that matter."

"Right," Leona said. "We'll get right on that."

"See you in the morning," Oliver said.

Reluctantly, Baxter and Darla made their way down the hall. Oliver closed the door and turned around. The twitch at the corner of his mouth kicked in.

"So they are not honeymooners," he said.

She wrinkled her nose. "It was a good theory."

"*. . . Follow me into the future . . .*"

Distracted by Vance's mesmeric voice, she focused on the rez-screen again. "Now what? We're not going to be able to sleep as long as that video is playing."

"In that case, maybe we should pay attention."

Oliver walked back across the room and sat down on the end of the bed. He studied the rez-screen, once again in his focused, academic mode. She hesitated, not sure how to handle the situation. He was probably right. They needed information. But she was in her *pajamas*. She thought about putting on her jacket but that seemed somewhat ridiculous under the circumstances. She reminded herself that he had seen her in far less clothing.

"Okay," she said finally.

She sat down beside him and started paying attention to the megalomaniac on the screen. Vance was holding up a palm-sized disc that dangled from a metal chain. There was a small crystal set into the pendant.

"*. . . You will wear the symbol of your loyalty at all times . . .*"

"He was very specific about the need for his followers to wear those pendants," Oliver said in a thoughtful tone.

"Yes, he was." She leaned back, braced her hands behind her, and contemplated the screen.

"According to the historians, the crystals were designed to resonate with the crystals of other followers," Oliver continued. "It was how the true believers of the cult recognized each other."

"The crystals in Vance's pendants and the one we saw on the dead caterer were transparent. No color." Leona touched the stone she wore beneath the top of her pajamas and then glanced at the crystal in Oliver's hand. "Where do the yellow crystals fit into all this?"

"Good question."

The rez-screen blinked off. The video winked out along with Vance's hypnotic voice. Leona shivered.

"Thank goodness that's over," she said. "Maybe we can get some sleep."

As soon as the words were out of her mouth, she realized she probably wouldn't be able to get back to sleep—and even if she did, the dream would be lying in wait for her.

"I don't know about you," Oliver said, "but I don't think I'll be able to sleep."

She exhaled heavily. "Whew. Thanks. Now I can say the same thing without embarrassing myself. That reminds me, earlier I could have sworn I saw a figure in the fog watching our rooms."

"I saw him, too."

"Him?"

"I think so," Oliver said. "But I didn't get a good look."

"Call me overimaginative, but I've got to tell you, this inn is getting creepier by the hour."

His brows rose. "Says the woman who was held prisoner in the Underworld by a bunch of artifact pirates."

"Yeah, well, between you and me, I may be suffering a little PTSD from that experience. But don't tell my family, okay? They already think my professional and personal lives are a train wreck."

"No surprise about the PTSD, given what you've been through."

She cleared her throat. "It wasn't just the kidnapping. There was also the little accident in the artifacts lab."

"The one that scared the crap out of your ex?"

"That one."

"Want to talk about it?" Oliver said, his voice absolutely neutral.

"It was sort of an explosion, but quite small, really."

"What, exactly, exploded?"

"A little Alien mirror. Harmless. It's not like I lost control or anything."

"Anyone hurt?"

"No," she said firmly. "At least, not seriously. My para-senses were singed a little and so were Matt's, but we both fully recovered. For the record, I was just really pissed off. I wasn't trying to kill him."

"Didn't think so."

She raised her brows at that. "What makes you so sure?"

Oliver surprised her with a sharp, dangerous smile. "Because you would have been successful. You aren't the half-measures type."

"Oh." She wasn't sure how to take that, so she forged ahead. "I cornered him in the lab because I was furious. After I was rescued from the kidnappers, I found out he had been cheating on me with a grad student. That was bad enough."

"You confronted him in the lab because of the grad student?"

"The reason I got him alone that day was because I had just discovered that he had used some of my work in a paper he had sent to the *Journal of Para-Archaeology*. He not only stole my research, he didn't even bother to credit me in the paper."

"Ah, the ultimate betrayal in the academic world," Oliver said. "No wonder you were pissed."

"Really, really pissed."

"Did he know you could work artifact energy?"

"No. I never told anyone. I'm sure Drayton and Grant, the two people who were kidnapped with me, had their suspicions. We spent a lot of time in close quarters together and we were working around Glass House artifacts, some of which were very hot. But they kept quiet after we were rescued."

"The three of you had developed a bond in captivity."

"Yes. It's not the sort of talent you advertise in the academic world. People worry that you could accidentally get them killed on a dig."

"I know. I'm in the same line, remember?"

She flushed. This was getting awkward.

"I suppose now that you're aware of my ability, you're a little concerned that I might be a hazard," she said stiffly. "I want to assure you that I—"

She broke off because there was a telltale twitch at the edge of Oliver's lips. It transformed into a grin and then a raspy chuckle.

"I'll bet you really did scare the hell out of Fullerton," he said.

"Yes," she said. "But when he recovered from the shock, he was furious. He threatened to tell my boss and everyone else in the department. My career would have been ruined. I tried to keep him quiet."

"How?"

"The old-fashioned way. Blackmail. I told him I would not go to the head of the department with the proof that he had plagiarized my work if he kept his mouth shut about what had happened in the lab."

Oliver nodded. "MAD. Mutually assured destruction. Good plan."

"I'm not proud of myself, but I was desperate."

"Understandable."

"Not that it worked," she said. "The rumors started to circulate anyway. I should have known it would be impossible to keep the incident in the lab a secret. There were some char marks that were hard to explain away as a normal lab accident. Still, I think my career would have survived if it hadn't been for the raid on the Society. That finished me at Hollister."

"Are you going to go through with your threat to accuse Fullerton of stealing your work?"

She groaned. "No. Accusations like that get messy fast for both parties involved. I didn't have any real proof. I was bluffing. And, as I said, I did singe Matt that day in the lab."

"As revenge goes, that's pretty pathetic."

"I suppose, but you know what they say about revenge. Two graves and all that. Anyway, I've got bigger problems. I doubt I'll ever work in the academic world again. My best option is to go private as a consultant. Most businesses doing work in the Underworld aren't terribly picky when it comes to talent. Corporations and private firms are profit-driven. All they care about are results."

"True. But going down that career path can be hazardous. There are a lot of shady operators working the ruins."

"I know." She gave him a steely smile. "I was kidnapped by some of those shady types."

He winced. "I guess you don't need any lectures on the dangers of running a small consulting business in the Underworld." He paused. "You'll miss the academic world, though, won't you?"

"Yes. It's the research and analysis that fascinates me. The sense of discovery. That's the mission of the academic world. Corporations and entrepreneurs are focused on profit and staying ahead of the competition. Different goals. Different mindsets."

"Your colleagues in the academic world sound like a tough crowd."

"True. I did learn one valuable lesson, however."

"What's that?" Oliver asked.

"I need to keep my personal and professional lives separate."

"Easier said than done."

"I know."

Oliver was silent for a moment. She assumed he was probably about to announce that it was time he went back to his own room. She didn't want him to leave, she realized.

She tried to think of a logical reason for asking him to stay. But he spoke first and turned the night—and her world—upside down.

He looked at her, his dangerous eyes heating. "What would you say if I told you that I want to kiss you?"

CHAPTER TWENTY-FOUR

She froze—but only for the seconds it took for her to catch her breath. Her intuition slammed into the caution zone, alerting her that kissing Oliver was going to prove risky in ways she could not predict. But the wild, independent, feminine part of her gave her intuition the middle finger.

I know he's dangerous. I don't care.

It was just a kiss. Not her first and, hopefully, not her last. Just a kiss. What could possibly go wrong?

"Yes," she whispered. "I would say yes."

He leaned toward her, not touching her with his hands. The kiss started out as a slow exploration. She understood that they were both determined to do their research—testing, sampling, feeling their way—before taking more intimate steps. They had each been burned in the past. They knew better than to make decisions that could not be unmade.

But it was as if she had touched a blazing-hot artifact of unknown power. Her senses soared. Energy shifted in the small space. Curiosity, followed by certainty, sparkled through her, igniting her blood.

She was intensely aware of the heat and power of his aura. He could handle his own energy field and hers, as well. She did not need to be cautious. She was free to fly.

"Leona," he said against her mouth.

It was not a question. It was a statement. A claim. He sounded satisfied, as if he was getting everything he had ever wanted or needed. No man had ever made her feel so incredibly desired. It was a thrilling experience.

The kiss went deep before she had time to adjust to the dazzling reality of the passion that was consuming them. Now his hands were on her, cradling the back of her head, holding her still so that he could ravish her mouth. She gripped his shoulders, savoring the sleek, hard strength of him.

His fingers found the buttons of the pajama top. She responded by slipping her palms under his T-shirt and flattening them against his taut, muscled back. Silently, she urged him closer. When his hand covered her bare breast, everything inside her clenched. The sudden, intense urgency was overwhelming. She could feel the liquid warmth between her legs. She tensed, suddenly, belatedly, aware that things were slipping out of her control. She was *always* in control.

He raised his head. "Did I hurt you?"

"No," she managed, tightening her grip on him.

He lowered his head to resume the kiss but an insistent chortle made them both go still.

"Roxy." Leona turned and saw the dust bunny on the windowsill. "She wants out again."

"She probably has better things to do than watch a couple of humans make out."

Oliver got to his feet and opened the window. With a cheery farewell,

Roxy bounced out onto the ledge, jumped to the drainpipe, and disappeared into the night.

Oliver closed the window and turned around to look at Leona. She saw the question in his eyes and knew it was the same one she was asking. Had the moment been irrevocably shattered? This was her opportunity to regain control.

But she did not need to be in control. Not with this man.

She smiled, very sure now. The question vanished from his eyes.

Together they turned down the bed. Out of nowhere a wave of awkwardness washed over her. She was suddenly conscious of the extremely unsexy flannel pajamas and her badly mussed hair. Then she remembered the vibrator she had left behind in her lingerie drawer. Stupid packing decision.

Along with the disconcerting hit of awkwardness came the doubts. Could she fake an orgasm well enough to fool this man? She had known him only a very short time, but she was certain that if she failed to climax he would feel responsible. Most men wouldn't notice if she did some acting at the end. Even if they knew she hadn't managed the grand finale they would attribute the problem to her lack of responsiveness, the ice water in her veins—not their poor skills in bed.

But Oliver wasn't like most men. He was the type who would take responsibility for her failure.

Of course you can fake it. Stop doubting yourself. Live for the moment.

She was trying to decide if she should get out of her pajamas before climbing into bed when Oliver took the decision out of her hands. Before she realized his intentions, he scooped her up in his arms and settled her on the sheet.

That settled the pajama question. She watched, fascinated, as he undressed in the shadows. Everything about him was hard, and the energy of his aura was unmistakably infused with the heat of sexual desire. It was intoxicating.

When he got into bed and reached for her, she went to him with an exhilarating rush of anticipation.

He finished unfastening the top of her pajamas and began to explore her, first with his hands and then with his mouth. She speared her fingers through his hair and arched against him. His warm palms slipped under the elastic waistband of the pajama bottoms. He peeled the garment over her thighs, all the way to her ankles. She kicked herself free. He cupped her heated core. She could have sworn she levitated.

"So wet and so hot," he whispered. "For me."

She was wet, she realized. Soaking wet. The tension deep inside her was both wondrous and unbearable. She reached for his rigid erection, circled him with her fingers, and squeezed gently. When she stroked him, he groaned.

"So hard," she said against his chest. "For me."

"Oh, yeah," he rasped.

He eased one finger inside her and then another, stretching her. She tightened herself around him. And then his thumb was pressing firmly against the exquisitely sensitive nubbin at the top of her sex.

The climax swept through her with an intensity that stunned her. She could not have resisted it if she had tried. The thrilling tension that had gripped her so fiercely was released in shivering waves of sensation. She opened her mouth on a silent shriek of surprise—she was breathless.

She clutched at Oliver's shoulders, hanging on to him as if he were a life raft in a storm-roiled sea.

He came down on top of her, caged her with his arms, settled between her legs, and pushed heavily, deeply into her. The muscles of his back were bands of mag-steel.

It was too much. She was already impossibly sensitized. A second wave broke over her just as Oliver's release pounded through both of them. Their auras flared. Resonated.

The room burned.

CHAPTER TWENTY-FIVE

"... *Molly didn't run away. She's my sister. She wouldn't leave without me. You have to find her* ..."

Leona's voice was soft, blurred by sleep and infused with desperation. A chaotic energy swirled in the atmosphere.

Oliver came awake on a surge of adrenaline.

"It's my fault she's gone ..."

He rolled onto his side and propped himself on his elbow. Leona was stirring restlessly. Her dreamstate anxiety electrified the room. The yellow crystal pendant was glowing more intensely than it had earlier in the evening.

"My fault. I wasn't paying attention. I was on the swing ..."

"Leona," he said quietly. "It's okay. Just a dream."

"... You have to find my sister ..."

He put what he hoped was a reassuring hand on her shoulder. Her eyes snapped open. Tension gripped her, rendering her motionless. He knew she was trapped in the strange, unnerving border between sleep and wakefulness. It was the territory where hallucinations and night terrors lurked.

"Wake up, Leona," he said.

He tightened his grip on her arm and generated a little energy, just enough to interrupt the sleep state paralysis. She shivered and then awareness returned to her eyes. The panic dissipated.

She looked at him with a wary expression and then she groaned and draped an arm over her eyes. "Sorry about that."

"There's nothing to be sorry about. You had a bad dream."

She pushed herself to a sitting position, evidently remembered she was naked, and grabbed the sheet to hold to her throat. "I fell asleep before you went back to your room. That's not supposed to happen. All I can say is that it's been a stressful couple of days. Make that a stressful week. Actually, it's been kind of a stressful month or two. Great. Now I'm making excuses."

He sorted through her words and focused on the ones that bothered him the most. "What do you mean, it's not supposed to happen?"

She glanced at him, bemused. "What?"

"You apologized because you fell asleep while I was still here. You said that wasn't supposed to happen."

"Oh, right. I told you, when we were younger, Molly and I decided to live our lives as free spirits. We made a couple of rules. Number one was that we would never date anyone who was married or registered with a matchmaking agency."

"A sensible rule."

"Number two was no sleepovers. No sticking around for breakfast in the morning."

"Because spending the entire night represents too much of a commitment?"

"And because it might set up false expectations. We were afraid that we might get too comfortable and start thinking there could be more to the relationship."

"And that would be a bad thing?"

"Realistically, yes," she said.

"Your sister, the other free spirit in the family, changed her mind."

"Yes." There was a short silence. "She did."

"Do you want me to leave?" He was not holding his breath. Okay, yes, he was holding his breath. Such a simple question. Why did it feel like so much was hanging on the answer?

She appeared to give that some thought.

"No," she said, "I don't want you to leave. This feels ... different."

He started to ask the next logical question—*Why is this different?*—but he changed his mind and shut his mouth. She had sounded bemused or maybe unsure. He decided it would probably be best not to push the issue.

He lounged against the pillows. "Do you want to tell me about your nightmare?"

"It was just a bad dream."

"You were talking in your sleep. Something about the need to rescue your sister."

For a moment he thought she was going to slide away from an answer, but she didn't.

"It's an old dream," she said. "It goes back to the day my sister was grabbed at the orphanage. I had that particular nightmare frequently when I was growing up but rarely in the past few years. It still comes back occasionally when I'm under a lot of stress."

"Do you know why the dream became less of a problem?"

"Sure. The moms taught me how to use lucid dreaming to rewrite the script. But in the past few weeks I've started having the dream again, and I haven't been able to get control of it."

"As you said, you've been under a lot of stress."

"Yes."

Oliver glanced at her pendant. The glow was rapidly fading.

"Your crystal was brighter than usual when you woke up a moment ago," he said.

"My crystal?" She touched the stone with her fingertips and then raised it so that she could get a close look at it. "I guess my dream energy rezzed it a bit."

"Interesting." He pushed the covers aside, got to his feet, and padded across the room. He picked up her messenger bag and brought it to the bed. "Let's take a look."

Leona opened the bag, reached inside, and took out the yellow pyramid.

The glow was fading, just as it was in the pendant, but the stone was still faintly luminous. He sat down on the side of the bed and took the pyramid stone from her fingers.

"Tell me about your dream," he said. "The one that seems to be rezzing these crystals."

"I told you the story. Molly was kidnapped by a madman, Nigel Willard. The moms rescued her. They had just opened Griffin Investigations. Molly was their first big case. The press loved it."

"Yes, but you never told me how the Griffins got involved. How did they know Molly had been kidnapped? Who hired them?"

"I did."

"You were six and a half years old. What made you call a private investigation agency?"

"I thought about calling the police but I was afraid Ms. Inskip, the director of the orphanage, would tell them I was just a kid playing with the phone."

"So you called an investigation agency instead. Why Griffin?"

"It was the only one I knew about. There was a sign on the other side of the orphanage fence. Molly and I could see it when we were on the swings. *Griffin Investigations. Want answers? We'll get them for you. Call now. No waiting.* There was a phone number. We had both memorized it because we had seen it so many times."

"You called the number and the Griffins believed you? A six-and-a-half-year-old kid?"

"I'm told I can be quite . . . forceful."

He smiled. "I have a thing for strong women."

She flushed. "Charlotte and Eugenie Griffin were at the door of the Inskip School less than thirty minutes later, demanding to talk to me. Ms. Inskip tried to stop them. She couldn't."

"So you were the one who rescued Molly."

"What?" Startled, Leona frowned. "No. I just told you, the moms did."

"You made the call to Griffin Investigations, and even though you were only six and a half years old, you convinced two adults to believe you. You launched the rescue operation and it was successful."

"I should have been paying attention. I didn't even notice Molly was gone until I turned around. I remember screaming—"

"I repeat, you were only six and a half years old. Even if you had been watching your sister every single minute, you could not have stopped a grown man from grabbing her. What matters is what you did when you realized what had happened. No question about it—you rescued your sister."

CHAPTER TWENTY-SIX

Last night was different.

Leona was still trying to analyze and organize her emotions the next morning when she and Oliver, accompanied by an enthusiastic Roxy, who had reappeared at dawn, went downstairs to breakfast. Yes, the sex had been amazing—unlike anything she had ever experienced. Eye-opening. She hadn't even needed the vibrator that was still sitting in her bedroom drawer in Illusion Town.

She had not had to fake anything with Oliver. Instead, she had been free to throw herself into the storm. In the end, there had been something beyond the physical involved. She would never forget that moment of breathtaking, incredibly intimate resonance. The word *transcendent* was overused but it was difficult to come up with another description for what had happened. The sense of a shared connection, however brief, was unique. Different.

The downside of discovering real passion was that, statistically speaking, it was extremely unlikely she would encounter another man who stirred her senses the way Oliver had. Maybe this was what Molly had discovered with Joshua.

On balance, there was no doubt that last night had been a life-changing event—at least for her—and not just because of the sex. He had given her a new perspective on the old sense of guilt she had harbored all these years. Her younger self hadn't failed to act when Molly was taken. She had launched what had proven to be a successful rescue. The moms had assured her that she had done what needed to be done, but somehow it sounded different coming from Oliver. It sounded logical.

When they reached the entrance of the small dining room, she gave Oliver a sidelong glance, once again trying to read his reactions to what had happened between them during the night. Once again, she was forced to abandon the attempt. He had awakened one hundred percent focused on the problem of Vortex and the upcoming interview with Norton Thacker. He was a man who understood priorities.

Until now, she had not realized how annoying priorities could be.

Edith Fenwick was pouring coffee for the paranormal investigators. Darla Price and Baxter Richey were seated at a table near the window. They waved a good-natured greeting.

"Good morning, you two," Darla sang out. "Any manifestation sightings last night in your room?"

"Afraid not," Leona said.

"Oh," Darla said, disappointed. "That's too bad."

"What about cold spots?" Baxter added, ever hopeful.

"Things were definitely not cold in that room last night," Oliver said, with more than a trace of masculine satisfaction.

Leona gave him a repressive look. He ignored it.

"Make yourselves at home," Edith said. She bustled forward with the coffeepot. "I was just telling the other guests that you are all going to be here for a while. The bridge got washed away last night."

Leona chilled. "The storm didn't seem that bad."

"No," Oliver said. "It didn't."

He did not appear surprised, Leona realized.

"Doesn't take much to wash out that old bridge," Edith said. "We lose it a couple of times every year. Don't worry, it will get fixed in a few days. Coffee?"

"Thanks," Leona said.

She sat down at one of the round tables. Oliver took the chair across from her. Roxy wriggled out of Leona's grasp and perched on the back of a vacant chair.

"Help yourself to the buffet." Edith poured coffee and smiled benignly at Roxy. "What do dust bunnies eat?"

"I think the real question is, what don't they eat?" Leona said. "Roxy will be fine. I'll fix a plate for her from whatever is on the buffet, if that's okay."

"There will be an extra charge," Edith warned.

"No problem," Leona said.

"All right, then," Edith said. "Let me know if you need anything else."

Oliver picked up his coffee and looked across the small room at Baxter. "Find any more evidence of Vincent Lee Vance's late-night visit?"

"We did, as a matter of fact," Baxter said, clearly elated. "The rez-screen in room three-oh-eight also came on. The door was unlocked so we took the liberty of checking inside. I hope that was okay, Ms. Fenwick? We didn't touch anything."

Edith Fenwick snorted. "Don't worry about it, but I can tell you right now you wasted your time. Those old rez-screens act up a lot at night. You can't blame it on Vance's ghost. The problem is Margo Gibbs."

"Who's Margo Gibbs?" Darla asked.

"She runs the station at the end of Main Street. She installed the rez-screens here at the inn. Must have done something to them that allows her to rez them remotely whenever she takes a notion—which is whenever she takes a notion to scare the tourists. The rest of us put up with it because channel one is the only rez-screen entertainment available in these parts."

Baxter looked crestfallen. Darla remained skeptical.

"Are you sure that's why the rez-screens came on last night?" she asked.

"Margo drinks." Edith grunted. "A lot. Says she likes to give visitors a little thrill. Claims they came to town to see a ghost, so she gives 'em one. She knew there were some guests here at the inn last night, so she must have cranked up that old Vincent Lee Vance video. Sorry it woke you up."

Evidently unconvinced or maybe just optimistic, Baxter and Darla went back to their meals.

Edith looked at Leona and Oliver. "This is your day to visit Thacker, isn't it? Remember what I said yesterday—you'll want to take a real close look at whatever he tries to sell you."

"We appreciate the advice," Oliver said.

Leona rose. "If you'll excuse me, I'm going to get breakfast."

Oliver stood, too. "Good idea."

Evidently realizing where they were headed, Roxy bounced up onto Leona's shoulder. From her perch she surveyed the muffins, eggs, toast, cereal, and fruit on the buffet. She chortled encouragingly when Leona selected a muffin.

"Okay," Leona said. "One for you, too."

Roxy chortled again.

"Right," Leona said. "Two for you."

Roxy chortled.

"Choose something else," Leona said in low tones. "We can't take all of them. The other guests might want some more." She continued on down the buffet table. "How about some eggs?"

Roxy chortled approval.

By the time they reached the end of the buffet table, there was a small mountain of food on Roxy's plate.

"It will be interesting to see if she actually finishes all that," Oliver remarked.

Roxy cleaned the plate. When she was done, she chortled, bounced off the table, and fluttered across the dining room. She disappeared into the kitchen.

"Uh-oh," Leona said. "I've got a bad feeling about this."

She jumped to her feet and hurried to the kitchen doorway. Edith was at the back door with Roxy, who was chortling.

"I'm not sure if I should let you outside," Edith said, wiping her hands on her apron. "Let me check with Dr. Griffin."

"It's okay," Leona said, relieved that Roxy wasn't running wild in the kitchen. "Dust bunnies like to explore. She'll come back when she's ready."

"Well, if you're sure," Edith said.

She opened the door. With a farewell chortle, Roxy tumbled outside and vanished.

"Thanks," Leona said.

She went back into the dining room and sat down at the table. "Crisis averted."

"For now," Oliver said.

"I wasn't worried."

"You were worried."

"Maybe a little." Leona lowered her voice. "What about the bridge? Aren't you concerned about the fact that it's washed out? You heard Edith. We could be stuck here for a few days."

"Now, that," Oliver said, "may be something to worry about."

CHAPTER TWENTY-SEVEN

The Thacker mansion loomed in the deep shadows of the woods, a gray stone bunker of a house. It was three stories tall and, Leona concluded, not at all graceful in its proportions. The windows were narrow and dark. The front door bore a strong resemblance to a fortress gate. There were no gardens, just a wide clearing around the structure and a long, graveled driveway.

"It's depressing," she announced, studying the big house through the windshield of the Slider. "I can't imagine living inside that place for any length of time."

"Judging by the stone that was used in the construction, I'd say it dates from the start of the Era of Discord," Oliver said.

"Vance's time."

"Yes." Oliver brought the car to a stop, rested one hand on the wheel, and contemplated the house. "Lawrence Thacker, the man who built the place, was convinced that the colonies were going to self-destruct in a civil war. He stocked up on food and water and weapons and then hunkered down with his wife and son to wait out the violence."

"A prepper," Leona said. "What happened to him?"

"When the rebellion was over, his wife and son left but Thacker stayed on. He became obsessed with the idea that Vance wasn't dead. When he died, the son inherited the mansion. It was handed down through the bloodline. About twenty years ago the Thacker we're going to meet today moved in and stayed. He never married."

Leona unfastened her seat belt. "This is going to be interesting."

Oliver opened the car door. "Remember the plan. I'm taking the lead. You're the outside consultant."

"Yes, right, I know. You're in charge. I got the message."

She opened the door, slipped out of the Slider, slung her messenger bag over one shoulder, and reached back for Roxy.

"Behave yourself," she ordered. "If you want to come inside with us, you're going to have to charm the housekeeper the way you did Edith Fenwick."

Roxy chortled, evidently confident in her talent for charm.

On the front steps, Oliver rezzed an old-fashioned doorbell. At first there was no response. Eventually Leona heard muffled footsteps. The door opened.

A tall, wiry woman dressed in jeans and a buttoned-up denim work shirt confronted them. Her graying hair was scraped into a thick braid that hung down her back. Her sharp features were set in stern, forbidding lines, and her pale eyes looked mean.

"What do you want?" she said.

She sounded mean, too, Leona thought. Roxy was going to have her work cut out for her if she wanted to charm the woman.

"You must be Ms. Harp," Oliver said, slipping into his professional persona.

"How do you know my name?"

"Edith Fenwick told us that Mr. Thacker had a housekeeper named Hester Harp. I'm Oliver Rancourt. This is Dr. Griffin, my consultant. I believe Mr. Thacker is expecting us."

"He's expecting you and the consultant, but not a dust bunny." Harp gave Roxy a piercing glare.

Roxy chortled and blinked her blue eyes. Harp did not look charmed.

Leona rezzed up a dazzling smile. "Edith Fenwick indicated that you were indispensable to Mr. Thacker."

"The dust bunny isn't coming into this house."

"Roxy won't be problem," Leona said. "She's a licensed emotional support dust bunny."

Roxy batted her baby blue eyes again.

"What's that ridiculous thing on its head?" Harp demanded.

"It's a fascinator," Leona said.

"A what?"

"A hat."

Harp was unmoved. "The dust bunny stays outside. No animals in the house. That's the rule. If you don't like it, you can get in your fancy car and leave."

Leona felt her temper kick in. She narrowed her eyes. "I explained that Roxy is a licensed emotional support—"

"I don't see any reason why Roxy can't stay outside," Oliver interrupted smoothly. He fixed Leona with a stern expression. "Leave her in the car if you're afraid she'll wander off and get lost."

"I'm not going to lock her up in the car," Leona muttered. She set Roxy down on the steps. "Run around and do some exploring," she said. "We'll be out in a while."

Roxy fluffed up, chortled, and bounced off, heading for the nearby trees.

"That's better." Harp stepped back and opened the door wider. "Thacker is in the library. Follow me."

Leona moved into the gloom-filled hall, aware that Oliver was right behind her.

She had been braced for strong currents of paranormal heat. Thacker was a collector, after all, and Edith Fenwick had called him a hoarder. But nothing could have prepared her for the sea of energy that churned in the hallway.

She glanced over her shoulder to see if Oliver was reacting to the seething currents.

"Hotter than a two-dollar mag-rez," he said in low tones.

Harp overheard him. "You get used to it. The Thackers have been collectors since the house was built."

It took a moment for Leona's eyes to adjust to the murky twilight that filled the mansion. When her vision sharpened, she almost regretted it. She had spent much of her career in the Underworld, but until now she had never been bothered by claustrophobia. The oppressive atmosphere inside the shadowed house was different. It closed in on her, rattling her nerves.

Stuff was piled everywhere. Alien artifacts, Old World and Colonial-era antiques, books, yellowed magazines, newspapers, paintings, and sculptures were stacked high on both sides of the hallway. There was only a narrow aisle available for walking.

The objects did not appear to be organized in any meaningful way. A dangerously high mountain of aging file folders sat atop a glowing quartz pedestal that was worthy of any mid-sized museum. Chipped and cracked dishes and cookware from the Era of Discord had been dumped into an open crate that also held rare and valuable quartz mirrors.

There was no doubting the paranormal provenance of many of the objects. In the dim light, the urns, crystals, and statuary that had come from the ruins radiated a familiar energy. Many of the other objects emitted currents that were not visible to the human eye, but they dazzled her senses.

Oliver looked around with an expression that was a mix of awe and disbelief. "This is . . . amazing."

"That's one word for it," Harp muttered. "But the pay is good. My mother had this job before me. Back then you could still see out some of the windows. Now they're all blocked off with what Thacker likes to call his collection."

"A lot of these objects are museum quality," Leona said.

"That's what Thacker claims." Harp stopped in front of a closed door. "Just so you know, the boss self-medicates with some herbs he grows in the basement."

"Thank you for the heads-up," Oliver said.

"Don't try to talk business with him. Just take a look at that old file he wants to sell. If you decide to buy it, call me. I'll take the money. I handle all of Mr. Thacker's finances."

That did not sound good, Leona thought, but she kept quiet.

"There will be documents to sign," Oliver said. He adjusted his glasses and gave Harp a sharp look. "Mr. Thacker's signature will be required."

"That's fine, just tell him where to sign," Harp said. "I'll handle the rest." She peered at Oliver. "You remembered the terms are cash only?"

"I remembered," Oliver said. He patted the messenger bag.

Harp opened the door and raised her voice. "The museum guy who wants to examine the Bluestone file is here, Mr. Thacker. He's got his secretary with him."

"Consultant," Leona said.

"Yeah, right," Harp muttered. "And a bit more on the side, according to what I heard."

"Excuse me?" Leona said, putting a lot of ice into her voice.

"Edith called to tell me you two were on the way here. She said you had booked two rooms but only used one last night."

Leona flushed. "Our private life is none of your business."

Oliver cleared his throat. "Uh, Leona, we're here to examine a file. We don't have time—"

She ignored him. A woman could take only so much.

"There seems to be a misunderstanding," she said through her teeth.

Harp ignored her. "I don't give a damn about your sleeping arrangements." She waved Leona and Oliver into the room. "Like I said, call me if you decide to buy the file."

Oliver gripped Leona's arm and steered her into the library. "What happens if we give Mr. Thacker the money?" he said over his shoulder.

"He'll stash it somewhere in the library," Harp said. "I'll never find it, so it won't get deposited. Might as well burn it in the fireplace. It will disappear either way."

She stepped back into the hall and closed the door with a thud that sounded uncomfortably like the crack of doom.

"What a dreadful woman," Leona fumed.

"Let it go. We've got work to do."

"Easy for you to say. You don't know how it feels to wake up one day and discover that everyone you know and some you don't are gossiping about you. I've already lost one career to the rumor mill at Hollister. I can't afford to have my new one sabotaged before it even gets properly launched. I need this new gig to work and I . . . Holy shit."

"My thoughts exactly," Oliver said.

CHAPTER TWENTY-EIGHT

The piles of artifacts, papers, books, and assorted junk stacked in the hallway had been merely the foothills, Oliver decided, the prelude to the towering mountain peaks and narrow canyons in the library. Footpaths that were barely wide enough to allow for single-file walking formed a maze across the room. The atmosphere was freighted with heavy waves of energy, a lot of which felt unstable.

"And we thought it was hot out in the hallway," Leona said. She sounded stunned.

The only good thing about the scene in the Thacker house library was that it had distracted her from the unfortunate exchange with Harp, Oliver thought.

"If the rest of the house is this bad, it's amazing the whole place hasn't exploded or caught fire." He looked around. "I've been in collectors' basements and vaults, and the storage rooms of a few museums that I thought were dangerously overcrowded, but this beats anything I've ever seen."

"There are rules and guidelines for handling antiquities," Leona said. "Every professional knows better than to pile so many objects of unknown power together in a confined space like this. Talk about a disaster waiting to happen."

He watched her out of the corner of his eye, trying to read her mood. She had been a mystery since they had awakened. He was reasonably certain the sex had been good for her, but he realized now that he had been expecting a change in their relationship this morning. He hadn't known what that change would look like—just something, *anything*, that indicated they'd had more than a casual one-night stand.

"Whatever you do, don't touch anything," he said. "Some of these piles look like they could topple if you even breathed hard on them. And if one of them goes down—" He did not finish the sentence. There was no need. Instead, he raised his voice. "Mr. Thacker? Oliver Rancourt here to see the Bluestone file."

"Yes, yes, I've been expecting you. I'm in the vault. Come on in."

The muffled voice came from somewhere in the back of the library. Unlike Harp, Thacker sounded welcoming.

"He probably doesn't get many visitors," Leona said.

Oliver raised his voice again. "Where, exactly, is the vault, Mr. Thacker?"

"Just follow the yellow brick road," Thacker called out. He chuckled. "You can't miss it. I marked the path myself after a guest got lost and panicked. Poor man was a basket case by the time I found him in the stacks. Claustrophobic, you know. Luckily he froze. No telling what might have happened if he had tried to escape by running blindly through the artifacts. Some of them are quite sensitive to human energy fields."

Oliver looked down. So did Leona. Sure enough, there was a strip of bright yellow tape on the carpet that led into the maze.

"Looks like we're off to see the Wizard of Lost Creek," he said. He went forward cautiously. "Follow me, stay close, and remember, don't—"

"—touch anything. Trust me, I won't. But this place hasn't been dusted in decades. Let's hope neither one of us sneezes."

"That would be a disaster."

The path marked by the tape twisted through the shaky-looking piles in what appeared to be a random fashion. But when Oliver rounded a corner, he found himself gazing through the doorway of a large walk-in vault that would have been equally suited to a bank.

Rows of steel-and-glass shelving were arranged in narrow aisles. Unlike the piles of chaotically stacked objects in the library and front hall, everything in the vault appeared to be organized. There was so much energy flooding the interior he was surprised there weren't a few small lightning bolts crackling in the atmosphere.

A small, thin, dapper man beamed at them. What little hair he had left was neatly trimmed. He wore a business suit that was accented with a polka-dot bow tie. The lenses of his wire-rimmed spectacles caught the light. His hands were sheathed in white gloves.

"Mr. Thacker, I presume," Oliver said. "Oliver Rancourt from the Rancourt Museum."

"Mr. Rancourt, a pleasure." Thacker put down the volume he had been examining and held out his hand. "I do hope you will be pleased with the Bluestone document. It really is an exceptional item, and given its history and provenance, it certainly belongs in the Rancourt collection."

"I'm looking forward to examining it," Oliver said. He shook hands and gestured toward Leona. "This is Dr. Griffin, my consultant."

"A pleasure, Mr. Thacker," Leona said. "You have an … amazing collection."

The atmosphere was so laden with conflicting currents of energy that it took a couple of seconds to process the transformation that came over Thacker. For a beat he gazed at Leona as if she were a magical creature who had just materialized in front of him. Astonishment and disbelief widened his eyes.

"Oh, dear," he said. "I see the rumors are true, then."

Leona narrowed her eyes in a warning look that Oliver was coming to recognize. He tried to think of a way to deflect her irritation but nothing sprang to mind. Of course not. Leona was a force of nature.

"If you're referring to the fact that those ridiculous paranormal investigators happened to find Mr. Rancourt in my room at the inn last night, I can assure you we were involved in a professional discussion. The rez-screens in some of the rooms had suddenly come on—"

"Yes, yes, the rez-screens." Thacker waved that aside. "They do that occasionally. Margo Gibbs drinks, you see. That's not what I meant. I was referring to the gossip about the bride."

"What bride?" Leona demanded.

"I'm told there's talk all over town that Vincent Lee Vance's bride has arrived and that she has the key," Thacker said.

Leona stared at him. "The key to what?"

"Why, the enhancement machine, of course," Thacker said. "According to the legend, Vance locked himself inside the device a hundred years ago, right after the failure of the rebellion. He promised his followers that the machine would keep him alive in a state of stasis until the time was right for his return. When the moment arrived, his bride would appear in Lost Creek and she would bring the key to the machine. She is the only one who can unlock it and free him to fulfill his destiny."

CHAPTER TWENTY-NINE

Hester Harp was right, Leona thought. Thacker was doing some serious self-medicating with some interesting herbs. Either that or he was delusional. Probably both.

Uncertain how to respond, she looked at Oliver for direction. But he was no longer in his antiquities-expert role. In its place was something very scary. He watched Thacker intently, cold fire burning in his eyes.

"What in green hell are you talking about, Thacker?" he said.

Thacker flinched and blinked a couple of times, unnerved. He made a visible effort to pull himself together.

"I d-didn't believe Ms. Harp when she told me that people in t-town were saying the bride had arrived," he stammered. "I was sure it was just another l-legend, you see. When it comes to Vance there are so many tall tales, aren't there?"

"Explain," Oliver said softly.

Thacker swallowed hard. "Surely you know the legend of the bride and the key?"

"No," Oliver said. "Please enlighten us."

This was not going well, Leona thought. Oliver was terrifying the poor man. Thacker looked as if he might faint from fright at any moment. That would only make things worse. Time to take charge.

"Don't pay any attention to Mr. Rancourt," she said, moving to step in front of Oliver. "He tends to get very intense when it comes to the subject of Vincent Lee Vance. Obviously he was not aware of the legend. I must admit I've never heard one regarding a bride and a key, either. Perhaps you could tell us more about it?"

Thacker tore his nervous eyes off Oliver and focused on her. She gave him a reassuring smile and he steadied.

"Yes, of course," he said, pulling himself together. "I just assumed both of you were aware of the story. Everyone here in Lost Creek knows it, but personally, I never put much credence into it. There are a great many conspiracy theories that feature Vance."

"Very true," Leona said. "Please go on."

She was aware that Oliver was waiting, as motionless as a crouched specter-cat, behind her, but he had the good sense not to interrupt.

"Yes, well, there are very few written records regarding the bride and the key," Thacker said. His self-confidence returned as he talked. "In fact, the only document I've viewed personally is a certain letter I found quite recently here in the house."

"I must admit I'm surprised you can locate anything in this collection," Leona said. "You obviously have a very unique filing system."

Thacker chuckled. "It does appear somewhat chaotic, doesn't it? I'm afraid it was like this when I took possession twenty years ago and it's only gotten worse. It's so hard to resist the impulse to add to the collection. I have been working my way through the various rooms, trying to identify the most important artifacts and documents. Whenever I find one, I make a point of relocating it here in the vault."

"Do you have the letter?" Oliver asked, impatience edging his voice.

"Yes, indeed." Thacker turned away and plucked a slim file off a shelf. "It was written by Vance himself."

Leona stilled. Behind her Oliver abruptly dropped the intimidating aura and slammed back into what she thought of as the real Oliver persona, that of a passionate researcher who hungered for answers. He had priorities. Evidently a genuine Vincent Lee Vance letter ranked a lot higher than the need to frighten Thacker. She smiled, amused by the quick shift.

"It was addressed to his followers here in Lost Creek," Thacker continued. "He called them the Guardians, you know."

"Provenance?" Oliver asked sharply.

"According to the notes in this file, it was found in the local post office a few months after the rebellion had been put down by the Guilds," Thacker said. "By then Vance had disappeared into the tunnels and was presumed dead."

"But the rumors and predictions of his eventual return were already getting traction among conspiracy buffs," Oliver observed absently. He did not take his eyes off the file folder.

"Indeed," Thacker said. "The rebellion fell apart immediately after the Last Battle of Cadence. Suddenly there were no more idiots running around claiming to be Guardians, that's for sure. No one here in town knew what to do with the letter, so my ancestor took it and filed it here in his collection. That's all I can tell you about the provenance."

"You said you only recently found it?" Leona asked.

"Yes," Thacker said. "It was pure chance. I was showing some Era of Discord documents to a visiting collector, an elderly woman from Frequency, and there it was, stuck in with some unrelated materials. I assumed it was just another example of Vance's rantings and ravings. By all accounts he was quite delusional toward the end. But I must admit I am now very intrigued and more than a bit concerned, truth be known."

"May I read the letter?" Leona asked.

"Certainly."

Thacker handed her a pair of white gloves. She pulled them on with practiced ease and took the letter from him. Oliver leaned over her shoulder to get a closer look. She was intensely aware of his prowling tension charging the atmosphere.

She did a quick visual examination. The paper appeared authentic to the era. So did the faded ink. She looked up. "I don't suppose you have another example of Vance's handwriting handy for comparison purposes?"

"Sadly, no," Thacker said. "But I've compared it to photographs of other documents attributed to him and it appears to be authentic."

Oliver removed his glasses to take a closer look. "Yes, it does."

Leona read the letter aloud, concentrating a little to decipher the hundred-year-old script.

To My Loyal Guardians:

I regret that I must leave you for a time, but know that the Great Cause is not lost. The Federation of City-states and the Guilds may claim victory for the present, but their triumph will be temporary.

I will return, and when I do, my powers will be enhanced a thousandfold. I will take my place as the leader of Harmony, and those who remain loyal will receive the gift that only I can bestow—paranormal talents beyond their wildest dreams.

Until the time is right for me to return to you, I will sleep in the Enhancement Machine. Do not fear. I shall be in a state of stasis. I will not grow old or weak. Instead, my powers will continue to develop.

You will know to expect my imminent return by these two signs:

First: The insignias of the Great Cause will be delivered to those who have been chosen to become the new generation of Guardians. I will communicate with the faithful telepathically from inside the Enhancement Machine. Only those who hear my voice and obey will be rewarded.

Second: When all is in readiness, my chosen bride will appear among you. She will find the Enhancement Machine and unlock it with the key. Thereupon I will awaken and lead you to our great victory.

Until that glorious day, I bid you farewell.

Leona looked up. "It's signed by Vance."

Oliver put his glasses back on. "It certainly is an interesting document."

"It's not interesting." Leona shivered. "It's downright creepy." She glared at Thacker. "What makes you so sure I'm the bride?"

"Well, I can't be positive, of course." Thacker sighed. "But Ms. Harp informed me that the rumors are circulating in town. Last night several people in Lost Creek evidently received telepathic messages from Vance confirming that you were the bride and that you had the key in your possession."

Leona shook her head in disbelief. "That's ridiculous. Absolute nonsense. I'm starting to wonder if this entire town is delusional."

Thacker frowned. "You're saying you're not the bride?"

"Yes, Mr. Thacker, that's what I'm saying."

Oliver clamped both hands very firmly on her shoulders, sending a silent message—*stop talking*. She reminded herself that he had a plan. Plans were all well and good until they fell apart. It wasn't her fault that things had taken a very strange twist.

Oliver looked at Thacker. "Perhaps you could show me the Bluestone file?"

"Of course, of course." Thacker appeared relieved by the change of subject. He picked up a large envelope and held it out along with a pair of gloves. "A fascinating document. The Bluestone Project was evidently one of the earliest attempts to investigate and harness the power of paranormal energy back on the Old World. It was a government program. Highly classified. Things went very much awry. They tried to shut it down and erase all record of it, but you can never make that sort of research disappear entirely."

"No," Oliver said. "You can't."

He started to pull on the gloves but gave up when it became obvious they were too small. Instead, he opened the envelope and carefully removed a document secured in a blue cover decorated with what looked like an official government seal.

He opened the document, gave it a cursory look, and inserted it back into the envelope.

"This will be a wonderful acquisition for the Rancourt," he said.

"Excellent." Thacker was clearly pleased. "You can pay Ms. Harp on the way out. She handles the finances."

"There's some paperwork to sign," Oliver said.

"Yes, yes, no problem."

Oliver opened the messenger bag and handed a document to him. "You'll want to read it before you sign."

Thacker chuckled and scrawled his name and the date. "Not necessary. If I can't trust a professional colleague, who can I trust?"

"Good question," Leona said.

"Precisely." Thacker peered more closely at her. "The name Griffin is familiar. I don't pay much attention to the news. The papers are always a few days late. But by any chance are you the para-archaeologist who was kidnapped several weeks ago?"

Leona winced. "That was me."

"I'm so glad you're all right. Pirates are a plague in the Underworld. The story caught my eye because it reminded me of another kidnapping involving a young girl. That was several years ago, of course."

Leona went still. "My sister, Molly. What made you remember us?"

"Something about the name."

"Griffin?"

"No, the name of the man who took the young girl all those years ago—Willard."

Leona got a screaming-loud ping. "Nigel Willard. Do you have some information about him in your collection?"

"Not a Nigel Willard, another Willard." Thacker raised his gaze to the topmost shelf. "I believe I have a journal—"

A muffled shriek of outrage reverberated in the hall.

"Oh, dear, that's Ms. Harp," Thacker said. "She sounds somewhat annoyed. It's never a good idea to upset her like that."

"Get out of there, you little monster," Harp screamed. "You're dead. Do you hear me? Dead."

"Shit." Leona whipped around, ducked past Oliver, and rushed back toward the door, following the yellow tape. "She's trying to murder Roxy."

CHAPTER THIRTY

Oliver watched Leona disappear amid the deep canyons and soaring peaks of documents, papers, books, and artifacts. He held his breath until he heard the outer door slam open. Only then did he allow himself to relax. She had made it into the front hall without setting off an avalanche.

Turning back to Thacker, he took the envelope and the signed paperwork and dumped both into the messenger bag. "You're certain you want me to give the payment to your housekeeper?"

"Yes, yes, yes." Thacker waved his hands. "Harp takes care of everything around here. I don't know what I'd do without her."

Oliver started to follow the path to the door but he paused. "Any chance you might sell the Vance letter?"

"Sorry, no. This collection is devoted to Era of Discord documents and artifacts. That letter belongs here. Don't worry, I'll keep it safe in the vault."

"Right. In that case, Leona and I will be on our way. Long drive back to Illusion Town."

"No rush," Thacker said. "I heard the bridge was washed out last night. The creek will be running very high by now. I'm afraid you and Ms. Griffin will be enjoying the amenities of our fine town for a few days."

"That may be a problem," Oliver said.

"I understand. You're welcome to come back here anytime to explore my collection."

"Thank you," Oliver said.

He retraced the route through the overstuffed library with great caution. The noise out in the hall grew louder as he got closer to the door.

Harp's shrill, infuriated voice echoed. "I warned you that beast was not allowed inside this house."

"If you'll get out of my way, I'll remove her," Leona said.

She was furious, too, Oliver thought. But her control was better than Harp's. She was on a mission to save Roxy. She was not going to get distracted by a screaming match with the housekeeper.

There was another sound now—the muffled rumble of an old-fashioned amber-powered motor. It sounded like it was coming from inside the walls.

There was no sign of the women, so he set out to find the scene of the crime. At the end of the hall, he rounded a mountain of papers and artifacts and turned into an intersecting corridor. At the far end a door stood open.

Harp's unpleasant voice came from inside the room.

"If you don't get that oversized rat out of here immediately, I will use my flamer," she shouted.

"I'm working on it," Leona said. "You're overreacting, Ms. Harp."

"I know everyone is saying you're the bride but I don't give a shit."

"I am not anyone's bride." Leona's voice was rising now.

Oliver arrived at the open door and found himself looking into a large kitchen filled with vintage appliances. Leona and Harp were confronting each other in front of the open door of what at first glance appeared to be an empty floor-to-ceiling closet. Harp gripped a large carving knife in one hand.

There were no shelves in the closet. No kitchen equipment. Nothing at all. The rumble of the motor and a faint, muffled chortle reverberated from somewhere inside.

"Is there a problem?" Oliver asked. Okay, stupid question—clearly there was a problem, but he had no idea what it was.

Leona swung around. "It's not a big deal. I was just explaining to Ms. Harp that I will take care of the situation. It's a matter of timing, you see."

"*There* is the problem," Harp announced. She aimed the carving knife at the closet.

The top of Roxy's ears came into view first, followed by the rest of her fluffy frame. She rose majestically upward on the platform of a dumbwaiter. She was chortling madly, evidently overcome with excitement.

When the device reached waist level it kept rising, heading for the floor above.

Leona made her move. She reached into the shaft with both hands and swept Roxy off the platform. The dumbwaiter continued upward.

Roxy chortled deliriously.

"It was just a game as far as she was concerned," Leona said, tucking Roxy into the crook of her arm. "She didn't cause any harm."

"If that dust bunny shows up here again, I'll use the flamer," Harp warned.

Leona was looking seriously dangerous now. Oliver stepped in quickly.

"Mr. Thacker and I came to an agreement," he said. "He confirmed that I am to give the money to you, Ms. Harp."

"What?" Distracted, Harp turned swiftly toward him. "Oh, it's you. Cash only."

"Right." He opened the messenger bag and took out the envelope that contained the money. "Feel free to count it. You'll find it's all there."

Harp snatched the envelope out of his hand, extracted the bundle of bills, and counted the money with impressive efficiency. It was not, he thought, the first time she had handled large amounts of cash.

When she was finished, she snorted. "The document is yours."

"I'd like a receipt," he said.

"I don't give receipts."

"Somehow that does not come as a surprise. How much are you skimming off the top of these sales?"

"Take the dust bunny and get out of here," Harp snarled.

"Don't worry," Leona said, "we're on our way."

With Roxy clutched close, she marched out of the kitchen. Oliver followed.

Neither of them said a word until they were in the Slider. Roxy wriggled out of Leona's arms and took up her favorite position on the back of the seat.

"I really do not like this town," Leona announced.

He put the car in gear and drove back toward the main road. "Can't say it's on my list of top ten vacation destinations."

She looked at him. "The Vance letter is a forgery."

"I know," he said. "So is the Bluestone document."

"There's something else," Leona said. "When I got to the kitchen, the first couple buttons of Harp's shirt were unbuttoned. When she saw me, she fastened the shirt right away."

"So?"

"She was wearing one of those Vance return cult pendants."

"I think that from now on we should assume everyone in town is involved in the cult until proven otherwise."

Leona fell silent for a moment.

"Thacker said he has a journal written by someone named Willard," she said.

"I heard. It might be another forgery."

"Maybe, but I need to see it."

CHAPTER THIRTY-ONE

Leona watched the narrow graveled road through the windshield. The gathering sense of dread that had been lurking at the edge of her awareness since arriving in Lost Creek was growing heavier.

"What is going on around here?" she whispered.

"Good question," Oliver said. "But I've got another one."

"What?"

"Everyone seems certain that the bridge washed out last night. We're going to take a look."

"Do you think people are lying about the bridge? Why would they do that?"

"Let's just say I'm curious."

They reached the end of the drive, but instead of turning left in the direction that would take them into town, Oliver turned right.

They drove the quarter mile to the creek and stopped. The water was running high and very swiftly. The bridge was gone.

Another chill zapped across the back of Leona's neck.

"Looks like everyone was telling us the truth," she said. "We really are stuck here."

Oliver unfastened his seat belt and opened the car door. "I'm going to take a closer look."

"At what?" she asked.

"I'll let you know when I get back," he said.

Sensing adventure, Roxy vaulted neatly onto his shoulder. Oliver walked down to the creek's edge. She watched the two of them examine the scene for a couple of minutes.

"Well?" she said when they returned to the car.

Oliver rezzed the car engine. "The bridge is gone."

"I noticed. I assume there's a punch line here?"

"Oh, yeah." He did a perfect three-point turn and drove back toward town. "The bridge was not swept away by the river. It was removed neatly and cleanly by someone with a very impressive set of tools. Probably a couple of someones."

Leona folded her arms around her midsection. "Sabotage."

"Yep."

"This is all about that yellow pyramid crystal, isn't it? The cult crowd thinks we have it and they really believe it's the key to resurrecting Vance."

"Looks like it."

"We need to do something. We need to act. We can't just hang around waiting for stuff to happen."

"I agree," Oliver said. "Tonight I'm going to pay a late-night call on the local rez-screen broadcasting station."

"Well, I suppose that's better than doing nothing."

"Thanks for your encouragement and support."

She winced. "You know what I meant."

His mouth kicked up in the little twitch that signaled amusement. "You're not the wait-and-see type, are you?"

"Apparently not." She glanced at the messenger bag in the back seat. "Why did you buy the Bluestone document if you knew it was a forgery?"

"Curiosity. I'd like to know who went to the trouble and expense of producing a fraudulent edition of a document relating to an Old World research project that was scrapped back in the twentieth century."

Leona got a ping. "How did you find out about it?"

"Another very good question. I rely on a handful of independent book and artifact scouts who work in the gray market."

"I see," Leona said.

"Are you going to go all judgy on me?"

"Nope. As you pointed out, every museum dabbles in the gray market from time to time. Goes with the territory. Are you saying you got the lead on the Bluestone document from one of your scouts?"

"Yes. It felt solid so I set up the appointment with Thacker. Meanwhile, I was also planning to attend the Antiquarian Society's reception to retrieve Pandora's box."

Another frisson of knowing shivered across her senses. "We are assuming that someone manipulated things to make sure that I was there, but they could not have known you would be there, too."

"No, pretty sure my presence on the scene was not part of the plan."

She glanced at him. "Regardless, we were both supposed to end up here in Lost Creek, weren't we?"

"Looks like it."

"Talk about a complicated strategy."

Oliver tapped a finger on the wheel. "There are two kinds of planners. Those like me, who prefer the simplest, least complicated approach—and then there are the jugglers."

"Jugglers?"

"They go for elaborate, complicated scenarios because it makes them feel smarter than everyone else. In control. But in reality, they are jugglers who pride themselves on keeping a lot of spinning plates in the air.

That works great right up until a plate falls off a pole. Lose one and the others become unstable."

"I don't like thinking of you and me as a couple of spinning plates."

"The good news for us is that our juggler lost control back at the start," Oliver said. "They just don't know it yet."

"What do you mean?"

"I'm sure the juggler never anticipated that we would become allies. If anything, we should have been rivals."

Allies. The word came as a shock. It shouldn't have, Leona thought. She wanted to tell him that they were not just allies, they were lovers. But now she had to reckon with the possibility that last night might have been a convenient interlude for him. This morning when she had awakened, she had hoped for more.

This was what came of breaking rule number two: *No sleepovers.*

She squared her shoulders. "Right. Allies."

Oliver shot her a quick, questioning look, as if he wasn't sure what to make of her cool, firm confirmation of the nature of their relationship. Then he turned his attention back to the road.

"Whoever is running this show must be here in Lost Creek by now," he said. "Things will start moving quickly."

"What makes you think that?"

"All of the elements of this very complicated project have been assembled in one place, and access to the outside world has been cut off. Our juggler knows they can't keep all the plates spinning indefinitely. It's time to bring the show to a close."

Leona considered for a moment. "I get that a bunch of delusional cultists are convinced that I've got the key to the enhancement machine where Vance has been hanging out all these years. But why lure you here?"

"I've been wondering that myself. Maybe I'll get an answer tonight."

"When you take a look at the local broadcasting studio?"

"Right."

"Roxy and I are coming with you."

"I've been thinking about that and I've decided—"

"You need me. I'm good with locks, remember?"

"I am, too. But I was about to say that I don't like the idea of leaving you alone at the inn, so you and Roxy are coming with me. I'm in charge tonight. Understood?"

"Has anyone ever told you that you may have control issues?"

"Often."

"What a coincidence. I get that a lot myself. It's annoying, isn't it?"

Chapter Thirty-Two

The community of Lost Creek shut down early but Oliver waited until midnight before leading Leona and Roxy out into the fog. They used the fire escape stairs at the rear of the inn. Roxy rode on his shoulder. Evidently she preferred the view from the higher vantage point.

There were no streetlamps, but the glow of the drifting mist was sufficient to illuminate the narrow sidewalks of the main street.

He did not like bringing Leona along for the foray to the broadcasting studio, but he had told her the truth earlier today—leaving her alone at the inn would have made him even more uneasy. It was clear now that she was at the center of this thing.

"It's a fine night for ghosts," Leona said softly. "The real kind."

He glanced at her. She was bundled up in an anorak, the messenger bag with the pyramid stone inside slung across her body. He could feel her tension but he was also acutely aware of her determination. He pictured her as a little girl, bravely defying the orphanage director to call a private investigation agency when her sister went missing. Then he remembered the wild escape through the tunnels the night of the Antiquarian Society reception. He would never forget the bloody evening gown exploding in flames. He wasn't going to forget the sight of her in her underwear and his evening jacket, either. And he would remember last night for the rest of his life.

They had spent so little time together and yet they had been through so much. He felt more intimately acquainted with her after knowing her for two days than he had with lovers he had known far longer. Closer than he had felt to Anna, even though they had been matched by an agency.

He yanked his thoughts away from that colossal mistake. He had only himself to blame for the fiasco of the non-marriage. Yes, Anna had been certain she was comfortable with his talent, but she'd had no real understanding of what he could do with it—neither had he, although he'd had his suspicions—not until the night when they had both discovered that he was one of the monsters.

"No such thing as ghosts, remember?" he said.

"I know, but I'm getting that vibe you get when someone is watching you."

"So am I."

She glanced at him. "Are we going to do anything about it?"

"Not yet. Pretty sure we're not in immediate danger."

"Why do you say that?"

"Roxy isn't worried."

She looked at Roxy. "You're right."

The small broadcasting studio at the end of the street was dark. Channel one had gone off the air at eight, as scheduled. Oliver stopped at the door and removed the lock pick from his pocket.

"I've got this," Leona said.

She touched the lock with her fingertips. He felt a whisper of her energy—it gave him a pleasant little rush—and then he heard the bolt slide open.

"You really are very handy to have around," he said.

"Thanks. It's always nice to be appreciated."

For a couple of seconds he tried to decide if she sounded irritated but gave up the effort. He just could not tell.

The interior of the studio was dark, thanks to the lowered shades. He took out the small penlight he had brought with him and rezzed it. The beam played over a jumble of vintage broadcasting equipment, an elderly swivel chair, and a heavy wooden desk. There was no sign of the alcoholic station manager. Evidently Margo Gibbs was drinking somewhere else tonight.

Roxy vaulted down to the floor and began to investigate.

Leona looked around. "What are we looking for?"

"Anything that looks or feels interesting," he said.

She turned slowly on her heel. Energy whispered.

"How about a floor safe?" she said.

"That would definitely qualify. Do you see one?"

"No, but I can sense the psi-lock." She walked across the room and stopped near a workbench that held an outdated microphone and a control box. She tapped the toe of one sneaker on the tiled floor. "I think it's under here."

"Let's take a look."

He crossed the room and went down on one knee to examine the section of flooring that had caught Leona's attention. It didn't take long to find the hidden button. He rezzed it cautiously.

One large floor tile popped open, revealing a vintage safe. Leona opened it without any effort. He aimed the light into the space. Together the three of them considered the video sticks inside. After a moment he removed one and focused the beam of the flashlight on the label.

"'Vance Speech Number Two,'" he read.

Leona took out the other two sticks. "'Vance Speech Number One' and 'Vance Speech Number Three.'"

"That explains the late night rez-screen programming on channel one. No ghosts involved." He took the video sticks from her, dropped them back into the floor safe, and got to his feet. A frisson of awareness raised the hair on the back of his neck. "I'm getting that vibe again."

"So am I." Leona closed the safe, stood, and picked up Roxy. "Maybe it's that guy with the mag-rez, the one named Burt."

"Time to find out."

"I assume you have a plan?"

"Always."

He explained it.

"No offense, but that seems like a very simplistic plan," Leona said.

"I'm a simple man. I like simple plans. I told you, I'm not one of the jugglers."

"You are not a simple man, but we can argue about that later. Let's do this. I don't like being watched."

He opened the door of the studio and led the way out onto the sidewalk. They walked quickly back toward the inn. The fog was heavier now. He heard footsteps behind them. The watcher was trying to close the distance.

When they reached the narrow alley between the general store and an amber tuning shop, he stepped into the dense shadows, stopped, and waited.

Leona kept walking, Roxy tucked under one arm. The footsteps of the person following her drew closer. A dark silhouette appeared at the mouth of the alley.

Oliver spoke from the darkness. "Looking for someone?"

The figure gave a violent start and swung around.

"I just want to talk to her. I wasn't going to hurt her."

A man, Oliver realized. Late forties. His long hair was tied back with a narrow strip of leather. The khaki trousers, well-worn boots, and scarred leather jacket marked him as ex-Guild. There was a set of headphones draped around his neck.

Oliver moved closer so that he was no longer concealed in the alley. "Why do you want to talk to my consultant?"

Before the watcher could respond, quick, light footsteps announced the return of Leona. She appeared out of the fog, still clutching Roxy, who was, Oliver noted, fully fluffed and unconcerned. The dust bunny did not detect an immediate threat.

"Who are you?" Leona asked.

She spoke in a calm, polite voice, as if she were accustomed to strangers following her in a fog-bound night. Some of the watcher's tension dissipated.

"Starkey," he said. He cast a wary glance at Oliver and then turned back to Leona, very earnest now. "Dwight Starkey. I wasn't going to hurt you, Ms. Griffin, but I need to know if what folks are saying is true. Are you the bride?"

"No," Leona said. "There is no bride, just a dumb legend."

"They're saying you brought the key. That you're here to open the enhancement machine and awaken Vance."

"Do you really believe Vance is going to make a comeback tour?" Oliver asked.

"Didn't used to." Starkey grunted. "Figured it was just a local legend for the tourists. But after Vance started talking to people here in town, making promises . . . Well, I started to wonder."

"Vance talks to people?" Oliver asked.

His voice must have had an edge, because Starkey flinched.

"He contacts his followers telepathically from the enhancement machine," Starkey said. "At least, that's what everyone around here thinks is going on. Personally, I don't buy that story."

"Are you one of his followers?" Leona asked gently.

"Shit, no." Starkey took a deep breath and seemed to stand a little straighter. "I'm fourth-generation Guild. My great-grandfather fought Vance's rebels at the Last Battle of Cadence. My granddad and my dad were members of the Cadence Guild. I joined when I was eighteen. I'd still be working in the Underworld if I hadn't gotten burned real bad by an artifact. Moved here a couple of years ago. I'm an artist now."

Leona brightened. "Are you, by any chance, the artist who signs his work Stark? The one who did that amber and metal specter-cat on display in the lobby at the inn?"

"Yes, ma'am," Starkey said.

"I love the piece," Leona said. "I'm going to buy it before I leave."

"Thanks," Starkey said. "Good amber in that cat. Tuned."

"I know nav amber when I see it," Leona said. "My work takes me into the Underworld, too."

Oliver cut in before the conversation could meander any further. "You're the one who was watching our windows in the fog last night, weren't you?"

"Yeah. Sorry. Just trying to figure out what in green hell is going on. I've got this feeling that the whole damn town is in danger. Most folks around here seem to be in some kind of trance."

"What do you think is going on around here, Starkey?"

"I don't know, and that's the honest truth." Starkey shook his head. "All I can tell you is that folks have been talking about the arrival of the bride for a couple of weeks now. They're sure Ms. Griffin here is her and that she's got the key."

"Do you think they will try to steal it from her?" Oliver asked.

"Doubt it," Starkey said. "At least not until she opens the enhancement machine. See, that's the thing. According to the Voice, she's the only one who can find the damned machine and unlock it. No one else can free

Vance. Shit, I can't believe I'm even saying that. I never believed any of it. Told myself it was just a scam."

"Who is running the con?" Oliver asked.

"Best guess is the acolyte."

"Who is the acolyte?" Leona asked.

"I don't know that, either." Starkey grunted. "When those pendants showed up on everyone's doorstep a while back, the Voice said they had been distributed by the acolyte. We were told to await the arrival of the bride."

"So you've heard this Voice?" Oliver asked.

"Sure. Comes from the pendants." Starkey pulled his out from under his jacket. "Gets in your head. When I realized what was going on I started listening to rez-rock on the headphones. That way I can still hear the Voice but it feels like it's coming from outside, not in my head."

Oliver glanced at Leona. "The pendants are communication devices of some kind."

"Apparently," she said.

Starkey frowned. "Not regular coms, I can tell you that much. They don't work both ways. You can't talk to the acolyte or anyone else with them. You just receive the messages. The Voice is hard to describe. It's like you hear it but not with your ears."

"Do you think Lost Creek really was Vance's headquarters during the Era of Discord?" Leona asked.

"Yes," Starkey said. "Wasn't sure when I moved here, but I do now. Until you showed up, though, I never believed he was coming back to lead another uprising."

"Don't worry," Leona said. "He's not coming back."

"I hope not," Starkey said.

"You're a Guild man," Oliver said. "You know the Underworld. So did Vance. His entire strategy was based on using the tunnels for his attacks.

If he did initiate the rebellion from here, he must have had access to the caverns. Any idea where that entrance was?"

"The Waterfall Cavern. Supposedly his enhancement machine is somewhere in the tunnels under Lost Creek, but no one has ever found it."

Oliver took the small locator off his belt. "We need the coordinates of the Waterfall Cavern."

"No problem. It's not that far. A thirty-minute hike." Starkey took out his own locator and sent the coordinates. When he was finished, he dropped it into a pocket and looked at Leona. "You're sure you're not the bride?"

"Positive," Leona said.

He nodded, evidently satisfied. "You two should probably get out of town first thing in the morning."

"I agree," Oliver said. Leona shot him a startled look. He ignored her. "This sounds like a job for the Guild and the FBPI. But there's the little matter of the bridge. It seems to have disappeared."

Starkey snorted. "That old trick. Should have known Burt and his pals would pull it. Don't worry, I'll take care of it."

"On your own?" Oliver asked.

"I'm not the only one in town who doesn't think it would be a good idea for Vance to return."

Chapter Thirty-Three

Leona waited until Starkey had disappeared into the fog before she spoke.

"Why did you let him think we'll leave in the morning?" she said, her voice low and fierce. "I don't know about you, but I'm not going anywhere until I get more information about the yellow crystals. We've barely scratched the surface. At the very least we need to check out that Waterfall Cavern. And I need to know more about that journal Thacker has."

He had known she would not be happy with his decision. Convincing her that he was right was going to take some work. He had two options— logical persuasion or brute force. He decided to try logic first.

"Calm down and listen to me," he said. "I realize this situation has rezzed a lot of strong emotions and you've still got questions, but—"

"Got news for you, Rancourt. Starting a conversation with the words *calm down* was your first mistake. You might as well forget the rest of whatever you were going to say."

"Let's face it," he said, determined to plow on. "We walked into a situation that is a lot bigger and a lot more dangerous than we assumed at the start. Right?"

"So?"

"Our team consists of one museum curator, one unemployed para-archaeologist, and one dust bunny. We're in over our heads. We don't have the resources to continue this investigation, but we've gathered more than enough information to get the attention of the FBPI and the Guild. Unlike us, they *do* have the resources to finish this job. They can tear this town apart and they can go into that cave Starkey told us about. They can follow the trail into the Underworld if necessary."

"The authorities will want to confiscate the pyramid crystal. If I give it to them, odds are it will disappear into an FBPI vault and I'll never see it again. I can't let that happen, not until I get answers."

"I can guarantee you it won't end up in an FBPI vault."

"What makes you so sure of that?"

"The Foundation has some strings it can pull."

"What if those strings don't work?"

"You need to trust me, Leona."

She sighed. "I know you mean well and I appreciate your good intentions."

"My good intentions?"

"But the bottom line is that you're the director of a small museum run by a foundation that no one seems to have heard of. I seriously doubt you or the organization you represent have the clout to override the Federal Bureau of Psi Investigation."

"Trust me, Leona. I'll make sure you get that damned crystal."

She did not respond until they reached the emergency exit door at the back of the inn.

"All right," she said.

He breathed a sigh of relief. "Thanks."

"If you want to thank me, just make sure I get that pyramid crystal when this is over."

"You have my word."

She opened the door before he could do it for her and went into the poorly lit stairwell, Roxy tucked under one arm. He followed, climbing the stairs behind her. The tension charging the atmosphere around her made him want to reach out and pull her into his arms so that he could comfort her. But something told him she would not welcome his touch at that particular moment.

Call me the sensitive type.

When they reached the second floor they went down the silent hallway and stopped in front of their rooms. It occurred to him that he had been assuming he would sleep in her bed again tonight. Now that the moment of decision had arrived, he wasn't sure how to ask the question.

"Uh, Leona—"

"No," she said. "I'm not in the mood. I'm sulking."

Before he could come up with a way to deal with that statement, she disappeared inside her room with Roxy. The door closed. Firmly. He heard the bolt slide home.

"This day just gets better and better," he muttered.

He rezzed the lock of his door and let himself into the shadowed room. Closing and locking the door, he walked toward the small desk, stripping off his jacket as he went.

The only warning he got was a glimpse of the small Alien artifact, a simple crystal bowl no larger than a soup bowl, sitting on the bed. The energy in the object was hot—dangerously hot.

He swung around, intending to dive for the door, but it was too late.

The explosion made no audible sound but the radiation enveloped him in a shower of senses-dazzling, silently screaming nightmares.

One crystal-clear thought hit him before he began to lose consciousness. He had the answer to the question he had been asking since he had picked up the fake Bluestone document at the Thacker mansion. He now knew why he had been lured to Lost Creek.

CHAPTER THIRTY-FOUR

The certainty that Oliver was in terrible danger came out of nowhere, icing her senses between one step and the next. For an eternity that must have lasted only a couple of seconds, she could not move. Could not breathe.

Roxy growled. Leona looked down and saw that the dust bunny was sleeked out. All four eyes and some teeth were showing. Nimbly, she vaulted to the floor and raced to the door, fascinator ribbons flying.

Leona tore herself out of the panicky paralysis and lurched toward the door. Oliver was in trouble. She had never been more sure of anything in her life.

She yanked open the door and flew out into the hall, Roxy at her feet. Together they raced to the door of room 204.

It was locked.

She steeled her nerves, concentrated, and caught the vibe of the lock. It was simple enough—it was just an old amber-rez room key in an old inn. No problem. She tweaked the vibe of her own key, essentially turning it into a passkey, and opened the door.

A storm of disorienting energy struck her senses. Vision, hearing, touch, balance—they all began to shut down in response to the sensory overload. Somewhere in the distance she heard Roxy rumble in a way that made it clear she was also affected by the silent, screaming gale. She scrambled up to Leona's shoulder and hunkered down. Two auras were stronger than one.

A single, coherent thought surfaced above the chaos. Leona grabbed on to it and held tight. This was Alien energy and it was coming from somewhere nearby. She focused through the yellow crystal pendant around her neck, seeking the source of the psi storm.

She found it almost immediately. At first glance, there was nothing extraordinary or alarming about the small crystal bowl on the bed. But she had handled objects like it while being held hostage by the pirates. It was from the newly discovered Glass House sector, and everything in those Underworld ruins was potentially dangerous.

She concentrated, found a path through the whirlwind, and worked her way to the source of the currents. When she was as certain as she could be that she had found what she was looking for, she sent back a neutralizing pulse with the goal of flatlining the energy of the bowl.

And then she held her breath because she was dealing with Alien energy, and the one truism about working with artifacts was that they were unpredictable. No one knew for sure what the ancients had intended when they tuned their objects. The crystal bowl on the bed could have been a medical device or a lethal weapon.

Roxy's paws tightened on her shoulder.

The bowl shut down just like any other engine that had been de-rezzed. Leona allowed herself to breathe again.

Oliver was on the floor at the foot of the bed. Motionless. His glasses had fallen beside him. His hands were clenched and his eyes were shut tight. His muscles were locked as though he were in mortal combat with unseen forces.

She rushed forward and crouched beside him. Roxy, apparently satisfied that the situation was under some semblance of control, hopped down to the floor and fluffed out. But all four eyes were still open.

"Oliver." Leona put a hand on his shoulder. It was like touching a tightly coiled spring.

His eyes opened halfway. He stared at her as if trying to bring her into focus. "Run. Find Starkey. He'll help you."

"I'm not running anywhere," she said. "Not without you."

"Go. Now."

She wanted to ask questions, a lot of them, starting with *What the hell just happened to you?* But this was not the time. The good news was that his pulse was strong and there was no sign of blood or physical injury that she could see. She had shut down the psychic weapon but damage had been done. Oliver was still battling invisible demons. He needed backup.

She tightened her grip on his shoulder and cautiously rezzed her talent. There were serious risks in deliberately attempting to interfere with another person's aura, especially if the target's energy field was as powerful as Oliver's. That went double when the target was in psychic combat mode. *Talk about unpredictable,* she thought.

Roxy muttered and pressed against her leg, offering the support of her sturdy little aura.

"Thanks," Leona whispered.

She opened her senses . . .

'. . . and nearly drowned in a tsunami of chaos.

Her throat closed. Her chest tightened. The shadowed room began to dissolve into a foggy dreamscape. It was a wonder that Oliver was not in a coma or dead. On some deep level he was sane, and he was in a mortal battle to stay that way.

She tightened her grip on his shoulder and plunged into the

maelstrom of fierce, sparking energy, seeking the strong, steady vibe at the heart of the storm. It had to be there—otherwise Oliver would have been lost by now.

She eased into the chaos in much the same way that she and Oliver had made their way through the towers of unstable artifacts and junk at Thacker's mansion, searching for the yellow brick road that marked the path to the center . . .

. . . and there it was. The currents that anchored his sanity were still strong but they could not hold out for much longer. She focused, trying to offer additional strength. It was the first time she had ever attempted such a tactic, but it was not unlike de-rezzing a complicated psi-lock.

Oliver seized on the lifeline she had tossed to him with such shocking strength that she almost fell into the chaos herself. Without warning, he took control. His energy field snapped back to full force, threatening to overwhelm her.

"Shit," she whispered.

She had never experienced anything like the sensation. The term *psychic vampire* came to mind. It was not a reassuring image. She reminded herself that Oliver was in the process of recovering from a near-coma and, quite possibly, a near-death experience. He was not trying to take control of her senses. He was a man coming back to the surface and gasping for air.

In the brief moment of panic, she fought the urge to fight back. If she did resist, she might accidentally flatline him the way she had the dangerous little bowl a moment ago.

Frantically she retreated, going full-dark with her talent in an attempt to sever the connection. The technique worked. She was suddenly free.

Oliver's hands unclenched. He opened his eyes, no longer a man trapped in hell. "Thought I told you to run."

"I'll get right on that." She stumbled to her feet and reached down to help him off the floor. "But you're coming with me. We both need to get away from this inn tonight."

He ignored the hand she offered, which was probably for the best because he was a lot bigger than she was and might have pulled her down to the floor. He got to his feet unsteadily but under his own power and looked around as if reorienting himself. For a second or two she worried that he would lose his balance, but he stayed upright.

"Flamers," he said. "We're not leaving without them."

"I've got mine." She patted the messenger bag still slung across her body. "Yours is in your messenger bag, remember?"

He shook his head, as if to clear it, and then appeared to realize he had his bag, too. "Right." He spotted his glasses on the floor and grabbed them. "Let's go."

"Right."

She went to the open door and started down the hall, heading for the emergency stairs at the back of the inn. She stopped when she realized Oliver was not following. She looked back and saw that he was rubbing his forehead with one hand.

"Are you okay?" she whispered.

"Yeah. Fine." He lowered his hand. "Just a little tired, that's all."

"No wonder. What about your senses?"

"Burned. I need some sleep."

He was beyond tired, she realized. More like exhausted. She had to get him to a safe place so that he could recover.

"Give me your locator," she ordered.

He blinked. "Why?"

"I don't think we're safe anywhere here in town. Our best bet is to disappear into the Underworld for a while. Starkey gave you the coordinates to the cave. He said there was a way down into the tunnels from there."

"I should have thought of that," he muttered.

He sounded thoroughly annoyed with himself. She understood.

"You're not operating at full-rez," she said. "You need time. Give me the locator."

He took the device off his belt and handed it to her. In spite of his exhaustion, the corner of his mouth twitched upward. "Did I ever tell you I've got a thing for strong, take-charge women?"

"Don't worry. In my experience, men with that particular issue always change their minds after a few dates with me."

"And then what?"

"They panic and run."

CHAPTER THIRTY-FIVE

The slog through the fog-dampened woods seemed endless. Each step felt like his last. Oliver wondered if it was possible to fall asleep on his feet. There had been plenty of times in his life when he had been tired. Times when he had mainlined caffeine to keep going. There were the times when he had resorted to Fast-Rez pills to stay alert in the Underworld while moving through dangerous, uncharted territory on an expedition. But never had he known the utter exhaustion that threatened to overwhelm him on the forever trek Leona was taking him on that night.

Her grip on his hand was the only thing that kept him vertical. She was using the physical connection to support his aura. Without it he knew he would have collapsed on the soggy ground and slipped into the dark dreamscape that beckoned.

"Not much farther," Leona promised, steering him around a tree.

"According to the locator, the entrance to the cave is only a few yards from here."

"You said that an hour ago," he said. He could barely get the words out.

"Not an hour ago. More like ten minutes, give or take. This time I really mean it."

"Should be there by now. Starkey said it was a thirty-minute hike."

"Not at the pace we're going."

"I just need five minutes of sleep."

"If you fall asleep now, you won't wake up for hours. I can feel the exhaustion in your aura. Just a few more yards. I think Roxy has realized where we're going. She's leading the way."

An encouraging chortle in the vicinity of his feet made Oliver look down. Roxy blinked all four eyes at him and then scampered ahead.

"Almost there," Leona whispered. "I promise. You've got to stay awake. Tell me something about yourself."

"I'm boring."

"Nope."

"Mostly I am." He paused, struggling to pull himself back from the edge of the dreamscape cliff. "Except when I'm not."

"Tell me about the times when you aren't boring."

"I'm scary."

"Because of your talent, do you mean?"

"Yeah."

"I don't know. Seems like a pretty cool talent to me. When I saw you slipping through the crowd at the reception, I assumed you were a clever artifact thief."

"Wasn't trying to be scary that night," he mumbled. "Just didn't want to draw attention."

"What are you like when you're scary?"

"You don't want to know."

"Yes, I do want to know."

"Why?"

"Because I'm curious about you."

"Why?"

"Lots of reasons," she said. "You're a very interesting person. I think we have a few things in common."

"Ever had to get a marriage annulled on account of your talent?"

"No. But I've never been married."

"Smart."

"Maybe. But now that my sister has found the right man, I'm starting to wonder—" She broke off and then started moving more quickly. "There's the cave. See the energy at the entrance?"

"No. I'm still psi-blind because of the explosion."

"You'll have to take my word for it. Energy is pouring out of the cavern."

She hauled so heavily on his hand he nearly went down. He managed, barely, to stay on his feet. He blinked a couple of times in an attempt to see through the glowing fog. Sure enough, he could make out a faint, shifting aurora spilling through a crack in the rocks.

The possibility that they had reached their destination gave him a small jolt of adrenaline.

"About time," he whispered. "I'm going to sleep now."

"Not quite. We can't risk sleeping in the cave. They might come looking for us. We have to get down into the Underworld. We'll be safe there."

She was right.

"Shit," he said.

"I agree. Current conditions are not optimal."

She draped his arm around her shoulder and helped him stagger through the narrow entrance into a cavern illuminated in a paranormal radiance. He heard more chortling. Roxy seemed to be enjoying the adventure.

The energy inside the massive cavern hit him like a ton of green quartz. He almost went down. He knew that if he had, he would have taken Leona with him. She struggled under his weight but she somehow managed to keep both of them on their feet.

He became aware of the low thunder of a nearby waterfall. He looked around and saw a wall of water tumbling out of the rocks into a pool.

"This place is really hot," Leona said. "It's the kind of energy that can cause hallucinations. Probably explains why the locals were so easily convinced that Vance will return."

He tried to take a closer look at the waterfall pool but he couldn't seem to focus.

"Roxy," Leona said, "where is the Underworld? Please, sweetie. Show us where the entrance is. We need to get Oliver down below where we can all hide."

Roxy chortled enthusiastically. Oliver wondered if she understood or if they were going to play hide-and-seek for the rest of the night.

"I'm really not up for that."

He did not realize he had spoken aloud until Leona glanced at him.

"What?" she said. "Never mind. Roxy has found the steps into the tunnels. Here we go. Almost there."

She guided him around the edge of the pool. When he looked down he could see that the waters were crystal clear. He also realized that he could not see the bottom. A chill of disturbing energy raised the hair on the back of his neck.

He must have somehow dozed off for a moment or two after that, because the next thing he knew, Leona was bracing him as they made their way down a spiral staircase. He recognized the familiar green quartz and the wide steps that had been designed for feet that were not quite human.

"You did it," he muttered. "You got us into the Underworld. You're good. Really, really good."

"The credit goes to Roxy," Leona said. She stopped at the foot of the twisted stairs and looked around. "We should be safe now. All we have to do is pick a chamber, any chamber. The only way someone could find us would be if they accidentally stumbled over us."

The buzz of Underworld energy gave him another little surge of adrenaline. He saw that they were in a rotunda that offered a choice of a dozen corridors.

"We'll take this one," Leona said.

She got him into one of the branching hallways and, a moment later, into a small chamber.

"Now you can sleep," she said.

He would have collapsed onto the hard quartz floor if she had not managed to control his fall. He ended up sprawled on his side and immediately closed his eyes. He was about to step off the cliff into the darkness when a memory made him pause.

"Forgot to tell you I figured out why someone went to so much trouble to get me to Lost Creek," he mumbled.

"Let me guess," she said. "Someone wants you dead."

"Yep. Thanks to you, they screwed up."

He stepped off the cliff and fell into the darkness.

CHAPTER THIRTY-SIX

She did not expect to sleep, but at some point she slipped into a dream involving a vault that held the answers that she and Molly sought. *A dark forest of towering stacks of papers, artifacts, and junk stood in the way. She kept getting lost. She desperately needed to find the right path.*

And then she saw the yellow crystal. It glowed in the shadows, just out of reach. All she had to do was follow it to the answers . . .

She opened her eyes and saw Roxy hovering over her, muttering. She was not sleeked out but there was no mistaking the air of concern.

"What's wrong?" Leona asked softly.

Roxy muttered again.

Leona sat up slowly, wincing when several muscles protested. She had fallen asleep next to Oliver, whose eyes were still closed. She reminded herself that this was not the first time she had spent a night on the hard quartz floors of the Underworld.

"It never gets easier," she said to Roxy.

She glanced at her amber-based watch and saw that it was a little after dawn. By rough calculation, she decided she and Oliver had slept about five hours.

Satisfied that she was awake, Roxy bustled to the messenger bag.

Leona pushed herself to her feet. "What's wrong?"

Roxy chortled—insistent now.

"Got it. You're hungry and you know there are some energy bars in my bag. I'll get one for you. Come to think of it, I could use one, too. And some water."

When she bent down to pick up her bag, Roxy growled. It did not sound like the cheery sound she made when she was anticipating a snack. More like a warning.

"What is it?" Leona looked at her. "What's wrong?"

When she got no response, she unzipped the bag with some care and peered inside. The pyramid crystal no longer glowed faintly. It pulsed with strong, slow-but-steady oscillating currents of energy.

She reached inside the bag and took out the stone. Now she could feel the energy as well as see it. "I wonder what—"

"The key to Vortex," Oliver said.

She turned and watched as he levered himself up to a sitting position. He did not take his eyes off the pyramid.

"The enhancing machine you've been searching for?" Leona asked.

"Maybe." Oliver got to his feet and moved to stand beside her. He took the crystal and examined it. "It's responding to a signal. But there's nothing in this chamber."

Leona opened her senses. "It's directional. Watch."

She retrieved the crystal and turned in a slow circle. The pulse of energy inside the stone got stronger when she aimed it at the entrance of the chamber.

"You're right." Oliver leaned down and grabbed his messenger bag. "Let's see where it takes us."

"Wait," she said. "How are you feeling?"

He blinked, briefly distracted. Then he switched his attention to her. His eyes heated. "Good. I feel good, thanks to you."

"You need food." She took an energy bar out of the bag and tossed it to him.

"Thanks."

"And you need to hydrate."

"I've got a bottle of water in my bag," he said.

Distracted, Roxy chortled. Leona gave her an energy bar and then took one for herself.

"You know," she said to Oliver, "whoever tried to kill you last night used an artifact as a weapon."

"I noticed. Not only can you activate some artifacts, you can flatline them, too. Nice. As I have already observed on more than one occasion, you are very handy to have around."

"My point is that it looks like there is someone else here in Lost Creek who can activate Alien artifacts."

"And whoever it is wants me dead for some reason." He peeled the wrapper off the energy bar. "Yeah, I get that. What's got me worried is that the juggler may be a multi-talent. Quite possibly a triple. We'll have to assume the individual is unstable."

She chilled. "What makes you suspect the juggler is a multi-talent?"

"Think about it. Assuming there is one person behind this operation, we can conclude that the individual has three powerful core talents—a high-level ability to plot an elaborate conspiracy involving a lot of moving pieces, a serious talent for some version of hypnosis—"

Leona frowned. "Hypnosis? Oh, you mean the so-called Voice that Starkey mentioned."

"Right. You've got to admit it's impressive. Our Vance wannabe is sending out hypnotic suggestions to several different people simultaneously by means of those pendants. According to the historians, Vance himself may have had that sort of ability. It's very rare but very powerful. It was how he made true believers out of so many people so quickly."

"It is an impressive form of hypnosis," she agreed. "So maybe the juggler does have at least two talents."

"And now we have discovered that our mini-Vance can also activate at least some Alien tech—namely, that crystal bowl."

"Unless the juggler is manipulating someone else who has that kind of talent," Leona said quickly. "Maybe using that person to work AUPs."

"It's a possibility." Oliver took a bite of the energy bar and munched, looking thoughtful. Then he shook his head. "But I don't think so. Too risky."

"Too risky?"

"As far as the juggler is concerned," he explained. "We think we've got a few control issues but we've got nothing on the mastermind behind this operation. We're dealing with a classic obsessive control freak who would never leave something as critical as the hypnotic manipulation factor to chance. Whoever it is wants me out of the way so they can get at you."

"Because I've got the key?"

"That's part of it, obviously. But I think the real motivation is deeper and more complicated. I think we've got an unstable triple who is obsessed with you on our hands."

"Why are you so sure the juggler is an unstable triple?" She realized her voice was rising. Not good.

Oliver looked at her. "Because they have concluded that you are a triple, too. What's more, you are clearly stable. That must be driving the juggler mad."

Her temper flared. "What if I told you that I *am* a triple?"

Oliver took another bite of the energy bar. "It's possible, but it depends on how you define the concept of core talent. The way I see it, you're basically a locksmith, one with the ability to unlock a lot of different things—psi-locks and even some artifacts, for example. You could call that two different talents, I suppose, but it seems more like a powerful version of your basic profile." He ate the last bite of the energy bar. "So, maybe you're a true double. Maybe."

"And if you're wrong? If I am a triple?"

"You believe you really are a multi-talent, don't you?"

"Yes."

He shrugged. "Okay, what's talent number three?"

She swallowed hard. "That's just it. I don't know. When I was in my teens, my family concluded that my ability to release the energy in some artifacts as well as resonate with them was my third. But now I think that's just a side effect of my locksmith talent. I can't escape the feeling that I've got a latent ability that has not yet appeared."

"What makes you think you have an undeveloped talent?"

"I can't explain it. I just know. The thing is, it could manifest itself at any time and I might not be able to control it."

"You'll be fine. Even if you are a true triple, you're stable. That's all that matters."

"But—"

"We can finish this conversation some other time. Right now, we need to find Vortex. Priorities, Leona."

He walked out of the entrance of the chamber. Thrilled by a promise of action, Roxy scurried to join him.

Leona gave up, slung her messenger bag over her shoulder, and hurried after the pair. When she moved into the hallway, the pulse of the pyramid crystal abruptly strengthened. She looked at it and kicked up her senses, feeling for the through line. And there it was.

"That way," she said, gesturing toward the far end of a seemingly endless green corridor. "The signal is coming from that direction."

They went forward together. Now that she was concentrating on the pyramid, she discovered it wasn't difficult to read the meaning of the pulses.

"It's similar to a locator," she said. "It's definitely responding to a strong signal."

"For you," Oliver said. "I can sense the energy in the pyramid. But I can't resonate with it."

She drew a deep breath. "Apparently I can."

They stopped at an intersection of five corridors. Again she turned slowly on her heel until she got the pulses that indicated one of the passageways. It led to the vaulted entrance of a green quartz chamber.

A large, clunky but ominous-looking machine stood in the center of the space. It was made of heavy-gauge steel and bore an unnerving resemblance to a metal sarcophagus.

Everything about it shouted Old World tech. The control panel was decorated with dials and switches—the kind that had to be operated manually, not rezzed on and off with a little psi. The long seam that ran the length of the metal machine indicated that the entire top portion was designed to open.

Like a coffin, she thought, unnerved.

There was a window of thick glass above the control panel. Behind it a yellow crystal pyramid pulsed with energy. Leona knew it was resonating with the crystal in her hand. She felt the hair lift on the back of her neck. Disturbing frissons arced across her senses.

Oliver went forward to get a closer look. Curious, Roxy joined him.

"Too bad we didn't bring a bottle of champagne," Oliver said.

She realized he was oblivious to the vibe of pure dread that she was getting. "Why?"

He smiled an ice-cold smile of satisfaction. "Because I'm pretty sure we just found the Vortex machine that Vincent Lee Vance used to turn himself into a multi-talent monster."

Leona swallowed hard against a sudden wave of lightheadedness. If he was right, there was a very real possibility that she was looking at the machine that had been used to create Molly and herself. Human monsters.

Chapter Thirty-Seven

For a long moment she just stood there and watched Oliver and Roxy prowl around the machine. She could not shake the heavy sense of incipient panic that had enveloped her, but Oliver was clearly intrigued by their discovery.

She reminded herself that he was the director of a museum that specialized in objects with an Old World paranormal provenance. He was an artifact hunter at heart. It was only natural that he was fascinated with Vortex. It was a relic he and his obscure organization had been chasing for a very long time.

She struggled to center herself. She would deal with her anxiety issues later. When you were in the Underworld, hazards were everywhere. You had to stay focused. She was a para-archaeologist. It was time to look at the scene from the viewpoint of a professional—the same way Oliver was looking at it.

Reluctantly she went forward, braced herself, and put the fingertips of one hand on the metal side of the machine. She rezzed a little talent and found the vibes that told her something about the history of the artifact.

"There's no question but that this is Old World tech," she said. "The only reason it hasn't rusted to pieces in the past two hundred years is because it's been down here in the tunnel. Nothing rusts in the Underworld. I wonder which of the First Gen colonists smuggled it through the Curtain."

Oliver grimaced. "For all I know, it was someone associated with the Foundation who couldn't resist running experiments here in an environment that has much higher levels of paranormal radiation than Earth. At some point, Vance got hold of it. He must have been unstable even before he climbed inside this thing and dosed himself with radiation from Old World crystals."

"I suppose so," Leona muttered.

"No question. No one in their right mind would take a chance like that." Oliver stepped back from the machine and surveyed the glowing chamber. He shook his head in disbelief. "And to do it down here where the para-rad is already intense and unpredictable. Talk about insane."

Leona tried not to dwell on that observation. She and Molly were not insane. They were not monsters, either. *We're not Vance knockoffs, damn it.*

Once again she forced herself to focus. She considered the pulsing pyramid crystal in her hand. "I think this stone is more than just a locator device designed to guide someone to the machine."

There was a flash of movement in the doorway. Belatedly she realized that Roxy was growling. She whirled around.

"You've got that right," Hester Harp announced from the entrance of the chamber. She had a flamer in one hand, and her eyes glittered with a disturbing energy. "It's much more than a GPS. According to Vincent Lee Vance, it's the key to Vortex. The key to the future. You are the bride, and you will unlock the enhancement machine."

CHAPTER THIRTY-EIGHT

Harp was not alone. Edith Fenwick was at her side, a flamer in her hand as well. Clustered behind them, Leona could see a small gaggle of people gathered in the hallway. She recognized several of them, including Burt, the man who had made a show of displaying his mag-rez in the diner. Luckily, his pistol would not function in the Underworld, but now he had a flamer. The bartender, the waitress, and the guys on the barstools were in the group, as well. Several were armed.

She was surprised to see Baxter Richey and Darla Price in the group. The paranormal investigators were wide-eyed and excited. Probably figured they were living the dream, about to get the story of the century.

Baxter had an old-fashioned amber-based video camera braced on his shoulder. The little red light indicated it was filming. Darla Price had a notebook in one hand, a pen in the other. She was no doubt scripting the next episode of their show, Leona thought. *Vincent Lee Vance Returns: Ex-*

clusive film and interviews. She wondered what would happen when Vance failed to make his big comeback.

Notably, two individuals were absent—the collector, Norton Thacker, and the Guild man, Dwight Starkey. Leona couldn't decide if that was interesting or ominous. Given the current situation, she was leaning toward ominous.

Roxy's low growl shattered the crystal-sharp tension. Leona looked down and saw her crouched beneath the Vortex machine. She was sleeked out and ready for combat—a pint-sized warrior with a fascinator.

The growl got Hester's attention. "It's that fucking dust bunny."

She raised the flamer and aimed it at Roxy.

"No," Leona said, suddenly frantic. "Don't shoot her. She's harmless. Roxy, please. Stop growling. Stay where you are, okay?"

Roxy stayed put but she did not fluff up. She kept all four eyes wide open.

"I wouldn't fire a flamer in that direction if I were you, Ms. Harp," Oliver said. He removed his glasses and began to polish them with a hand-kerchief. In the process, he slipped effortlessly into his Museum Guy persona. "Even if you've got very good aim, you'll hit Vortex as well as the dust bunny. There's no telling how that sort of energy would affect the machine. After all, it's Old World tech that has been sitting down here in a sea of para-radiation for a very long time. It's no doubt highly unstable."

The lecture worked. Harp swung the barrel of the flamer away from Roxy. Leona's relief was short-lived, however, because the weapon was now aimed at Oliver.

He carefully repositioned his glasses on his nose. "You all went to a lot of trouble to lure Dr. Griffin and me to your quaint little town."

"We don't need you," Edith Fenwick declared. "You're a damned nuisance."

"I got that impression last night when someone tried to murder me with an artifact," Oliver said.

"You're a problem, Rancourt," Burt warned.

"Because I was chasing Vortex," Oliver said. "The juggler knew that sooner or later I'd find my way to Lost Creek, so they decided to issue an invitation in the form of an Old World document I couldn't resist, the Bluestone Project file."

"Juggler?" Burt snorted. "What the fuck are you talking about?"

"You know the juggler as the Voice," Oliver said.

"The Voice wanted you out of the picture," Burt shot back. "It said the artifact would take care of you last night, but the next thing we knew, the two of you had disappeared."

"How did you find us here in the Underworld?" Leona asked.

Harp chuckled. "The pyramid crystal, of course. The Voice told us there's a tracking code on it."

"The Voice has known where you were every step of the way," Edith Fenwick said. "When we realized you were heading down into the tunnels last night, the Voice told us to wait. For hours there was nothing. Figured you were asleep. But this morning the Voice said you had found the enhancement machine."

"Interesting," Oliver said. "Vortex has been down here all along but you couldn't find it, could you?"

"It was part of the legend," Harp said. "Over the years plenty of folks have searched for it. But once something disappears into the tunnels with no tracking device, it's lost forever unless someone stumbles over it by accident. The Voice told us that Vance's bride could resonate with the key and use it to lead us to the machine."

"And only the bride can open it and awaken Vance," Baxter Richey said. His voice thrummed with anticipation. He aimed the video camera directly at Leona.

"All of which means we don't need Rancourt anymore," Burt announced. "I'll strip his amber and dump him in the tunnels."

Oliver regarded him as if the threat was mildly irritating but not particularly relevant.

"No, wait," Leona said quickly. "You've got what you wanted. I led you to Vance's machine. Trust me, you do not want to kill anyone. I can guarantee you that if either Rancourt or I vanish here in Lost Creek, our families will make sure the FBPI and the Guild turn this town upside down until they find out what happened."

"She's got a point," Oliver said in the same deceptively mild tone.

"You don't even know for sure if I can unlock the machine," Leona continued. "If I really am the bride and if I do awaken Vincent Lee Vance, he can decide what to do with Oliver."

Oliver looked at her, brows slightly elevated. She was certain she saw the edge of his mouth twitch in one of his silent laughs. In that moment she knew he had a plan. That was a good thing, because she did not have one.

"She's right," Baxter said. "Let's see if she can unlock Vortex." He swiveled the camera toward the machine and back to Leona.

"Yes," Darla Price said eagerly. "Let's find out if she can unlock it."

The crowd rumbled agreement.

Edith and Harp exchanged looks and then Harp nodded once. Decision made.

"Do it," she ordered.

Well, shit, Leona thought. *Now what?*

She looked at Oliver. He inclined his head in the smallest possible nod. *Go for it.*

Evidently, unlocking Vortex was part of plan A.

Another unnerving possibility occurred to her. Maybe his professional curiosity had gotten the better of his common sense. Maybe he couldn't resist finding out what was inside the machine.

She shot him a warning glare. He did not seem to notice. She stifled a sigh and turned to the audience gathered at the entrance of the chamber.

"I would like to remind everyone that this situation began when someone opened an artifact known as Pandora's box," she said.

"The Voice said you're the one who opened it," Harp reminded her.

"Ah, but I wasn't the first one to open the artifact." Leona held up a finger. "Someone else did that before me. Whoever it was put the pyramid crystal inside. I have been assured by an expert that the stone was not part of the original collection of objects inside the box. Someone screwed around with Pandora's box. That was probably not a good idea."

"Shut up and open Vortex," Burt shouted. He was sweating heavily now and his eyes were feverish.

"Awaken our leader," the bartender shouted from the back of the crowd.

The others took up the chant. *"Awaken Vincent Lee Vance."*

Leona glanced at Oliver one last time, searching for some indication of a plan.

He shrugged. "Might as well see what's inside Vortex," he said. "We've come this far."

"Fine," she muttered. "But when this is over, you and I are going to have a serious conversation about the importance of having a backup plan."

"Count on it," he said.

She tightened her grip on the pyramid crystal, clapped one hand against the side of the machine, and rezzed her talent. For a moment she was confronted with a storm of chaos. But it was human psychic chaos—not Alien. There was nothing particularly complicated about the vibe that had been used to lock Vortex. But there was an element of violent madness.

If it was Vincent Lee Vance who had designed the lock, he had, indeed, been insane.

Insane, yes, but in his own twisted fashion, he had been clever. The lock was dangerous. She had no way of knowing what kind of trap Vance had created, but she knew it would probably be lethal.

She set her back teeth and eased her way into the currents of energy, searching for the pattern. There was always a pattern.

Energy—a lot of it—shifted in the atmosphere. She heard the crowd in the doorway start to murmur uneasily. Maybe they were finally starting to wonder if the whole Vincent Lee Vance return cult thing was a good idea after all.

"Too late," she said under her breath.

She got the crystal-clear ping that told her she had flatlined the lock. There was a metallic crack that seemed as loud as thunder. It was followed by a grinding groan as the heavy lid of the coffin-like machine slowly opened.

A glary, hellish yellow light spilled out.

The crowd in the doorway froze. Their excitement and obsessive anticipation was now infused with something close to panic. It was one thing to buy into the expectation of the return of Vincent Lee Vance—it was another thing altogether to be in the chamber where a man who was supposed to have died a hundred years ago might actually sit up in his coffin.

The townsfolk clogging the doorway weren't the only ones who were unnerved, Leona thought. She did not like the feel of the radiation streaming out of Vortex. It was intense and unstable.

She took several hasty steps back and came up against Oliver's solid frame. He put a hand on her shoulder, sending a silent message that she interpreted as *get ready*.

About time, she thought.

Roxy, fascinator ribbons streaming behind her, darted out from under the machine, vaulted lightly up onto Oliver's shoulder, and hunkered down. The team was once again ready for action, Leona thought.

The glare from the interior of Vortex was senses-dazzling, almost blinding. She could just make out that the light emanated from dozens of pyramid-shaped crystals that lined the interior of the machine.

Old gears rumbled to life. A transparent crystal platform rose. There was a figure clad in tattered clothing on top of it. Leona's throat tightened in horror. Oliver's hand abruptly tightened on her shoulder. She knew he had not seen this coming, either.

CHAPTER THIRTY-NINE

The body on the crystal platform did not move. For a moment no one moved. It was as if the room had been locked in ice.

"Well, this is interesting," Oliver said, shattering the silence. He was in his Museum Guy mode, but Leona could feel his battle-ready tension. Keeping his grip on her, he guided her calmly across the room to study the motionless figure on the platform. "If this individual thought he was climbing into a paranormal enhancement or preservation chamber, I'd say that what we have here is a case of failed expectations."

An agitated murmur swept over the crowd. Roxy rumbled.

Oliver reached up to touch her lightly with his free hand. "Not yet," he said very softly.

Roxy stilled but she kept all four eyes on the crowd at the entrance.

Leona used one hand to partially shield her eyes against the blazing crystals and tried to examine the corpse inside the chamber with a detached, academic eye. Because it was definitely a corpse.

The body was that of a man who appeared to have been in early middle age when he died. There was no obvious injury. For whatever reason he had apparently lain down in the chamber, sealed the lid—and died.

The most disturbing thing about the dead man was that he was chillingly well-preserved—a testimony to the power of the crystals, perhaps. But the effect had been a form of mummification, not hibernation or cold storage.

There was no mistaking death, she thought. The dead were truly silent in every sense. A corpse had no energy field, because the life force was gone. But the *act* of dying left traces behind—a forensic psychic stain that provided evidence of the manner and time of death. In this case, the interior of the chamber was saturated with a dark energy. The man inside Vortex had not died quickly.

His eyes were wide open, as if he had gazed at some unseen horror in his final moments. His face was a true death mask, the mouth drawn back in a terrible grin. Leona shuddered. Her intuition told her she was looking at a man who had realized too late that he had locked himself inside a coffin and that there was no escape.

She turned away from the grisly sight. Roxy took no interest in the body at all. She was still keeping watch on the crowd.

Oliver switched his attention to the audience. Leona sensed another shift in his energy field. Between one heartbeat and the next, he was in command of the room. In some indescribable way he had metamorphosed from glasses-polishing Museum Guy to the Guy in Charge.

The crowd stared at him, riveted, and awaited his verdict.

"I've got good news or bad news, depending on your point of view," he said. "I can assure you of two facts. The first is that this man is very dead. The second is that it is not Vincent Lee Vance."

That news produced gasps of disbelief, followed by confusion. Leona thought that at least a few people looked relieved.

Harp recovered first. She fixed Oliver with a suspicious glare. "What makes you so sure it's not Vance?"

Oliver gestured toward the figure on the platform. "See for yourself. The body is well preserved, so it's obvious he looks nothing like the images of Vance in the photos and videos from the Era of Discord. The clothes this individual was wearing when he went into the Vortex machine are definitely post–Era of Discord. I'd say they date from about forty years back—definitely not from a century ago. Finally, there is no sign of Vance's signature crystal pendant."

"Face it," Leona announced. "You've all been scammed. In fairness, it's not because you are natural-born dumbasses—at least not entirely. Someone has been using the crystals in those pendants you're so proud of to hypnotize you."

Fury roiled through the crowd.

"Pissing off the people with the pitchforks was not part of the plan," Oliver said in low tones.

Leona ignored him because the crowd was in the process of turning into a full-blown mob.

"That's a fucking lie," Burt yelled. "No one could hypnotize me. I'm too strong."

Harp grunted. Her eyes narrowed. She touched the pendant that dangled around her neck. "For all we know, you two are the ones who are trying to hypnotize us. You don't want us to know the truth. That's it, isn't it?"

"They're both lying," the bartender shouted.

"She's still got the key," Edith said. "We need to get it."

Baxter aimed the camera at Leona. "Darla, are you getting all this?"

Darla did not respond. She stared at the dead man, stunned.

Harp raised the flamer, aiming it at Leona. "Give us the key."

"I suggest we all calm down," Oliver said in his Guy in Charge voice.

But this time it had no discernible effect on the crowd. There was too much energy churning the atmosphere, Leona realized. The powerful human emotions of rage and confusion were being enhanced by the paranormal atmosphere and the senses-blinding glare of the Vortex crystals.

"Get the key from her," Edith shouted.

The crowd, with Harp at the forefront, surged forward.

"This is not going quite the way I had planned," Oliver said. "We need a distraction."

He plucked the pyramid crystal from Leona's fingers and tossed it into the Vortex chamber.

"It's all yours," he announced to the crowd.

Harp swung toward the machine. The others followed. Mob mentality was a powerful force, Leona thought.

"This is our cue to exit," Oliver said.

He released his grip on her shoulder, seized her hand, and hauled her toward the entrance, which was no longer clogged with people. She felt a shiver of heavy energy envelop her and recognized the vibe of Oliver's aura. She knew he had gone into his nothing-to-see-here persona and had wrapped her and Roxy inside the invisible cloak of his talent.

The crowd ignored the three of them, intent on recovering the pyramid crystal.

She glanced back once just as Oliver was pulling her through the doorway. It seemed to her that there was something different about the energy pouring out of Vortex. The instability was rapidly growing worse. She could feel the mounting danger in the wildly oscillating currents.

And then they were through the doorway and racing down the glowing green quartz corridor. Roxy, riding high on Oliver's shoulder, fluffed out and chortled.

"We need to find a better hobby," Oliver said. "Running away from the bad guys is getting old."

"This is plan B?" Leona asked, breathless. "We run for our lives? I was expecting something a little more sophisticated in the way of an exit strategy."

"Actually, this is plan C," Oliver said. "Plan B went to green hell when you pissed off the crowd by calling everyone dumbasses and informing them they had been scammed and hypnotized."

"It was the truth."

"That's not the point."

Screams and panic-stricken shouts interrupted Leona before she could defend herself. She turned to look over her shoulder and saw a gaggle of frantic people scrambling through the doorway.

The intensity of the glow at the entrance of the Vortex chamber was stronger now.

The explosion sounded as if it came from the depths of the sea, but the light show and fireworks cascading through the entrance were dazzling. Roxy chortled approval and bounced up and down on Oliver's shoulder.

Oliver halted, dragging Leona to a stop. They turned to survey the disaster. The stampeding crowd swept toward them, intent on escape. They flattened themselves against the tunnel wall to avoid getting trampled. Roxy chortled again, evidently cheering on the runners.

When the last of the stampeding herd had passed, they turned back to look at the entrance of the chamber. The explosion was slowly diminishing, but a nerve-rattling energy continued to illuminate the entrance.

They watched in silence until the doorway abruptly went dark. Well, not technically *dark*, Leona thought. The energy emanating from inside the chamber was once again the familiar acid green of Alien quartz.

Silently they walked back to the doorway and contemplated what was left of Vortex.

The machine had melted down into a huge lump of molten metal.

"The body—" Leona said. She stopped.

"Incinerated by the explosion," Oliver said.

Jagged shards of crystals littered the floor. None of the pieces glowed with energy. What was left of the pyramid stones had not been simply flatlined, Leona thought; they had been shattered.

She released Oliver's hand to bend down and pick up a chunk of crystal. It felt like a piece of glass in her hand.

"Dead," she said quietly. She chucked it back down onto the floor. "No one could tune it, not even my sister."

Oliver looked satisfied. "Good."

She glanced at him. "You knew this would happen when you tossed the pyramid crystal into the machine, didn't you?"

"There was no guarantee," he said. "But it was obvious the energy inside was unstable. Figured it wouldn't take much to push it over the edge."

"Don't get me wrong, I'm very glad we escaped that mob, but now you don't have a machine to study."

"It would have been interesting to examine it, and I would give a great deal to know the identity of the body inside. But the end goal was always to render the damn thing inoperable."

She looked at the small mountain of still-molten steel that had once been Vortex. "In that case, mission accomplished."

"Definitely. Now, we can only hope that Starkey came through on his promise to fix the bridge. If so, we're getting the hell out of this burg. The FBPI and the Guild will take charge of the scene. That's their job."

"Fine by me, but we need to pick up our things at the inn and then we have to make one stop before we leave town."

"I know where this is going and it's a bad idea."

"You came here on a mission and you've been successful," she said. "I came here for a purpose, too. I'm not leaving until I accomplish my goal. One thing is clear: a man named Willard kidnapped my sister, and we know he was involved with the yellow crystals. I need to get a look at the document Thacker mentioned, the one he said was linked to someone named Willard."

"I was afraid you were going to say that."

"I just thought of a potential problem."

"Only one?"

She ignored that. "What if Burt and the others try to stop us? Maybe they will sabotage your car or something."

"The Slider has good onboard security. I doubt if they can damage it. But if necessary we'll steal a car. Burt's truck will work fine."

"Have you ever actually stolen a car?"

"No, but I've got you, and you're pretty good with locks."

"Just so you know, I've never had any practical experience in car theft."

"How hard can it be?" Oliver checked his locator, hitched his messenger bag on his shoulder, and started walking. "Let's go."

"Wait," she said. "That's the wrong direction. According to my locator, the entrance to the cave is behind us."

"I don't think it would be a good idea to exit the way we came in. If the locals are still pissed off at us, it would be the ideal location for an ambush."

"Good point." She hurried after him.

"The locator is showing another exit up ahead," he said. "Maybe a half-hour hike."

"There's no way to know where it comes out," Leona said, falling into step beside him. "It might be somewhere deep in the mountains."

"Exactly. Which means that Burt and the gang won't bother to cover it. They'll assume we'll do the obvious and leave the way we entered. After all, we're not from around here, remember? We don't know the territory."

Roxy chortled, enjoying the new adventure. From time to time she catapulted off Oliver's shoulder to briefly explore a glowing chamber or a chunk of quartz that she spotted on the floor. But she never disappeared for more than a moment.

"Everything's a game to you, isn't it?" Leona said to her at one point when she tumbled out of a vaulted chamber waving a small unpolished crystal in one paw.

"Until it's not," Oliver said, watching Roxy dash ahead to check out an intersection.

Leona remembered Roxy sleeked out and ready to rumble when the three of them were confronted by the mob of townspeople. "They've definitely got a live-in-the-moment mindset. Humans could probably learn a lot from dust bunnies."

"That mentality works fine for them, but humans need plans," Oliver said. "And backup plans."

CHAPTER FORTY

Some twenty minutes later they stopped at a vaulted door-way that looked exactly like countless other doorways they had passed.

Oliver checked the locator. "This is the exit point."

Leona followed him into a cavernous, high-ceilinged quartz chamber. She stopped and looked around. "This is amazing. But then, I say that a lot in my work."

Oliver's mouth twitched in brief amusement. "So do I. Hazard of the job."

"Yes, it is." She smiled. They really did have a few things in common.

A deep channel of crystal-clear water some nine or ten feet wide flowed out of an opening in one wall, curved gently across the floor of the vast space, and disappeared into a tranquil pool on the far side. Twin rows of quartz pedestals topped with faceted crystals lined both sides of the waterway.

Elegant little footbridges crossed the indoor river at various points. Blocks of quartz that looked a lot like park benches were placed near the edges.

A graceful, gazebo-like structure stood on the far side of the water feature. Inside, a tightly wound spiral staircase twisted upward and vanished into the ceiling.

A crystal-clear sculpture the size and shape of a one-person canoe was displayed on a platform anchored in the wall above the opening where the river emerged. Two sets of quartz steps, one on each side of the channel, led up to the artifact.

"This place looks like a city park or a space for contemplation," Leona said.

Oliver walked toward one of the little footbridges. "I'd like to take a closer look at that crystal canoe, but we need to keep moving. Let's find out what's at the top of that staircase."

She started toward the footbridge. Belatedly it occurred to her that Roxy had gone uncharacteristically silent. She looked around.

"Roxy? We're leaving. Where are you? This isn't a good time to play hide-and-seek."

A faint chortle sounded from the far side of the chamber. Leona turned toward it and was just in time to see Roxy vaulting up one of the flights of steps that led to the crystal canoe.

"She's got a thing for boats, doesn't she?" Oliver said.

Leona ignored him. She hurried along the river's edge, heading for the steps that led to the canoe.

"Roxy, *no*."

Roxy was already inside the canoe. She waved a paw and chortled.

Leona was almost at the steps. There was no handrail, so she flattened one palm against the wall to steady herself as she climbed toward the platform.

"Roxy, we don't have time for this. Please, sweetie. Get out of the boat."

A faint hum sounded from inside the wall. The platform with the crystal canoe and Roxy began to move.

"Shit," Leona yelped. "Stupid talent."

She yanked her hand off the wall but she knew it was too late. She had accidentally activated a mechanism concealed in the quartz.

The platform glided downward and lowered the canoe into the water.

She tried to grab Roxy out of the vessel but she missed. The canoe settled gently into the artificial river, where it was immediately carried gently away by the current.

"I've got a bad feeling about this," she said.

"She'll be okay," Oliver said. "She's probably just going to get wet again."

"Do something," Leona said, scrambling back down the steps.

"Yes, ma'am."

Oliver walked toward the far end of the river.

The slow current was carrying the canoe toward the opposite end of the chamber and the serene pool.

"Jump off, Roxy," Leona shouted. She ran alongside the river, but she knew she would not be able to catch the canoe.

Roxy chortled, buzzed, and ducked as the vessel floated under first one footbridge and then three more. There was only a single bridge left before the river flowed out of sight into the unknown.

Without warning, a section of the quartz wall on the far side of the pool dissolved. As if a dam had been breached, the once-calm water abruptly rushed through the opening.

Leona glimpsed a nightmarish blue energy storm on the other side. Lightning flashed in the depths of the wild currents. Paranormal fire flared and roared.

The canoe was headed straight into the hellish furnace. Roxy would not survive the terrifying flames. Even if she jumped overboard now it would be too late. The once gently flowing river had become a fast-moving torrent.

For the first time Roxy seemed to realize that she might be in trouble. She was no longer chortling. Her fur stood on end and all four of her eyes snapped open.

Oliver walked out onto the middle of the last footbridge, crouched, and deftly plucked her out of the canoe just before it passed underneath.

Roxy chortled ecstatically, thrilled with the conclusion to the game. Oliver turned to watch the crystal canoe glide into the fiery blue energy storm. The gate closed, once again becoming a solid quartz wall.

For a moment Leona stared at the blank wall where the canoe had just disappeared. Then she took a deep breath.

"So, I'm going to take a big leap here and go way out on a professional limb," she said. "The first rule of para-archaeology is, don't assume anything, and I absolutely agree that we have no way of knowing how the Aliens used this chamber. Nevertheless, I don't think that what we just witnessed was a theme park ride."

Oliver walked off the little footbridge, Roxy on his shoulder. "Speaking as one professional para-archaeologist to another, I'm inclined to agree. Got a feeling we're in an Alien funeral parlor."

Leona swallowed hard. "That crystal canoe?"

"A coffin."

"And the blue firestorm?"

"The crematorium."

Leona shuddered. "If you hadn't grabbed Roxy—"

"Try not to think about it," Oliver said.

"Right." Leona strode toward the gazebo and the spiral staircase. "Like I'm not going to have nightmares about sailing into a crematorium. Let's get out of here."

Roxy chortled and looked back at the river to Alien hell.

"No," Leona said. "You don't get another ticket for that ride. But I promise that when we get home I'll take you on a very cool boat cruise."

"How are you going to do that?" Oliver asked. "Illusion Town is in the middle of the desert."

"I've got a plan."

He smiled. "Plans are good."

CHAPTER FORTY-ONE

The ancient staircase wound upward for what must have been the equivalent of three or four stories. It was a tedious climb because, as was always the case in the Underworld, the steps were a little too wide and a little too far apart to be comfortable for humans.

The other issue, Oliver knew, was that he and Leona had been through a lot recently. The five hours of sleep he had gotten last night had restored his senses, but he needed more rest in order to get back to normal. Same with Leona. Luckily, they had started out in good shape, but they could not keep going indefinitely. He had to get them somewhere safe, preferably off the damn mountain, by day's end.

"Do you think the Aliens ever figured out how to build elevators?" Leona grumbled at one point.

"If they did, we've never come across one," Oliver said.

"Then again, would we recognize an Alien elevator if we did find one?"

"There is that."

"I wonder—" She rounded another twist in the staircase and stopped. "Here we go."

"Aboveground ruins?"

"No. A hole-in-the-wall exit sealed by a vault door. No telling what's on the other side."

Oliver followed her around the final twist in the staircase and saw that she was looking up at a mag-steel door in the ceiling. A vintage ladder provided access. That meant that at some point in the past—evidently decades earlier, judging by the ladder—someone else had discovered the exit and secured it with a locked door.

More unknowns.

"Just one surprise after another here in Lost Creek," he said. "I'll take a look."

Roxy had been bouncing up the staircase under her own steam. She chortled and her ears perked up.

Leona glanced down at her. "Little adrenaline junkie. I would have thought you'd had enough excitement for one day."

Roxy was practically vibrating with anticipation.

"She doesn't look worried," Leona said. "That's a good sign."

Oliver reached the heavy trapdoor and studied the lock mechanism. "This is old. Era of Discord tech, or maybe even earlier."

Leona studied the door. "I wonder if it was intended to be an emergency escape hatch for Vance."

"Maybe." He tested the door. "It's locked."

"Want me to open it?"

"Thanks, but I've got this."

He took the lock pick out of his jacket pocket and eased it into the hundred-year-old keyhole. Cautiously he pulsed a little energy. There was a distinct click when the lock gave way. He slipped the pick back into his pocket and took out his flamer.

He cracked the trapdoor. Light—the familiar kind used by humans to illuminate their homes and offices—appeared in the narrow opening.

"Who's there?" Norton Thacker yelped. "What's going on? This is a private residence. No trespassing. I've got a flamer."

Great, Oliver thought. The mansion was crammed with flammable materials—a real tinderbox—and the owner had a flamer.

"It's Rancourt," Oliver said. "Dr. Griffin is with me." He opted not to mention Roxy. "Sorry to intrude like this, but things got complicated last night."

"Rancourt?" Thacker pulled the trapdoor open and looked down at them. "And Dr. Griffin. I wasn't expecting you. Do come up."

"Thank you," Oliver said. He stepped off the ladder and into the library vault. "About the flamer."

Thacker chuckled. "Not to worry. I was afraid you were an intruder bent on raiding my collection. I wanted to scare you off. I wouldn't think of having a flamer around so many valuable books and documents and papers."

"That is very good to know."

Leona climbed up to the top of the ladder and moved into the vault. Roxy bounced up behind him and chortled at Thacker.

"You must be the dust bunny," Thacker said, chuckling. "Ms. Harp mentioned you. Evidently you caused a bit of a to-do in the kitchen. Best behave yourself. My housekeeper was in quite a state after you left last time. It's never a good idea to upset Ms. Harp."

Roxy blinked her blue eyes and chortled. She was in full adorable mode, Oliver thought, and Thacker looked charmed.

Leona smiled. "I'm starting to feel like Alice in Amberland. Another day, another dust bunny hole. You never know where you'll end up."

CHAPTER FORTY-TWO

Thacker beamed. "Lovely to see you again, Dr. Griffin."

He did, indeed, appear happy to see her, she thought, but his expression switched immediately to one of concern.

"I must admit I've been a bit anxious all day. Ms. Harp was acting rather strangely yesterday evening and she did not show up for work this morning. I had to make my own breakfast. Tell me, did you find the Vortex machine?"

"Yes, as a matter of fact, we did," Leona said.

"Oh, dear, I was afraid of that." Thacker sighed. "I don't suppose you were able to open it?"

"I did," Leona said.

"I was even more afraid of that."

"No need to worry," Oliver said. "There was a dead body inside but it wasn't Vance. Things got complicated, and in the end, Vortex melted down into a slag heap."

Thacker appeared greatly relieved by that news. "Excellent, excellent."

He tut-tutted. "And not the least bit surprising. Old technology can be extremely problematic. Well, that takes care of the rumors about Vance's return. I really ought to offer you both tea, but as I said, Ms. Harp did not show up today."

"Hard to get good help, isn't it?" Leona said.

"Just as well," Oliver said quickly. "No time for tea, I'm afraid. We need to get on the road. Long drive."

Leona ignored the unsubtle hint. She had been lucky enough to get another crack at Thacker's collection and she was not about to surrender the opportunity.

She rezzed up her most polished smile and turned it on Thacker. "The last time we were here—yesterday—you mentioned you had a journal written by someone named Willard."

Thacker brightened. "Willard. Yes, indeed. I found it years ago and moved it in here because it referenced some Old World theories concerning the prediction of outcomes associated with various approaches to paranormal enhancement. Predicting the results has always been the problem, you see. Methods of enhancement have been developed over the years but the vast majority have failed."

"We know," Oliver said. He checked his watch. "We're under a time constraint here."

Leona pretended she hadn't heard him. "Any chance I might examine the Willard journal?"

"Of course, of course," Thacker said. "Hang on, I'll fetch it for you."

He slid the movable stepladder into position, climbed the rungs to the top, stretched out an arm, and pulled a slim, leather-bound volume off the shelf.

Roxy's low growl was the only warning they got before Harp appeared in the doorway of the vault, a flamer in her hand. Her eyes glittered with rage.

"You two destroyed the future," she snarled.

"Ms. Harp," Thacker squeaked. "I wondered when you'd show up. I say, you'd better put the flamer away—"

He lost his balance on the stepladder. In a frantic effort to recover and avoid a fall, he dropped the volume and grabbed the handrails.

Leona snatched the falling book out of midair. Roxy chose that moment to launch herself from under a nearby shelf. Sleeked out, eyes and teeth showing, she dashed toward Harp.

"I've had enough of that fucking dust bunny," Harp shrieked.

She swung the flamer toward Roxy, trying frantically to aim at the fast-moving target. But Oliver had somehow moved alongside her without being noticed. *You never see him coming,* Leona thought.

He grabbed the arm Harp was using to hold the weapon, forcing it upward, deflecting the shot. An instant later, he snapped the flamer out of her hand.

"Roxy, it's okay," Leona said. "You don't need to bite her."

Roxy scrambled to a halt. Harp drew back a booted foot in preparation for a savage kick. Leona swooped forward and grabbed Roxy.

Off-balance now, Harp toppled backward. There was a sickening crunch when her head struck the edge of a bookcase. She landed on the floor and did not move.

Leona clutched Roxy close. "It's okay. Everything's under control."

"Actually, things are not under control," Oliver said. "We need to get out of here. Now."

Leona suddenly smelled smoke. She looked up and saw flames leaping from the top shelf. Harp's errant shot had struck a stack of documents.

"My library," Thacker wailed. "Ms. Harp, what have you done?"

He started gathering up books and files willy-nilly. Several cascaded to the floor.

Oliver gripped Leona's shoulder and propelled her toward the entrance of the vault. *"Go."*

He was using his Guy in Charge voice. It was effective. She rushed toward the door of the vault, Roxy clutched under one arm, the Willard journal in her hand. She glanced back once and saw that the flames were rapidly consuming the top shelving. Sparks landed below, igniting other shelves filled with highly flammable materials.

"Oh, shit," she whispered.

"Yep," Oliver said.

He did not elaborate. Instead, he hauled a near-hysterical Thacker away from a flaming pile of papers and shoved him toward the door. Dazed and panicked, Thacker followed Leona out into the crammed library.

"What about Harp?" Leona called.

"I'll take care of her," Oliver said. "Just go."

Leona looked down to make sure she was on the yellow tape path and then raced through the canyons formed by the towers of artifacts, books, objects, and assorted junk that had been accumulating for a century. She could hear Thacker behind her, stumbling and panting as he struggled to run with his armload of books and files.

Evidently grasping the scope of the danger, Roxy remained sleeked out and wide-eyed. There was no cheery chortling now, Leona noted.

She swerved around a sharp corner, saw the open door of the library, and dashed out into the hall. Thacker followed, dropping a couple of his precious books in the process. When he bent down to retrieve one, he lost another volume.

Oliver emerged from the library, Harp slung over his shoulder. "Outside. This place is going to go up like a bonfire."

Leona ran down the narrow aisle formed by the stacks that lined the hallway, wrenched open the front door, and burst outside into pouring rain. Thacker and Oliver followed.

By the time they reached the safety of the driveway, the entire first floor of the mansion was exploding in flames.

"This should be far enough," Oliver said. "The stone walls and the rain will keep the fire from spreading. I think."

They all staggered to a halt and turned to watch the big house implode. For a time no one spoke. Eventually Oliver dumped Harp on the wet ground and looked at Leona and Roxy.

"Never a dull moment around you two," he said.

Leona studied him closely, but in the end she could not decide if the corner of his mouth had kicked up in his edgy micro-smile or not. Considering the circumstances, probably not.

She tightened her grip on the journal and opened her senses. She realized Oliver was watching her, waiting for the verdict.

"It's authentic," she said. She looked at Thacker. "I really need this document. How much do you want for it?"

"What?" Thacker jerked his attention away from the burning mansion and glanced at her. He appeared bewildered by the question for a few seconds and then his expression cleared. "Oh, right, the Willard journal. It's yours, Dr. Griffin. I'm happy to give it to you. Least I can do."

Leona cleared her throat. "Sir, your house and your entire collection are currently in the process of burning to the ground. You'll need money to rebuild."

Thacker chuckled. "No need to worry about me. Money isn't a problem. Inherited a fortune, you see. Besides, you and your sister have a much stronger claim on that journal than I do."

"Thank you. I am truly grateful. But why did you say that giving me the journal was the least you could do?"

"You're a legend come to life, Dr. Griffin." Thacker beamed. "You're the bride who brought the key to Vortex to Lost Creek, opened the machine, and proved that Vincent Lee Vance was not alive inside."

"Setting the legend crap aside," Leona said, "I would remind you that the body inside Vortex was not Vance."

"Exactly," Thacker said. "And in the process, you broke the spell that has gripped this little community for the past couple of months."

CHAPTER FORTY-THREE

"The bridge is back where it's supposed to be," Starkey said. He planted a hand on the roof of the Slider and leaned down to talk to Oliver through the open window. "It's early afternoon, so you shouldn't have any trouble getting down off this mountain and back to Illusion Town in time for dinner."

"I used the landline in the inn to contact the FBPI and the Guild," Oliver said. "They'll be on-site as fast as they can scramble a team together. I expect an advance team will be here later today. Meanwhile, you're in charge."

"I'll keep an eye on things until the Feds get here," Starkey said. "Shouldn't be a problem. Those damned pendants have gone dead. No one's hearing the Voice. People are coming out of the fog."

Leona sat quietly in the front seat of the Slider, the Willard journal on her lap. Roxy was perched on the back of the seat, eager for another road trip.

Earlier, when they went upstairs to grab the suitcases, there had been no sign of Edith Fenwick or the paranormal investigators. Oliver had checked Baxter Richey's room and the one that had been used by Darla Price. Their car was gone. It was clear they had packed up and left.

Starkey looked like a new man today. He was not wearing the headphones and he no longer had the air of a lonely, tormented artist who felt compelled to walk the night in an effort to protect his community against the ghosts of the past. He was a Guild man with a mission.

Leona smiled at him. "I bought your beautiful specter-cat. I love it. There was no one at the front desk so I left the cash on the table near the stairs. You might want to collect it just in case Edith Fenwick forgets to pay you."

Starkey chuckled. "I'll do that." He took his hand off the roof of the Slider and stepped back. "Drive safe."

"Thanks," Oliver said.

He put the vehicle in gear and drove out of the parking lot. Leona took one last look around Lost Creek. Main Street was even quieter than usual. The grocery store and the diner were closed.

"I wonder how Baxter Richey and Darla Price will explain this episode to their audience," she said. "I suppose they could recast it as a myth-busting story. *Vincent Lee Vance Cult Exposed.*"

"Don't count on it," Oliver said. "It's more likely they'll go with *The Bride of Vincent Lee Vance Returns.*"

Leona shuddered. "That is not funny. A story like that would destroy whatever hope I have of firing up a new career as a private consultant."

"That just goes to show how little you know about consulting work. Trust me, that kind of press would do wonders to launch your new career. People love a good legend."

"I am not a legend."

"Yes, you are, at least in this town."

Oliver smiled his edgy little smile.

"What?" she asked, instantly suspicious.

"It just occurred to me that I'm sleeping with a legend. Not a lot of people can say that."

"If you want to survive until we get off this mountain, you will not mention the word *legend* again."

"Got it," he said. "You know, it occurs to me that we haven't eaten anything except a couple of energy bars since dinner last night. We've had a lot of exercise since then. I'm hungry."

"Don't worry, the road food arrangements have been handled."

She unhooked her seat belt and leaned into the rear compartment to grab the paper sack she had placed there. Settling back into the front seat, she reached inside the sack and took out two large cups of coffee. She slipped the cups securely into the holders on the console and then she removed the box of muffins.

Roxy chortled approvingly.

"I'm impressed," Oliver said. "Where did you get the coffee and muffins?"

"Roxy and I went into Edith Fenwick's kitchen while you put the luggage in the car. We figured Edith owed us something after what happened last night."

"In other words, you two stole the coffee and muffins."

"Got a problem with that?"

"Nope. Pass the muffins."

When they were off the mountain and on their way back to Illusion Town, Leona opened the journal and took a closer look at her prize. Shock jolted through her.

"I don't believe it," she whispered.

"What's wrong? A fake after all?"

"No, it's genuine," she said. She looked up from the cramped writing.

"Thacker was right. This isn't Nigel Willard's journal. It's his brother's. Cyrus Willard."

"Is that a problem?"

"We didn't know Nigel had a brother."

"Interesting that he turned up in Lost Creek," Oliver said.

"Yes," she said. "It is. He also had a sister. Agnes."

"Any indication she was interested in Vortex?"

"No way to know. She was institutionalized at a young age, according to this journal. Evidently, she was highly unstable. A danger to herself and others."

"Anything else?"

"Yes. All of the Willard siblings were convinced they were descendants of Vincent Lee Vance."

CHAPTER FORTY-FOUR

Hours later, back in her apartment, Leona contemplated Cyrus Willard's journal. It was now lying on the coffee table next to the little specter-cat sculpture. She had spent the long drive from Lost Creek studying the contents.

She picked up her glass of wine and considered what she had learned.

"It did answer a couple of very interesting questions," she said. "We now know the identity of the body we found inside the Vortex machine. Cyrus Willard, twin brother of Nigel Willard, the man who kidnapped Molly all those years ago. I didn't recognize him because the mummification process distorted his features. The last entry in the journal is about his plan to climb inside the Vortex machine. He was convinced he would emerge with all of Vance's powers and the stability needed to control them."

Oliver reached for the last slice of pizza. "Thus proving he was unstable before he went into the machine. Only a deranged individual would have climbed into that thing without making sure there was an exit strategy."

"I wonder if the Willards really were descended from Vance."

"It's possible. Vance ran a cult and he was a womanizer. By all accounts, he had more than one lover."

"A biological connection to Vance is not something most families would advertise. Definitely not the kind of thing you want to put down on a matchmaking agency questionnaire."

She had called Molly and the moms to give them a full report and assure them that she and Oliver and Roxy were okay. They had wanted to see her when she arrived but she had pleaded exhaustion and promised to get together in the morning for a full accounting.

The first thing she had done after leading Oliver into her apartment was open a bottle of wine and order an extra-large pizza from Ollie's House of Pizza. *All four food groups in each delicious bite.*

She and Oliver were now kicked back on the sofa in her apartment. The pizza box was empty and they were making their way through the last half of the wine. Roxy was on the table polishing off her final slice of pizza.

There were answers in the journal, and some of them were unsettling. Talking about them with Oliver was complicated, Leona thought, because they edged too close to the Griffin Family Secret. She had tried to go there when she told him that she was sure she was a triple, but he had seemed unconcerned, maybe because he didn't believe her. The fact that she did not know the nature of her third talent made the claim hard to prove.

Still, the question of whether or not she had three talents had been raised, at least. It was no longer a secret. The mystery of her birth and the reasons why she had cause to believe she was a triple, however, were still a deep, dark family secret.

Molly had taken the huge risk of confiding the truth about their origins to Joshua, but that was different. She and Joshua had been through a lot together. They trusted each other. They were going into a Covenant Marriage. They were making a lifelong commitment.

She and Oliver, on the other hand, were merely sleeping together. Correction—they'd had a one-night stand.

She drank some wine and thought about that. When you got right down to it, they were not even involved in a serious romantic relationship. Yes, they had been through some bad stuff together and survived—which probably explained the hot sex. But they were nowhere near family secret territory. Maybe at some point in the future . . .

Great. Now she was sliding into a brooding mood. *Achieving Inner Resonance* strongly advised against allowing that state of mind to take control. Besides, this was not the time to contemplate the possibility of a future with Oliver. They both had too many other things to focus on. Priorities.

"It might be interesting to do a genealogical search on the Willard family," Oliver said.

Clearly he was focusing on priorities. She suppressed a sigh.

"Good idea," she said, trying for a bright and professional vibe. "The moms conducted one on Nigel Willard after he kidnapped Molly, but they didn't get far. He was a real loner. There was certainly no mention of a twin or a sister. They found enough mysterious dead ends to conclude that he had gone to a lot of trouble to erase most of his history. That made them think that there was probably a streak of psychic instability in the bloodline. Families will go to almost any length to conceal that kind of thing."

"Discovering that Nigel Willard had a twin and a sister will give your mothers some new leads," Oliver said.

"When you think about it, it doesn't matter if they were Vance's descendants." Leona swirled the wine gently in her glass. "Both brothers have been dead for years, so we won't be getting any more answers from them."

"The sister may still be alive, though. If she is, she will probably be living in an asylum under an assumed name."

"The moms will find her. They are very good at that kind of research."

Roxy chose that moment to bounce off the coffee table and hustle over to the balcony door. A dust bunny with places to go and things to do.

She stopped and chortled. Leona pushed herself up from the sofa and crossed the room to open the door. Roxy dashed out onto the patio and disappeared into the night, fascinator ribbons flying.

Leona smiled. "She's back in town and ready to party." She closed the door, flopped down on the sofa, and yawned. "Wish I had her energy."

"So do I." Oliver rested his head on the back of the sofa and contemplated the ceiling. "We've resolved several issues, but we don't have the answer to the most important question."

She looked at him. "We don't know the identity of the person who put together the complex schemes that lured both of us to Lost Creek."

"No, but we know that the individual was in Lost Creek," Oliver said. "Hiding in plain sight."

"Think it was someone we met while we were there?"

"Probably, but maybe not. We also know that person was at the Antiquarian Society reception, too."

"Whoever it was murdered the waiter."

"Right. So the Feds are looking for someone who was in both places. That should narrow down the list of suspects."

Leona thought about that. "Well, they've got a town full of suspects, but it's hard to see any of those people in Lost Creek as a good fit for the role of mastermind killer juggler."

"The juggler was there, and by now they will be seriously pissed and very, very frustrated."

Oliver sounded pleased. Satisfied.

"How is that helpful?" she asked.

"Rage and frustration are massively destabilizing emotions, even if your profile is strong and stable. Emotions like that cause people to make mistakes. That's a good thing as far as law enforcement is concerned. Trust me, it's just a matter of time before the Feds make an arrest."

"You know, there was one person we never met in Lost Creek who was always there in the background," Leona mused. "Margo Gibbs, the owner of the local rez-screen station. Everyone said she drank, but—"

"But that makes for a good cover. I agree. I also think the Bureau will take a close look at Thacker. He knew more about Vance's connection to Lost Creek than anyone else, and he was obsessed with the history."

"I don't know," Leona said. "He seemed genuinely happy that Vance hadn't emerged from the Vortex machine."

"Who knows how he really felt? He's weird, even for a collector."

"What about the waitress at the diner? Or the bartender, for that matter? Harp? Edith Fenwick? Burt?" Leona groaned and rested her head against the back of the sofa. "Forget it. Everyone in town is a suspect, except maybe Starkey."

"Huh. That's a thought."

"No, I can't imagine Starkey is our master juggler."

"Why not?"

"I don't know," she admitted. She looked at the specter-cat on the coffee table. "But I'm too tired to think logically tonight."

"So am I." Oliver finished his wine and leaned forward to set the empty glass on the table. "I should go back to my apartment and get some sleep."

There was a short silence. Leona knew the next move was up to her. She reminded herself that she was falling in love with a man who did not know all of her secrets. That was not smart. More importantly, it was not fair to him. After what they had been through, she owed him the truth, even if it meant the end of their relationship.

"You're welcome to stay here," she said.

He turned his head to look at her. His eyes burned, this time with the kind of heat that set fire to her senses.

"I'd like that," he said.

"But there's something you should know before you make the decision. There's a reason why I was obsessed with the pyramid crystal."

"Is this where you tell me that you think you and your sister have a history that involves getting dosed with Vortex radiation and that's why you think you're triples?"

She stilled. "You know?"

He shrugged. "Not the details, but it wasn't hard to put the big picture together."

"I don't think you understand."

"I'm listening."

She took a deep breath. "Molly and I are the results of Vortex-type experiments that were conducted on our birth mothers. They were both pregnant and single. Alone in the world. Nigel Willard tricked them into taking jobs in his lab. He irradiated them with yellow crystals without their knowledge. Claimed it was a lab accident. And then he injected them with a serum that he told them would protect them against any ill effects of the radiation."

"But in reality, Willard was attempting to enhance the para-profiles of the babies?"

She swallowed hard. "Well, yes. That's pretty much it. Our birth mothers escaped and left their infants on the doorstep of the Inskip orphanage. But Willard tracked down both women and murdered them. He found Molly and me, too, but he left us at the orphanage to be raised."

"While he monitored you from afar? Is that it?"

She nodded. "He kidnapped Molly when she was six and a half to run some tests on her. He planned to take me next. But the moms ended that plan. Willard died in the tunnels. Molly and I grew up to become triples. We were raised with the understanding that the only logical thing to do was keep the family secret a, well, a secret."

"Given society's attitudes toward triples and enhancement experiments, that was a perfectly sensible decision. Can we go to bed?"

She studied him, eyes narrowed, trying to get a handle on his reaction. "I'm not making this up. What I just told you is the truth. Molly and I are the result of some bizarre experiments conducted on our birth mothers."

"I believe you. But when you think about it, we're all experiments of one kind or another. That's how evolution works. You and Molly survived and you are both stable. That makes the two of you success stories."

"You really don't care, do you?"

"About how you came to be you? Nope." He did his edgy, telltale smile and his eyes got hotter. "For what it's worth, I really like the way you turned out. *Now* can we go to bed?"

She touched the side of his face with her fingertips. "Yes."

He got to his feet, swept her up off the couch, and carried her down the hall. When they reached her shadowed bedroom, he stood her on her feet beside the bed. He wrapped one powerful hand around the back of her head and pulled her close.

"For a while back there on the sofa, I thought we'd never get here," he said.

"You're not afraid of me, are you?" she whispered.

"No. Are you afraid of me?"

"No."

"To paraphrase an Old World movie, this looks like the start of a beautiful relationship."

His mouth came down on hers before she could start to question his definition of *relationship*. He wasn't afraid of her, and he wanted her, and she could trust him. It was more than enough. For now.

CHAPTER FORTY-FIVE

The day after she and Oliver returned to Illusion Town, Leona decided to fulfill her promise to Roxy. Doing so gave her a convenient way to spend some together time with Molly. The plan seemed simple enough, but the attendant in charge of the gate of the River of Alien Nightmares ride at the Underworld Adventures theme park looked doubtful.

"I'm not sure it's okay to let you two take a couple of dust bunnies with you on the ride," he said.

Leona gave him a glowing smile and tightened her grip on Roxy. "Don't worry, these are emotional support dust bunnies."

"They are licensed," Molly added, clutching Newton.

Roxy and Newton chortled and batted their innocent blue eyes at the attendant, who continued to look skeptical.

"I dunno," he said.

"We'll hold on to them," Leona added. "They're just dust bunnies. What could possibly go wrong?"

This being Illusion Town, she sweetened her assurances with a couple of gracefully palmed twenties.

This being Illusion Town, the attendant made the gratuity vanish with an equally smooth move. "Well, okay, I guess."

He opened the gate and ushered them onto the first in a line of self-piloting vessels designed to take passengers along the artificial river and through the dark ride.

Leona stepped aboard first. The small craft wobbled a little. She sat down on the bench. Molly followed with Newton.

The attendant lowered the safety bar. The boat took off with a small jolt. It moved faster than Leona had anticipated, whisking them toward the entrance of the tunnel of Alien nightmares.

Thrilled, Roxy wriggled free of Leona's grip, fluttered to the front of the boat, and clutched the side with two paws. The ribbons of the blue fascinator flew in the light breeze. Newton hurried after her, so excited he bounced a little.

"I'm not sure this is a really great idea," Molly said.

"Here's the thing," Leona said. "I promised Roxy I would take her on a real boat ride when we got back to Illusion Town. Given that this city sits in the middle of a desert, there aren't a lot of options."

"Fair point," Molly said. "Actually, I'm glad you suggested we do lunch and this ride today. I needed a break. Between the increased business at Singing Crystals and all the wedding preparations, I'm feeling a little frazzled."

"I understand." Leona put her arm around her and hugged her. "You're happy, though, aren't you? Really, truly happy?"

"Yes. Joshua is the one."

"I'm so glad."

"What about you?"

"Truth? I'm sort of holding my breath."

"Well, you've only just met Oliver," Molly pointed out. "There's no rush."

"I know. I'm holding my breath because part of me is afraid to believe I've met the right man."

"If it makes you feel any better, the moms and I had a long talk about the wisdom of your relationship with Oliver Rancourt."

Leona flinched. "You did?"

"Of course we did. We're your family. We concluded that the fact that you've broken the rules for him indicates he may be the one. Looks like the Griffin free spirit sisterhood is about to be officially closed due to lack of membership."

"Nothing will ever be the same now that I've met Oliver, that's for sure. I don't think I could go back—"

She broke off because the gates of the dark ride's tunnel abruptly opened in front of the boat. Roxy and Newton chortled madly as the craft sailed through the entrance. When the gates slammed shut again, utter darkness descended. Leona could no longer see her hand in front of her face.

The special effects and scary scenes started appearing and disappearing immediately. Leona thought she was prepared but she yelped in spite of herself when a ghostly spider flew at them out of the darkness. It was followed by a monstrous creature with a mouthful of jagged teeth.

She was not the only one who jumped.

"Yikes," Molly said. "So much for the 'moderately scary' ranking on this ride."

The creature with the big teeth reached out with long claws, barely missing Leona's shoulder. She shrieked again. An instant later, the boat whipped around a sharp turn and plunged down a short waterfall. Strange sea creatures, mouths agape, waited at the bottom.

Roxy and Newton were ecstatic. Their chortling reverberated inside the dark tunnel.

Leona caught glimpses of their silhouettes occasionally, but that was about it. For the most part, she could not see them or anything else except the frightening special effects.

Shrieks and yelps of surprise echoed from somewhere in the deep shadows behind them. Another boat had entered the dark ride.

A mad scientist wielding a huge syringe filled with glowing green fluid appeared at Leona's side. She screamed. The figure disappeared as the boat rounded a bend in the river.

"You know, you'd think it would not be so easy to freak out a couple of women who have been through what we've been through in recent weeks," Molly said.

"I just hope Roxy doesn't realize that this theme park sells yearly passes."

More screams and startled laughter sounded from other people on the ride. There was another sharp twist in the river. Water splashed over the side of the boat, dampening Leona's jeans.

She was about to ask Molly if she had gotten wet, too, when she became aware of the sudden silence at the front of the small boat. She stilled.

"Roxy?"

There was no response.

"Newton?" Molly called softly.

More silence.

"This is probably not good," Leona said.

"Probably not."

A short time later the boat shot out of the exit, heading back to the dock. For several seconds the abrupt shift from deep darkness to bright desert sunlight made it hard for Leona to focus. When her vision settled down, she saw that she and Molly were alone in the vessel.

"Definitely not good," she said.

"Nope."

The screaming started then—real screams. A sense of dread whispered through Leona. She and Molly turned to look at the boat that had followed theirs into the dark ride. The two passengers, a young couple in their teens, mouths agape in horror, eyes glazed with shock, clutched the safety bar that pinned them to their seats.

"Did you see it?" the woman shouted to Leona and Molly. "There's something in that tunnel. Something real."

"Uh, no, no, we didn't see anything," Molly said.

"Probably just a trick of the light," Leona offered.

She turned around quickly in the seat. The boat came to a halt at the gate. The attendant opened the safety bar.

"What happened to the dust bunnies?" he asked.

The young couple in the following boat arrived before Leona and Molly could explain. They started shouting, talking over each other in a frantic attempt to make the attendant understand.

". . . Something weird inside the tunnel," the man said. "For sure it's not one of the special effects."

"They were, like, for-real monsters," the woman said. "They had four eyes. That's all you could see in the darkness."

Another boat emerged from the tunnel exit. Two women were yelling. The man with them looked grim.

". . . Really huge rats, I think," he said to the attendant. "You need to shut down the ride and get an exterminator in there before you send anyone else through."

Molly looked at Leona. "I believe we have the answer to your earlier question."

"What question?"

"Your exact words were, 'What could possibly go wrong?'"

"Oh, yeah, that question. All I can tell you is that I had a plan. Seemed like a good idea at the time. Oliver is right. One should always have a plan B."

CHAPTER FORTY-SIX

"We haven't been able to prove or disprove that the Willard brothers and their sister were descended from Vincent Lee Vance," Eugenie said. "But we've turned up a few interesting details, one of which is that the twins attended a private boarding school that claimed to have a unique method for educating high-talent children with symptoms of psychic instability."

"Interesting." Leona put the phone on speaker and set the device on the kitchen counter, freeing her hands so that she could spoon freshly ground coffee into the coffeemaker.

She and Roxy were alone in the apartment. They had just finished a light lunch of cheese-and-pickle sandwiches, and she was getting ready to hit the grocery store to stock up. When you had a man around the place, you had to make sure there was food on hand.

A man around the place. She wasn't clear on the definition of the phrase. Like *relationship*, it was a frustratingly vague concept, at least when applied to Oliver and herself. But whatever was going on between them was vastly different from what she had experienced with Matt Fullerton or his predecessors. No question about it, her days as a free spirit were over. For now.

They had returned from Lost Creek the day before yesterday, and even though Oliver had not officially moved in, their lives together had begun to take on a domestic routine. After breakfast, he had left for his office at the museum. He had called an hour ago to let her know that he had heard from his contact in the Bureau, who had informed him they were still actively investigating the scene in Lost Creek. As of yet, no one had been arrested.

"Anything else on the Willard brothers?" Leona asked.

"Some bits and pieces," Charlotte said. "Cyrus tried to erase all traces of his branch of the family tree, too, but he was not nearly as thorough as his brother. We were able to track down the sister, Agnes Willard. The poor thing was committed to an asylum at an early age because of severe psychic instability. She was deemed to be a risk to herself and others. Turns out she died a few months ago."

"All of which goes a long way toward explaining why the Willard brothers tried to make their ancestry records disappear," Eugenie added. "Just the rumor of psychic instability severe enough to require permanent hospitalization is enough to destroy a family. In any event, Nigel and Cyrus managed to get through college and launch careers as scientific researchers. But they apparently had a falling-out at some point, and for all intents and purposes, Cyrus disappeared."

"That's probably when he went to Lost Creek, found Vance's notebook, and eventually the Vortex machine," Leona said.

"There's one more item of interest," Eugenie added. "Nigel appears to have died without issue. But we're not sure about Cyrus. We're looking into the possibility that he may have had offspring."

"Thanks," Leona said. "Keep me informed, okay?"

"Will do." Eugenie switched into her Mom voice. "Will you be seeing your new friend, Oliver, again?"

"Yes," Leona said, bracing herself for the inquisition. "As a matter of fact, he'll be here for dinner tonight." There was no need to add that he would be spending the night.

"Dinner?" Eugenie's voice sharpened. "At your apartment?"

"Yes."

"Sounds lovely. As it happens, Charlotte and I are free tonight. We could join you. We'd love to meet Mr. Rancourt."

Panic struck Leona. It was too soon. She needed more time to get used to the idea of living with Oliver. Time to make sure that what they had was going to last.

"Well—" she began.

"I'll bring my famous lasagna," Eugenie said.

"I'll bring the wine," Charlotte added.

I'm doomed, Leona thought. It was going to be Meet the Parents Night. She had to warn Oliver.

Mercifully, the security system buzzed, announcing a caller at the lobby door.

"Sorry, Moms, gotta run. There's someone at the downstairs door."

"Who?" Eugenie demanded.

"I don't know. Bye."

"Leona, make sure you know who is on the other side of that door before you open it," Charlotte said.

Leona groaned. "I'm not an idiot, Mom." She rezzed the button that activated the video monitor. A familiar face appeared. For a beat she was off-balance. Bewildered. "It's okay, I recognize him. Bye."

She ended the phone call and rezzed the audio on the monitor. "What are you doing here, Matt?"

Matt Fullerton glared at the street-level call box screen with the expression of a desperate man. Not a typical look for him.

"Let me in, Leona," he said quietly. "I need to talk to you right now. There's been an accident in the Underworld directly beneath the Antiquarian Society mansion. Lives are at stake."

"That's horrible." Leona stared at the screen, stunned. "But the Guild has experts who deal with situations like that. Why do you need me?"

"Because this incident involves artifacts of unknown power—a room full of AUPs, in fact. We don't know which object rezzed the problem. Even if we did, none of us has the talent to de-rez it. There may be other people who can handle this, but I don't know of anyone except you, and time is running out."

CHAPTER FORTY-SEVEN

"Whose idea was it to charge through that doorway straight into a room full of hot AUPs without making sure the entrance wasn't trapped?" Leona asked.

Matt's jaw was rigid. "There was no indication of a gate or a trap. The doorway looked clear."

She opened her mouth to launch into a lecture on basic protocols for dealing with artifacts of unknown power but stopped herself at the last instant. This wasn't the time or the place. It dawned on her that she was actually feeling sorry for Matt. He had been lucky enough to snag the position of team leader for this project. His future at Hollister depended on how well he handled it. She knew that he must have been truly desperate to come to her for help—desperate and genuinely concerned about the fate of the people trapped on the other side. He wasn't a monster, just a very ambitious academic. There were a lot of those around. She ought to know.

The two of them were standing in front of a quicksilver gate that now blocked the entrance to the Antiquarian Society's Underworld storage chamber. Roxy was on her shoulder, fluffed out with all four eyes open. Two more members of the Hollister Department of Para-Archaeology hovered nearby. They looked worried. They had reason to be. Three of their colleagues were locked on the other side of the strange gate.

Matt had ignored the speed limit driving across town and into the exclusive neighborhood on the hillside overlooking the city. The mansion that housed the Society's headquarters was no longer a crime scene, but it was a busy site. A security company had been hired to protect the artifacts until they could be cataloged, photographed, and removed by the Hollister team. Vehicles bearing the logo of a professional transport company that specialized in valuable and potentially dangerous objects were lined up in the long, sweeping driveway.

An entrepreneur had set up a catering truck. A small scrum of reporters had gathered around it, cameras at the ready, on the off chance that something exciting happened. They had not yet been informed of the disaster under the mansion. Matt had made it clear that Hollister did not want that sort of publicity.

He had done his best to shield her from view as he rushed her out of the car and into the mansion. She knew the last thing he wanted was to have the press get wind of her presence on the scene. Officially, Hollister had severed all connections to her. That hurt, but she refused to let the pain show. She had a job to do. She was a professional consultant now. Time to act like one.

Matt raked his fingers through his hair and stared at the quicksilver gate. "What do you think?"

She answered the question silently in her head. *I think there is no telling what we're going to find on the other side of that gate. We don't even know if the people who got trapped in there are still alive. I think you took a risk you should not have taken. I think you should have followed procedure.*

The temptation to say it all aloud was nearly overwhelming. She exerted some serious willpower and managed to resist. This was not the time for revenge. It was time to think positive and apply the principles of chapter six in *Achieving Inner Resonance*, "Opportunity Is a Flower That Blossoms in the Shadows." If she was successful, the university might become a future client.

She rezzed up what she hoped was a cool, confident consultant's smile.

"I think it's time to open the gate and free your colleagues," she said.

She centered herself, went into her talent, and cautiously flattened one hand on the gate . . .

. . . and nearly choked on a hastily swallowed shriek. It was like touching a live wire.

Shit. That hurt. She managed to grit her teeth and keep her mouth shut. *I'm a professional. Don't try this at home.*

On her shoulder, Roxy growled and tightened her grip.

The quicksilver energy dazzled and flared with wild currents and sparks of lightning that appeared chaotic. It was always this way, she reminded herself. Okay, this was an extreme version of an Alien lock, but nevertheless, the laws of para-physics applied—she hoped. There was an anchor current—there was always an anchor current.

She slipped into the storm, searching for the pattern and the vibe that would guide her to the center.

There it is.

Gently she sent out the flatlining currents.

And then she held her breath, because while the laws of para-physics were believed to be immutable and universal, there was a lot that humans did not know about those laws. They knew even less about how the Aliens had engineered them into their technology.

The quicksilver gate flashed, brilliant and fierce, in a recoil that threatened to dazzle her senses. Her hair lifted in a wild, spiky halo around her head. Roxy's fur stood on end. Matt and the others took several steps back.

For a beat there was no reaction from the gate. Then in the blink of an eye it dissolved. There was a moment of fraught silence during which she frantically tried to blink away the visual aftereffects of the sharp, hot recoil. She was vaguely aware of Roxy chortling, and then she heard a lot of cheering from inside the chamber.

When her vision cleared, she recognized her former colleagues who had been trapped. They were making an effort to project a just-another-day-at-the-office vibe, but they could not disguise their relief. They hustled out of the cavern and into the glowing green corridor.

"Leona," Margery Bean exclaimed. "Don't tell me Matt had to get you to rescue us. That must have pissed him off."

"He's right here," Leona said. "Ask him."

Matt looked at her. "Thanks," he said quietly.

She gave him a very shiny smile. "Anytime. I'll send you my bill first thing tomorrow."

He winced.

Margery chuckled. "Thanks for the rescue. You're the best when it comes to handling hot artifacts. I'm so glad you're back on the team."

"Oh, I'm not on the team," Leona said. "I've gone private. I'm a consultant now. Which reminds me." She turned to give Matt another bright smile. "In addition to my standard rate there will be an extra charge for emergency callout services."

"Fair enough," he said.

She took that as her cue to make her exit. "I'd better be on my way. I had to squeeze this job into my schedule, which means I'm now running late for my next client."

There was no next client, but image was everything in business.

"Wait," Matt said. "How long will this gate stay open?"

"There's no way to know," Leona said. "It's an Alien gate. By definition, that means it's unpredictable. There's a lot of volatile energy in the artifacts stored inside that room. If I were you, I'd hire a professional gatekeeper to stand by while you're cataloging those objects."

Matt grunted. "Bullinger won't like that. You know how he is when it comes to budgets."

"I know," she said. "But Bullinger is not my problem anymore."

"You're right. Thanks, again, Leona. I'll walk you back upstairs to the entrance. I would drive you home but I can't leave until things get organized here. You'll have to call a car. There aren't a lot of taxis cruising this neighborhood."

"I'll put it on the bill."

He escorted her up the quartz steps and through the hole-in-the-wall below the mansion. It was not the same opening that she and Oliver had used to escape on the night of the raid. This one was larger. She assumed it was the exit point the caterers and staff had used to escape the FBPI raid.

Inside the big house they went past the pantry. The door was open. The dead waiter's blood had dried to a terrible brown stain on the floor. Leona was aware of the disturbing whisper of dark energy, the unmistakable evidence of violent death. Roxy muttered.

"I know, I don't like it, either," Leona said.

Matt glanced at her. "What don't you like?"

"Nothing," she said.

"Leona, there's something I need to say."

"I figured that's why you insisted on escorting me out of the mansion. What is it?"

"You haven't filed a complaint about my failure to give you credit in that paper that the journal is going to publish."

"I've been busy."

"Are you going to do it?"

"No. It wouldn't do me any good now that I've been fired by Hollister.

It would look like petty revenge. We both know I can't prove that I should have had credit."

"Maybe not, but a formal complaint would create a real headache for me."

She did not respond.

"You weren't fired," he continued. "Technically speaking, your contract was not renewed."

"Semantics."

Matt nodded. "I know. Thanks for not filing the complaint."

"You didn't tell anyone that I had rezzed that artifact in the lab. I know it was the scorch marks that started the rumors."

"Can we call off the cold war?"

"Yep. Revenge is all about looking back. I don't have the time. I've got a future that needs planning."

"I appreciate it."

They reached the front door of the entrance. Leona stopped.

"You've said what you wanted to say." She took out her phone. "You can go back to your team. I am quite capable of calling a ride. Good luck with the rest of the project."

"Thanks," Matt said. "It's a big one."

"Don't forget to hire a gatekeeper."

He smiled. "It's at the top of my to-do list."

He turned away and disappeared back into the mansion. Leona walked outside and took out her phone to book a car.

She thought about what had just happened down in the tunnels and smiled. She had saved the team. This time she had not been too late.

Chapter Forty-Eight

Roxy chortled and bounced off her shoulder. By the time Leona looked up from her phone, the dust bunny was racing toward the food truck parked in the long driveway.

"What could possibly go wrong?"

Oh, yeah. Right.

"Roxy, come back, sweetie. The car will be here soon. Time to go."

But Roxy had arrived at the food truck. She vaulted up onto the ledge in front of the order window and went into adorable mode.

The server chuckled and handed her a bag of pretzels. "There you go."

Roxy chortled in delight and went to work opening her prize. The bored reporters were amused.

Leona groaned and walked toward the truck. "How much do I owe you?"

"No charge," the server said. "Worth it for the entertainment."

"How are things going in there?" one of the reporters asked, angling his head to indicate the mansion. "Are they finding anything interesting?"

"You'll have to ask the people in charge," Leona said. "I'm an outside consultant. I never comment on my clients' projects."

A woman carrying a microphone stepped in front of her. "Why did they think it was necessary to bring in an outside consultant?"

"It's routine to call in specialized talent on major projects like this one. Don't worry, I'm sure the director, Dr. Fullerton, will hold a press conference later today. You'll have to excuse me. I've got an appointment with another client."

She scooped up Roxy and hurried back to the front steps of the mansion.

Her phone rang. She recognized the familiar code and took the call.

"Hi, Mom. What's up?"

"We just finished running the genealogical search using the data about the Willard brothers and their sister, Agnes," Eugenie said.

"It was a complex search," Charlotte added. "We won't bore you with the details. Suffice it to say that the real clues were in the files of the asylum where Agnes was hospitalized. We told you that she died a few months ago. Turns out there wasn't much in the way of an estate, but what she did have—mostly her personal effects—went to the only surviving relative, a niece."

"So Cyrus Willard had a child?"

"Yes," Eugenie said. "But he never knew her. Evidently he needed cash at some point, so he sold his sperm to a fertility clinic. It took some doing—Charlotte had to hack the sperm bank records—but we think we tracked down the daughter."

"Got a photo?"

"Yes," Eugenie said. "That wasn't easy, by the way. No social media presence. Evidently she likes to keep a low profile. A DMV shot was the best we could do."

"Text it to me."

"Sending now," Eugenie said.

A silver-gray car with heavily tinted windows turned into the drive. Roxy chortled, enthused about the prospect of a ride.

"Hang on, my car just arrived," Leona said. She hurried down the steps.

"Where are you?" Charlotte asked.

"At the Antiquarian Society mansion. Meet the new consultant on the block. I just concluded a job for the Hollister team. And get this, Matt Fullerton is in charge of the project. Having to call me in on an emergency project was very hard for him."

"Revenge is sweet," Eugenie said.

"Not as sweet as I expected," Leona said. "It was kind of a letdown, to be honest. But that chapter of my life is definitely closed. I saw the flower of opportunity blossoming in the shadows and I grabbed it."

"What does that mean?" Eugenie asked.

"It's advice from a book I'm reading," Leona said.

She tucked Roxy under one arm, jumped into the back seat of the vehicle, and closed the door. She focused on her phone, waiting for the photo.

"You made good time," she said to the driver without looking up from the screen. "I'm glad because I'm—" She broke off because the photo had appeared on the screen. "Oh, shit."

"What is it?" Charlotte asked, her voice sharpening.

"I recognize Agnes Willard's niece," Leona said.

The phone went dead as the car pulled away from the steps. Roxy was suddenly sleeked out and growling. Leona looked up. For the first time, she saw that a glass window separated the driver's compartment from the rear seat.

She grabbed the door handle but the automatic locks had clicked shut, trapping her. She could unlock them but it would take a moment.

She needed her talent to pull off that particular trick, and her talent was seeping away like water down a drain.

An unfamiliar, unpleasantly herbal scent wafted in the atmosphere. Roxy was no longer growling. She had gone limp. Not asleep, Leona realized. Roxy was unconscious.

She would be soon, too, because the scent was growing stronger. She tried to cover her mouth and nose with the sleeve of her jacket but it was too late.

The driver did not turn his head to look at her, but she could see his eyes and a portion of his face in the rearview mirror. Baxter Richey was no longer playing the role of naïve, enthusiastic paranormal investigator. He drove like a robot at the wheel—or as if he were in a hypnotic trance.

He was not alone in the front of the car. There was a woman in the passenger seat. A baseball cap concealed her hair. She turned around to peer through the glass barrier. Her eyes glittered with barely controlled fury.

"Darla Price," Leona whispered, her voice thick from the effects of the drug.

"That name was for the Lost Creek portion of the project, the part you fucked up. You can call me Melody Palantine."

CHAPTER FORTY-NINE

She came awake to the familiar radiance of green quartz. That answered two questions. She was alive and she was in the Underworld. *Gotta think positive.*

It took her a moment longer to realize that she was lying on the floor of a tunnel chamber. She pushed herself to a sitting position and looked around with blurry eyes, trying to orient herself. Hope sparked briefly when she realized she still had her nav amber in the form of her bracelets and earrings, but when she pulsed a little energy, she realized they had been flatlined.

Her crystal pendant was gone.

She looked around. "Roxy?"

Melody Palantine appeared in the doorway. She had a flamer in her hand. The fierce, volatile energy of her fury charged the atmosphere.

"Forget the fucking dust bunny," she said. "I told Baxter to get rid of it."

"If he hurts her—"

Melody snorted. "You'll do nothing. And if you're thinking of making a run for it, forget it. I used a handy little gadget fresh out of my company's labs to flatline your amber and the yellow crystal in your pendant." She pulled the necklace out of her pocket and held it up. "Your sister did a very good job of locking in the codes, by the way. She's definitely a high-rez tuner—I'll give her that—but she's a failure as far as Uncle Willard's experiment goes."

"How do you define *failure*?"

Melody dropped the necklace back into her pocket. "She's not a multi-talent. A double, at best. Certainly not a triple."

"Do you think I'm a triple?"

"That's what I've been trying to decide. But it's difficult to measure psychic energy, especially if someone is concealing a third talent. And that's what any smart, stable triple does, right? Conceal the full range of their profile? We all know how society fears people with high-rez talents. People like us."

Leona managed to push herself awkwardly to her feet. A wave of dizziness almost overwhelmed her. She took a few deep breaths in an effort to steady her senses. "What makes you think I might be a triple?"

"No need to play dumb. According to my dear dead aunt's journal, you and Molly are the results of her brother Nigel Willard's experiments. He developed his own version of the enhancement process, you see. His goal was to create stable multi-talents. I need to know if he was successful with his approach. You and Molly are the only evidence available. He never got a chance to run any more experiments after he irradiated your mothers."

"My para-psych profile is almost identical to Molly's. You've already determined she's not a triple, so obviously, I'm not, either."

"I'm not so sure about that."

"Why are you obsessed with finding out whether or not I'm a multi-talent?"

"Because you're *stable*," Melody snapped, "like me."

"Well, you're not in an asylum, but I wouldn't go so far as to call you stable."

"I'm a direct descendant of Vincent Lee Vance." Melody's voice rose. "I inherited his enhanced talents and his para-psych profile—his quartz-solid, *stable* profile."

"You're sure about the stability thing?"

Melody's face tightened into a mask of rage. She aimed the flamer at a point slightly to the right of Leona's head and fired. The bolt of fire struck the wall, doing no damage to the nearly indestructible quartz, but the shot came so close, Leona felt the heat. She flinched and instinctively stepped sideways.

"Yes, I'm fucking sure I'm stable," Melody rasped. "Just like Vance."

Leona took a deep breath. "Right. In that case, why are you worried about me?"

Melody took a breath and appeared to steady herself. "There have been some minor setbacks with the approach to enhancement that my people have been using in our labs. I need to know if Nigel Willard's methods were more successful."

"I see. This is all about you trying to build Vortex 2.0."

"Let me explain it to you in simple sentences," Melody said. "Whoever controls a reliable, successful enhancement process will hold all the power."

"And you intend to be the only one in control of that process, is that it?"

Melody raised her chin. Her eyes heated. "I am going to succeed where Vincent Lee Vance failed. I have a destiny to fulfill."

"You think you can do that because you're his descendant?"

"Yes, and because I am a stable multi-talent." Once again Melody made a

visible effort to regain control. "Back at the start I assumed I had the inside track. I discovered that the head of Spooner Technologies was working on a modern Vortex machine. When I realized that Spooner had it tucked away in a secret lab in the tunnels, I went to work for him. I became his trusted administrative assistant. Spooner is now in an asylum. I control the company and the Vortex experiments. I was certain we were on the right track until my aunt died and I got her diary."

"Did you know your father was the dead man we discovered in the Lost Creek Vortex machine? His name was Cyrus Willard."

"I figured it out," Melody said. "Believe it or not, I wasn't even aware of that side of the family until I got the box containing Agnes's personal possessions. In addition to the diary, there were several letters from Nigel and Cyrus. Lab notes, really. They were both obsessed with Vortex. They are what led me to Lost Creek and Thacker."

"You were the elderly woman who made sure that Thacker found the fake Vance letter, the one about the so-called legend of the bride and the key. And then you used the pendants to manipulate half the town of Lost Creek with the Voice."

Melody smiled. "I am, among other things, a very, very good hypnotist."

"Obviously. You were also the mysterious acolyte. You found the Vortex machine in the Lost Creek tunnels, didn't you? But you couldn't open it."

"Sadly, a talent for paranormal locks is not one of my abilities. But when I found Vance's machine, I also discovered the key crystal. Cyrus Willard's papers made it clear the pyramid was the secret to unlocking the machine, but I couldn't resonate with it."

"You were desperate, so you tracked down Molly and me."

"According to Nigel's notes, he had used the same kind of crystals in his own machine to irradiate your mothers and the babies they were carrying. When I realized that you and your sister both wear tuned Vortex crystals, I knew there was a high probability you could resonate with them. Neither of you is the type to wear untuned stones."

"The Griffin sisters were on your psi-dar for two reasons," Leona said. "First, because you wanted to know if we were stable triples. Second, you thought one of us might be able to use the pyramid key to unlock the machine in the Lost Creek tunnels. Initially you went after Molly, but when your overly complicated plan fell apart, you tried to set me up at the Antiquarian Society reception. But there was a serious flaw in your plan, right from the start."

"There was no way I could have known about the fucking FBPI raid," Melody shouted.

"That wasn't the flaw. That was a twist, a glitch. Instead of letting it throw you off balance, you should have seen the flower of opportunity that was blossoming in the shadows."

Melody was suddenly so enraged, Leona was afraid she might burst into flames.

"Don't quote that stupid book to me," Melody screamed. "*Achieving Inner Resonance* is fucking ghost shit. Every fucking word."

"You read it?" Leona asked. "I'm on chapter six. I admit I had my doubts about the positive-thinking theory, but—"

"It's all a fucking lie. That crap about thinking positive is a cruel joke. I tried it. Look what happened to me. Someone should sue the author."

"I'm not sure you can blame the author for your own screwup. That was just poor planning."

"I did not screw up," Melody cried.

"Your big mistake was stealing Pandora's box from the Rancourt Museum. That got Oliver Rancourt's attention."

"I had no choice." Melody managed to regain some self-control. "I had to have a suitable artifact to submit to the Society. I needed an object of power that the board would not be able to resist. When it comes to AUPs, no museum has a finer collection than the Rancourt. I had no way of knowing that Oliver Rancourt would be able to track down the missing artifact."

"People tend to underestimate Oliver," Leona said. "He was certainly right about you. You're obsessed with the intricacies of your own plans. You make them so complicated that you can't adapt them to unexpected twists."

"That's a lie." Melody raised the flamer again. "I have Vincent Lee Vance's talent for strategy."

"He failed, remember?"

"Because the Guilds ambushed him," Melody shrieked.

"And he had no backup plan. Right. Okay, you've got a talent for strategy and one for hypnosis. I'm assuming your third talent is your ability to rez some Alien artifacts."

"Yes," Melody said. "Like you."

Baxter Richey appeared in the doorway behind her. His expressionless face and blank eyes made it clear he was still in a trance.

"Where's Roxy?" Leona asked. "What did you do to her?"

Baxter did not react to the question.

"I had to put him in a very heavy trance," Melody explained. "He can only respond to direct demands or questions from me." She raised her voice slightly. "Baxter, what happened to the dust bunny?"

"Lost," Baxter said in his flat voice.

"What the fuck?" Melody began. Then she gave Leona an amused smile. "I believe my exact instructions were, *Lose the dust bunny*. People in a trance take commands very literally."

Leona knew a rush of hope. Maybe Baxter actually had lost Roxy and not murdered her. She glanced at the pendant around his neck. The stone in it glowed.

"You used those pendants to transmit hypnotic commands to the members of your Vance return cult," she said.

"It was the same technique Vance used to control his Guardians."

"Why did you murder the waiter, Astrid Todd, at the reception?"

"Turns out not everyone can be hypnotized. Todd had some serious talent herself. She actually tried to scam *me*. She pretended to be a true believer, but she figured out what was going on and just played along."

"What happened at the reception?"

"I arranged for her to get the job on the catering staff that night because I thought it might be useful to have someone I could trust to handle the unpleasant stuff in the event I ran into a problem. I knew the Society would have a lot of security for the event."

"You wanted someone to take the fall if things went wrong."

"But the stupid woman turned on me. Tried to blackmail me—*right there in the mansion*. I couldn't believe it. That's when I realized she was not under the control of the Voice. She threatened to tell the head of the Society that I was a thief who was there to steal some of the artifacts. She demanded that I transfer a fortune into her bank account."

"You panicked, grabbed the nearest weapon—a kitchen knife—and killed her."

"I did not panic. I did the only thing I could under the circumstances. I had to kill her. She gave me no choice."

"Nope, you definitely panicked." Leona tut-tutted. "Oliver is right. You're an overplanner. A juggler. One little spinning plate falls off a pole and you lose control."

"That's a lie." Melody's face was a blotchy red. "I had things under control. Then I heard someone coming down the hall."

"Me."

"I hid in the restroom. The next thing I knew, Rancourt was with you in the pantry. I was trapped and the raid was in full swing. I knew it wouldn't be long before the Feds were swarming down that hallway. And then you actually came into the restroom to wash your hands. I thought you would never leave. When you did, I left the restroom, grabbed Todd's pendant, and escaped through the kitchen door. There was an agent watching that exit, but I used my hypnosis talent to make him forget he had seen me. In the darkness, no one noticed the blood on my clothes."

"When things settled down you realized that, in spite of everything, your plan had worked to some extent."

"*Yes.* Exactly." Melody looked visibly cheered. "I knew the box had been stolen and opened, and that someone had been able to resonate with the pyramid because I put a tracker code on it. When I got the ping from your address, I realized you were the thief. Stealing the artifact was a very impressive move, by the way."

"It wasn't quite like that, but never mind. Details. Before you stole Pandora's box from the museum, you knew that, sooner or later, Oliver Rancourt would become a problem because he would investigate the loss of the box. You wanted him out of the picture, so you set up a plan to lure him to Lost Creek."

"The Foundation has been chasing Vortex clues much longer than I have," Melody said. "Generations. I knew that once Pandora's box disappeared, Rancourt would contact his connections in the gray market. He can afford to pay for information, so sooner or later, he would become a nuisance."

"What you didn't expect—didn't allow for in your strategy—was that Oliver and I might join forces and work as partners."

"When Richey and I saw him in your room that night at the inn, I figured he had seduced you so that he could manipulate you."

"See, that's your problem, Melody. You're good at keeping a lot of spinning plates in the air, but you have a habit of miscalculating when it comes to people and their emotions and motivations. That makes you a failure, just like Vance."

"I am not a failure. I found Vance's Vortex machine and I found you, the one person who could open it."

"That machine is now a useless lump of metal. The yellow crystals, including the key, have been destroyed. But the worst part is that you still don't know if I'm a multi-talent—if I'm your competition. That's why you haven't killed me or dumped me into the tunnels without nav amber. You really, really need to know if I'm a successful multi-talent."

"I'm rapidly coming to the conclusion that you're just a double, like your sister. You're an impressive locksmith, and judging by the way you were able to flatline that little bowl I used to take down Rancourt, you apparently have a talent for working some Alien artifacts. But I've seen no evidence of a third talent."

"You want a demonstration? No problem. I'll give you proof if you agree to hire me."

Melody looked dumbfounded. "Why would I do that?"

"Because we both know you're not going to quit until you've fulfilled your destiny. A woman in your position needs a reliable fixer, someone she can count on to handle the pesky little problems that are bound to crop up along the way. You've been trying to go it alone and it's not working."

"You're serious."

"Absolutely. You need me. Let me demonstrate my third talent and then we can talk."

Melody snorted in disbelief but there was intense curiosity in her eyes. "All right, show me what you can do."

"I'll need a volunteer from the audience."

"You're expecting me to volunteer?" Melody laughed. "Don't hold your breath."

"Baxter, there, will be perfect. I'll need physical contact, however. You'll have to send him over here."

Richey did not react. He continued to gaze at nothing.

Melody frowned. "What are you going to do to him?"

"I can flatline him for you. You're planning to get rid of him anyway, right? He knows too much and eventually the trance will wear off. He'll start talking—assuming he's still alive."

"Are you telling me you can kill someone with your talent?" Melody asked, her eyes widening.

Leona smiled. "You can see why I haven't wanted to publicize that particular aspect of my para-psych profile. It's not a great thing to put down on a résumé or a matchmaking agency questionnaire."

"You're lying."

"Allow me to demonstrate."

Melody hesitated and then shrugged. "All right." She went into her hypnotic command voice. "Baxter, walk toward the woman. I will tell you when to stop."

Baxter obeyed, crossing the chamber until he was close enough for Leona to touch.

"Baxter, stop," Melody ordered. She did not take her eyes off Leona. "Go ahead, show me your third talent."

Leona put her hand on Baxter's arm. He appeared unaware of her fingers gripping him. Cautiously, she rezzed her talent to get a sense of his energy field. It was partially locked. No surprise. The first step was to free him. She sent out a little energy, just enough to counteract the trance.

It was as if she had flipped a switch. The tension evaporated from his body in a heartbeat. He looked around, bewildered.

"Where am I?" he said. He realized she was holding his arm. "Dr. Griffin? What are you—"

"You said you were going to flatline him," Melody snapped. "You lied."

"Not exactly," Leona said. The physical contact with Baxter allowed her to focus through his nav amber. "I said I *could* flatline him for you. But I'd much rather flatline you."

She sent a pulse of hot energy through Baxter's tuned amber, channeling it through the heavy atmosphere of the tunnels, and aimed it at Melody's energy field.

Melody screamed. Rage, horror, and panic twisted across her face as the intense currents hit her with the force of a flamer. She stared at Leona.

"Not possible," she gasped. "No one can work Alien energy that way. No one."

Her eyes fluttered. A terrible shudder went through her. She collapsed without another word.

Leona stared at her, wondering if she had just murdered another human being. Before she could process that possibility, Richey collapsed slowly, gently, to the floor. She crouched beside him and breathed a sigh of relief when she realized that his pulse was strong.

A flash of bright blue appeared in the doorway. Roxy raced into the chamber, chortling madly, the ribbons of the fascinator streaming behind her.

"Roxy." Leona scooped her up and held her very tightly. "I've been so worried."

Oliver materialized at the entrance. He glanced briefly at Melody's very still form and then looked at Leona.

"Are you all right?" he asked.

His voice was so cold and so controlled she knew he was channeling a lot of intense emotion. It was all there in his specter-cat eyes.

"Yes," she whispered. She took a breath and tried again. "Yes, I'm okay. I'm burned out for now. It will take me a few hours to recover, and I'll probably have a panic attack later, but right now I'm . . . okay." She looked down at Melody. Another rush of horror zapped through her. "I may have killed her. I didn't mean to, but I've never done anything like that before and I—"

"You didn't kill her," Oliver said. "Trust me, you would know if you had."

He was right. She pulled herself together and reminded herself that the energy of violent death was unmistakable. There was no hint of that vibe around Melody Palantine.

Oliver crouched near the unconscious woman and checked for a pulse. "She'll definitely wake up. Not sure what kind of shape her para-psych profile will be in, though."

A familiar figure appeared at the entrance.

"Assassin," Burt roared. He had a flamer in his hand. He aimed it at Leona. "You killed Vincent Lee Vance and now you've murdered the ac-olyte."

"Put the flamer down," Oliver ordered quietly.

Burt did not acknowledge the command. It was as if he didn't even see Oliver, Leona thought, and this time Oliver was not trying to be in-visible.

She tightened her grip on Roxy, who was sleeked out and trying to escape her grasp.

"He's still in a trance," she said quietly. "With Palantine unconscious it will eventually wear off, but at the moment—"

"It's a problem," Oliver said. "Yeah, I can see that."

Leona felt energy shift in the atmosphere and knew that Oliver had just cloaked himself in his talent. He glided up to Burt, snapped the flamer out of his grasp, and then moved back.

Burt whirled around and launched himself at Oliver. *"You can't be al-lowed to interfere with the Vance destiny. With the future."*

"No," Leona shouted. "Stop."

But it was clear Burt had no intention of stopping. His trajectory and his crazed determination combined with the raw power of his heavily muscled body should have ensured that he slammed into Oliver. And he would have if Oliver hadn't sidestepped him.

Burt scrambled to a halt and circled around his target, preparing for another charge.

"We don't have time for this," Oliver said quietly. "We've got dinner with Leona's parents tonight. My first time. I need to make a good im-pression. You know how it is."

Leona sensed lightning-hot energy crackling in the atmosphere. With it came a thrill of stark panic so overwhelming it left her unable to move. She could barely breathe. In that moment she could not have run or even screamed if her life had depended on it.

She knew she was only getting the backwash of the terrifying currents that struck Burt. He stared at Oliver, horror shattering his entranced aura.

"Monster," he rasped.

Leona was suddenly stricken with a panic unlike anything she had ever known.

She was locked inside a transparent coffin that was being slowly propelled into a furnace of blazing blue fire . . .

In the next instant Burt collapsed, unconscious, next to Melody Palantine.

Oliver looked at Leona. It was clear he was braced for her reaction.

She broke free of the dreamscape, damp with perspiration. Relief descended on her with such force it was all she could do to remain on her feet. She planted one hand against the nearest quartz wall.

"Okay," she said, drawing a deep breath. "That's one hell of a talent you have, Rancourt. Do you have any idea what Burt just saw?"

"He saw what I wanted him to see: his worst nightmare."

She frowned, trying to process that. "But what, exactly, did he see?"

"I don't know. Everyone has their own nightmares. I just rez them. I don't see them."

"That explains it, then."

"You saw a nightmare, too, didn't you? I tried to focus on Burt but you were not that far away, and the energy down here is so strong and so unpredictable—"

"It's all right, Oliver." She took her hand off the wall and rezzed up a shaky smile. "I can handle a bad dream. Griffin women can take care of themselves."

Some of his tension eased. "Yeah, I can see that. I know you've been through a lot, but the Guild and the FBPI will be here at any minute. We need a good story to explain three unconscious people, one that doesn't involve us being scary monster talents."

"Right. But first I want my pendant back. Molly can retune it."

She crossed the room to where Melody lay sprawled on the floor, reached into the pocket of the woman's jacket, and retrieved the yellow crystal.

She slipped it over her neck and looked at Oliver.

"Now we can work on our story."

CHAPTER FIFTY

Leona unlocked the door of her apartment and led the way inside. "I've been meaning to ask, how did you find me so quickly today? Palantine flatlined my nav amber and my yellow crystal."

"I found Roxy first," Oliver said, following her into the small foyer, "thanks to that ridiculous fascinator. She was just waking up from the effects of the drug Palantine used on the two of you."

"Right." Leona smiled at Roxy, who bailed off her shoulder, landed on the floor, and fluttered toward the kitchen. "Molly tuned the blue crystal butterfly in the fascinator. She gave it a nav code primarily because she was afraid the hat might get lost, but also because I spend a lot of time in the Underworld and you can never have too much nav amber and crystals."

"Evidently it never occurred to Palantine that anyone would bother to tune a fascinator. Roxy led me straight to you."

Roxy bounced up onto a dining counter stool and then up to the counter. She chortled.

"I think she's hungry," Oliver said. "So am I."

Leona checked the time as she followed Roxy into the kitchen. "We've got dinner with the moms in an hour. Will some pretzels hold you over?"

"Pretzels and a large glass of wine. I need the booze to fortify myself for dinner tonight."

Leona took the lid off the pretzel jar and doled out two small bowls of pretzels. She started to close the lid, changed her mind, and filled a third bowl for herself. She set one bowl on top of the counter for Roxy.

Oliver opened the refrigerator and grabbed the open bottle of inexpensive red. Closing the refrigerator, he took two glasses out of the cupboard and carried everything to the dining counter.

Making himself at home, she thought. But it felt right. It was as if the apartment had been waiting for him. There had always been something missing in the decor. Now the place felt complete.

The interview with the FBPI had gone smoothly, thanks to Oliver's connections. Explaining the three unconscious people had taken a bit of creative thinking, but the Feds appeared to have been satisfied with a story involving a delusional, multi-talent, would-be cult leader who had gone insane. The paranormal atmosphere of the Underworld had overwhelmed her fragile, unstable senses.

In the process of self-destructing, the Vance wannabe had taken down the two innocent men she had hypnotized. Burt and Baxter Richey had both recovered, but they had no memory of how they had become involved in the kidnapping or of the events in the Underworld that had followed—at least, that's what they claimed. Leona believed them.

She and Oliver had been content to let both men plead innocent due to having been in a hypnotic trance. The important thing was that Melody Palantine was now in a secure cell in a para-psych prison hospital. She was awake but still delusional. The doctors did not know if her paranormal senses would ever recover, but they were prepared to administer psi-suppressing drugs if necessary.

Meanwhile, money was already pouring into the tiny community of Lost Creek, thanks to the arrival of the FBPI, the Guild, and a lot of obsessed para-archaeologists. The inn would soon be booked solid, Leona thought. The diner would be busy.

She sat down across from Oliver and picked up a glass of wine. "You said the moms called you when I disappeared in the middle of my phone conversation with them?"

"Yes." Oliver munched a pretzel. "They told me you had been in the process of getting into a car at the mansion and that you had just recognized the woman in the photo. Then your phone went dead. They were worried when they couldn't reconnect. They sent the photo to me."

"You recognized Darla Price, aka Melody Palantine."

"Immediately. Eugenie and Charlotte filled me in on what they had learned about her. It was more than enough to send her straight to the top of the suspect list. But I couldn't track her because her amber was locked. Yours had gone dark."

"I see." Leona started to drink some wine and stopped when she got a ping. "Eugenie and Charlotte? You're on a first-name basis with my moms?"

"I am." Oliver swallowed some wine and reached for another pretzel.

Leona cleared her throat. "We will get back to that. Moving right along, I gather that when you realized my amber had been flatlined, you started tracking the crystal in Roxy's fascinator."

"Yep." Oliver's eyes glinted with admiration. "Not that you needed rescuing. You had the situation under control when I arrived."

She shuddered. "Maybe. Barely. Until Burt showed up."

"Got a feeling you could have handled him, too. Griffin women can take care of themselves."

She shook her head. "No, my senses were exhausted after I took down Melody Palantine. They still are."

"You would have figured it out." Oliver munched on the pretzel. "What, exactly, did you do to Palantine?"

Leona met his eyes. "I'm not sure. But I think I can now say I finally discovered my third talent."

"What do you think happened?"

"Somehow I was able to use Baxter Richey's amber to pull energy from the quartz around me and channel it straight at Melody's aura."

Oliver paused in mid-munch. Then he smiled. "Damn, woman. That's amazing."

"No," she said, "it was a terrifying sensation. Like channeling lightning. It was painful in a way I can't explain. I wondered if I was incinerating my own talent in the process. I can't begin to imagine how it felt on her end. And poor Richey fainted."

Oliver watched her for a moment. "But you're okay now?"

She nodded. "I think so. My senses are recovering. I definitely do not want to have to pull that trick again anytime soon, though."

Grim understanding appeared in his eyes. "I know the feeling. I don't like using my talent to the max, either."

"Burt called you a monster."

"He was right. I could have killed him with my talent."

"But you didn't."

"No," he said. "I didn't."

"Was that the reason your marriage was annulled on the grounds of a fraudulent para-psych profile? Your wife witnessed your talent in action?"

Oliver's mouth twitched in a wry smile. "No wife involved, remember? An annulment means we were never married. But yes, she saw that side of me, and so did I."

"You mean you didn't know what you could do?"

"Not until I had the need to do it. I went on instinct and intuition."

She sipped some wine. "I understand."

"My non-wife and I were attacked on our honeymoon. One of those wrong place, wrong time things. A couple of high-grade talents carrying mag-rez pistols. I nearly flatlined both of them."

Leona got another ping. "Your non-wife was shocked to see what you could do with your talent. She never understood that wasn't your real talent."

He frowned. "What are you talking about?"

She smiled. "You are a decent, honorable man. The kind of man who does the right thing when the chips are down. I know you would have my back in a bar fight, and you would show up with bail money if I got arrested at two in the morning. That's the kind of talent that really matters, at least to me."

He had been about to swallow some wine but something went wrong. He choked on a laugh and spewed drops of the drink into the air and across the table.

"Damn," he rasped, grabbing a napkin. "Sorry about that." He laughed again as he mopped up spilled wine. "When was the last time you got into a bar fight or were arrested?"

"It's been a while," she admitted. "Like forever. But I don't doubt you'd be there for me."

"Always." His eyes met hers. "You'd be there for me, too."

"Yes. Always."

"I'm in love with you, Leona. I started falling for you that night at the Society's reception when I found you in that lab, setting the dust bunnies free. I've been falling ever since. I'm all the way in now. There's no going back, not for me."

Joy sparkled through her senses. "I'm so glad, because I'm in love with you. I wasn't sure what was happening. I've never been in love. It changes everything."

"This is new to me, too. You're right. It changes things." His eyes heated. "But it's been only a few days. We need a little time."

"Time to be sure?"

"No, I'm very sure."

"So am I."

"It's our families who will want us to take some time. They need to be reassured that we're a good match."

She winced. "True. They will insist we go through a normal dating relationship."

He smiled. "Eugenie and Charlotte, being moms, are way ahead of you. I've been meaning to tell you that we have an appointment at the Banks matchmaking agency tomorrow."

Leona stared at him. "What?"

"It was probably my fault. Late this morning, while you were busy rescuing the Hollister team, I went to the offices of Griffin Investigations to introduce myself."

"They must have been floored when you walked through the door. I'll bet they never saw you coming."

"They are your mothers. Of course they saw me coming. Just so you know, I didn't simply introduce myself. I told them that I would be asking for your hand in marriage at some point in the near future. I wanted to give them a heads-up. Figured it was the traditional thing to do."

"Wow. So that's why we've got an appointment at the Banks agency tomorrow."

"Tomorrow evening we will be having dinner with my family. We will continue to go through all of the conventional steps to a Covenant Marriage because that will satisfy everyone involved. But in the end, we will get married."

"What happens if the Banks agency doesn't think we're a great match?"

"That's not going to happen," Oliver said.

"But if it does happen?"

"You and I got away with Pandora's box and the key crystal the night of the reception. We avoided getting swept up in an FBPI raid. We found a long-lost Vortex machine—to say nothing of dismantling a cult and taking down a killer megalomaniac who was trying to become the next Vincent Lee Vance. We can figure out how to hack a matchmaking computer."

She relaxed. "So you have a backup plan."

"Always. For everything except for you. I don't have a backup plan for any scenario where you are not in my life."

She went into his arms with a sense of certainty that thrilled all of her senses. This was the right man.

"I love you, Oliver."

"That's all I need," he said.

CHAPTER FIFTY-ONE

The positive match from the Banks matchmaking agency (*When it comes to Covenant Marriage, you can bank on Banks*) came through twenty-four hours after they registered. Oliver was in the process of moving his things into Leona's apartment when the news arrived on his phone.

Late that afternoon he took a break from arguing about which side of the walk-in closet would be his to pick up a bottle of champagne at a nearby wine shop. A small, private celebration was in order.

Leona smiled at him over the rim of the glass. "No backup plan required."

"I told you we wouldn't need one," he said. "Sometimes you know when things are real."

"Yes."

The champagne led to an intimate dinner for two at a nearby restaurant and more champagne. Neither of them noticed when Roxy disappeared.

CHAPTER FIFTY-TWO

When the chaos ended, the attendant at the River of Alien Nightmares ride told the media that he never saw the dust bunnies coming. He pointed out that it was midnight and the Underworld Adventures theme park was thronged. He never had a chance to stop the pirates.

The dust bunnies materialized out of the shadows beneath the Great Wheel and a nearby row of food stalls and rushed the gate in what appeared to be a coordinated assault. "There was no way to secure the little suckers with the safety bar," the attendant said. "All I can tell you is that the ringleader was wearing a blue hat with a lot of ribbons on it. I think it may have been a licensed emotional support dust bunny."

Estimates of the actual number of pirates involved varied widely, but certain facts were not in dispute. The uninvited guests breached the gate at the dock and piled into one of the self-driving boats before the attendant realized what was happening. The vessel shot off on the artificial river and disappeared into the dark ride. Much excited chortling could be heard.

The boat was empty when it appeared at the exit of the ride. The screaming began as soon as the next vessels filled with paying customers entered the tunnel. In the end, the hero of the night proved to be the server at the pizza stand. She and her team leaped into action and raced to the rescue. They set several pizzas into an empty boat. The attendant sent the vessel into the dark ride. The strategy worked. When the boat emerged at the exit point, it was crammed with dust bunnies dining on pizza.

Upon arriving at the gate, the pirates grabbed slices of leftover pizza and vanished back into the shadows. After all, the night was young. More adventures awaited down in the Underworld. On Harmony, the real excitement came after dark.

ANOTHER NOTE FROM JAYNE

Thanks for joining me for another adventure on Harmony. The rumors are true. The dust bunnies have taken over my Jayne Castle world. In hindsight, all I can tell you is that I never saw them coming.

If you got this far, you know that Leona Griffin has a sister with whom she shares a mysterious past. You can read Molly's story in *People in Glass Houses*.

Did the name Oliver Rancourt ping a memory? That's probably because his ancestor back on Earth was Harlan Rancourt. Harlan's story is in *Lightning in a Mirror* (written under my Jayne Ann Krentz name).

Interested in some of my other books? Check out the list at the front of this book or head to my website, jayneannkrentz.com, where you will find all sorts of information, including a list of my novels sorted by series.

Waving from Seattle,

JAYNE

Do you love fiction with a supernatural twist?

Want the chance to hear news about your favourite authors (and the chance to win free books)?

Christine Feehan
J.R. Ward
Sherrilyn Kenyon
Charlaine Harris
Jayne Ann Krentz and Jayne Castle
P.C. Cast
Maria Lewis
Darynda Jones
Hayley Edwards
Kristen Callihan
Keri Arthur
Amanda Bouchet
Jacquelyn Frank
Larissa Ione

Then visit the *With Love* website and
sign up to our romance newsletter:
www.yourswithlove.co.uk

And follow us on Facebook for book giveaways,
exclusive romance news and more:
www.facebook.com/yourswithlovex

PIATKUS